Novels by Annabelle Lewis

The Carrows Family Chronicles

Charlotte McGee, Book One

Titan Takedown, Book Two

Carrows Justice, Book Three
(Available January 2019)

Titan Takedown

BOOK 2

THE
Carrows Family
CHRONICLES

ANNABELLE LEWIS

This book is a work of fiction. People, characters, places, events, and situations are the product of the author's imagination. Some historical and celebrity names appear in the novel in order to place the story in a historic or modern cultural perspective, but these names are used in an imaginary context and do not suggest that any of the incidents ever happened.

Contact Annabelle at annabellelewisauthor@gmail.com

ISBN-13: 978-0999336816
ISBN-10: 0999336819

First Edition

Publisher:
PePe Press

Cover Design:
Keri Knutson
Alchemy Book Covers and Design

Editors:
Erin Liles and Alida Winternheimer

Interior Designer:
Pikko's House

Dedication

For Lane. The best guy in the whole world.

Prologue

____

Henry Carrows Sr., or Hank, as he was better known, was born in 1905 and began his life as would his progeny, lucky and gifted. Too young to serve in World War I, from his early years, he worked with his father, who ran a hotel and livery business. His father had been a partner with Elias J. "Lucky" Baldwin and was exceedingly prosperous. In his early twenties, Hank took advantage of a natural offshoot of the hotel and livery business and ran a liquor operation during Prohibition. Prohibition was a gift bestowed on many who were willing to break the law and run risks. Hank was born to the job.

If he wasn't rich before, he became so during those years. He was fearless, which as it happens, is a necessary characteristic of a grifter, and he likened himself to a pirate. He enjoyed himself immensely with the ridiculous opportunity that Prohibition had handed him. A United States law prohibiting a product that everyone wanted, to the extent that even, and sometimes especially, law enforcement turned a blind eye to its sale, was a business opportunity for anyone open to the dangerous speculation. Hank had the resources, the business know-how, and the charm it took to keep everyone around him happy and successful. He prospered beyond his wildest dreams.

Then the Depression hit. And again, this was not a setback for Hank but only an opportunity. He set his eye to the Pacific coastline. He knew that the scenic land next to the ocean would be extraordinarily valuable, and in 1930, he purchased a large section of it. The land that would later be named Whispering Cliffs, nestled in a high bluff overlooking the Pacific Ocean and sharing acreage with Topanga State Park, was purchased for a song. Not a steal exactly but close enough. He hired architects, artisans, and laborers, who were both cheap and plentiful, and began building his home. The mansion became legend not only in the area but throughout the nation. It was a treasure. A perfect monument. A perfect, private monument in paradise.

While he completed his project by the sea, Hank enjoyed further success as he branched out into mining, steel manufacturing, fishing and canneries. He also endeavored in Coca-Cola, tobacco, and obtained the patents for several lucrative aeronautical concepts. But he became bored with the lack of hijinks and risks that these industries offered. Prohibition had been fun, and he missed being a pirate.

His next opportunity for adventure came again from the United States government when in 1934 they legalized pari-mutuel gambling. He became a partner in building the Santa Anita Racetrack and found a new home. When World War II came around, Hank's usual luck held when he was officially diagnosed with flat feet, a gift he didn't fully appreciate until that time and which would later be handed down to his son, Henry.

By the time Henry was born, Hank was forty and well established at Whispering Cliffs but was now spending most of his time in Pasadena and the Santa Anita Racetrack. His wife of five years was a contented dreamer and was delighted when they finally conceived a child. Henry would be the only one. Hank typically left his small family of two alone by the sea and lived in another home he built in Pasadena close to his beloved racetrack. The excitement of the sport and the women who were obliging to him as their generous benefactor and intimate companion, along with the gambling and corruption at the track, filled Hank's lust for life.

But Hank loved his young son, Henry, and eventually felt it was his duty to spend time with the boy and bring him into his inheritance. Not the monetary kind, but that of grifting, gambling, and hijinks.

From the age of about five years, Henry Carrows spent most of his time at the racetrack with either his father, bookies, jockeys, or other moneyed and questionable characters. The safety of five-year-old Henry Carrows as he ran loose around the Santa Anita Racetrack was never an issue. Everyone knew Hank and eventually his son. Young Henry started as a stooper. He basically snatched old tickets left around the seats and on the floor in the hopes someone had mistakenly tossed a winner. This almost always paid off because the complex rules of racehorse betting sometimes confused the better. This was intended.

Hank also instilled in Henry the differences between being a con man and a grifter.

"A con man always gets caught, kid. A grifter will get away, and the best part is, the mark will never know it was you who set them up."

Hank impressed his son. He was Henry's hero. As the years went by, Hank taught Henry everything he knew about his tricks. They styled themselves as businessmen, supremely confident in their destiny. Gambling on the backs of others and their fearless games of cat and mouse were the wellspring of their life source. They lived to play games and had the finances to do it well.

Chapter 1

Charlotte Carrows considered her life to be entering its third chapter. The first chapter was when she was raised at Whispering Cliffs, the second after her daughter, Petunia, was born, and now she was in the next chapter with her love, Alex Macchi. Brought into her life by a twist of fate and under dark circumstances, he succeeded brilliantly in helping to cast off David Torres, Petunia's biological father, an ugly and threatening person. More importantly, Alex brought joy back into Charlotte's life.

She lay back on her bed, the phone cradled next to her ear. Alex lived on the opposite coast, in California, and their nightly calls were the highlight of her day.

"Did you file the paperwork with the attorney?" Alex asked one evening, his voice so comforting, even thousands of miles away.

"Yes. I'll officially once again become Charlotte Sophia Carrows, and Petunia's legal name will be Petunia Sophia Carrows. The McGee will be officially gone."

"Good for you."

Charlotte rolled over and stared at the empty pillow beside her. "We've got to make a decision, Alex. It's been too long since I've seen you."

"I know. I can't live like this either," he groaned.

"Petunia will be in first grade next year. If I'm moving to California, then we've got to make that decision soon."

"I talked to Oliver about us today," he said.

Charlotte smiled, thinking about Oliver Baach and his stoic nature. She could hear the amusement in Alex's voice. "And what was his advice?"

Alex laughed. "He straightened his tie and changed the subject. I don't think my boss, and Henry's best friend, is comfortable giving me advice about my love life. Nor about me moving to New York."

Charlotte laid her hand softly on the pillow and smiled.

Since their very first encounter, Alex and Charlotte were good together. And good to each other. He appealed to Charlotte on many levels. Tremendously dedicated, kind, and respectful, he'd proven himself to be trustworthy and discreet. He was a good man with a great sense of humor, and he wasn't hard to look at. Charlotte's mother, Julia, always said Alex reminded her of Goran Visnjic, the actor who played a doctor on *ER*, and while there was something about his kind eyes that reminded Charlotte of him as well, she thought if they had to reference the screen, he looked more like Clive Owen.

She rolled over in frustration and stared at the ceiling. She gathered up her long dark hair, moved it to the side, and slid her hand beneath her head. "Don't you miss the city, Alex? Just think of it. Bundled up in your winter jacket, freezing, walking the streets of Manhattan again. As spoiled as you are with the weather in California, I know you secretly miss it."

"It was sunny and seventy in the city of angels today, my love. If you and Petunia lived here, we could have spent the day together outside. Without jackets."

She closed her eyes, trying to imagine how she would feel living in California again. Alex's job as a private investigator for a law firm was important to him. Extremely successful, he'd built a home and reputation as someone who could be counted on for personal and business situations that required a delicate hand. His services were in demand, his case load extremely full. But they'd been dating for nearly two years and almost all of it from a distance. They both realized that things needed to change.

"But I love New York, Alex. I love the city and the people. They treat me like I'm just one of the crowd. For the most part. New Yorkers have a way about them, you know that."

"I know. We'll figure it out. How about we make the decision next week when I'm out there?"

Charlotte's green eyes widened, and she sat up. "A deadline. I like it. Next week. But promise me it won't be by a flip of a coin."

"Hey, of course not," he protested.

She stretched her long legs out in front of her and

smiled. "Maybe I'll call Isabella and your mom and tell them that now's the time to apply pressure if they want you to move home."

"Sure. Pit the family against me. I won't stand a chance." He laughed. "Speaking of, is my sister going to be at Mom and Dad's when I'm in town? Did you talk to her?"

Charlotte wiggled her toes, examining them as she thought about her conversation with Isabella, Alex's only sister.

"I don't think so. She and Finn are stretched really thin. They want to get some work done on the barn repairs. She said it's coming along, but it's taking up most of their time. Maybe we can help them, Alex. Hire some contractors or something?"

"My sister and her husband can fend for themselves, honey. I mean, it's nice of you to want to help, but it was their decision to buy the farm. It was their dream to live in the country."

They were both quiet for a time, as lovers sometimes are when conducting conversations on the phone, each holding the tenuous connection through the airwaves like a soft embrace.

Charlotte broke the reverie. "We're wasting so much precious time living apart, Alex. All I know is that I miss you. I want you here with me all the time so we can have a proper relationship, so we can really be together."

"I feel the same. Next week we'll make the decision. Now, how about you tell me more about your day? This time start with the part where you wept for me. Tears shed, thinking about me, maybe in the shower, this morning before you left for work."

She smiled. She loved this man.

But their plans abruptly changed a few days later when Alex's father, Anthony, unexpectedly passed away. His death had come out of nowhere and much too soon. The days following the death had been brutal. Upon hearing the news, Alex had taken the first flight out of Los Angeles. Charlotte met him at the airport, and the two of them had gone directly to the Macchi home in Bay Ridge, Brooklyn, where he was met by his family with love, heartbreak, and tears.

The funeral over, Charlotte sat on a long brocade sofa in the family's formal living room the afternoon of the service, holding Isabella's hand and staring at the family, who were not themselves. The home was filled to capacity with friends and relatives, speaking in quiet groups, eating, drinking, and remembering the man who had built a wonderful family. The Macchis, typically a colorful group of people, often laughing and unafraid of expressing their love physically, looked now to be wandering around lost, as if they were ghosts.

Physically striking, all of them handsome in their dark formal wear, they were as one tragically serious. Isabella, suffering from lack of sleep, reached over to the coffee table in front of them for her saucer and cup that a passing relative had just refilled with coffee. Her leg jumped as she sipped the hot beverage. "Uncle Ted," she said to Charlotte, her eyes indicating a man across the room, "is the family lawyer. He said he'd read the will later after everyone has gone."

Charlotte scanned the room, her eyes drawn to her beloved Alex as he said something to his mother, Marie, and kissed her tenderly on the cheek. That simple gesture, the look between them, seemed to give them each a moment of comfort. Alex, with his careless elegance, appeared strong, but she knew he was held up by a thread. The evening before, he had cried bitterly in her arms, letting the pain wash over him privately, away from the rest of the family.

Charlotte caught his eye as he took a seat next to his listless mother and gave him a small smile. She turned to Isabella. "Alex thought I should stay for the reading, but if you think I should leave, I can go upstairs while he speaks with you all?"

Isabella placed her cup back on the table and said, "No. Of course not. We're glad you're here, please don't leave. You're practically family, and if Alex wants you here, then this is where you should be."

Isabella sat back and laid her head on Charlotte's shoulder, gently tucking her hands into Charlotte's arm, and said softly, "I'm so glad you met him, Charlotte. I'm glad you had a chance to get to know him, and us, before this happened. I don't think we'll ever be the same."

Charlotte placed a hand over Isabella's and looked over her head at Finn, Isabella's husband and childhood sweetheart, sitting on the other side of them on the sofa. They shared a look, but Finn, too, seemed far away. Looking toward the large kitchen, she saw Tony, the oldest of the Macchi children, murmuring with a group of men. So many people she had yet to meet. They could be relatives, friends, or some of the cops from Tony's precinct. Tony's wife, Abby, pregnant with their first child, had gone upstairs to lie down.

The house was filled with the aroma of comforting food, warm bread, coffee, and spices. She heard the voices of children nearby and turned to look in the dining room and saw Michael, Alex's younger brother, by the buffet helping his wife and two young daughters, Leonora and Andria. The two girls had become close friends with Petunia. This day, being too much for Petunia to understand, Charlotte had left her in the care of friends.

A bar had been set up in a corner, and Nick, the youngest of the boys, gathered with a group of young adults, partaking in the refreshments. Nick, like Alex, had the Macchi eyes. Almost sad, or conveying wisdom, they now looked haunted.

Isabella lifted her head off Charlotte's shoulder and, closing her eyes, rolled her neck slightly from side to side. "It's been a long day. I don't think people are going to stay much longer. Maybe I should get up and start thanking them all for coming. Look at Mom, she needs to lie down."

It was true. Marie Macchi, sitting across the room, was considering the face of someone Charlotte didn't know, accepting their condolences, Alex still beside her. She looked exhausted.

"Has Alex told you when he's going home?" Isabella turned to Charlotte with a worried look.

Charlotte stared back and gave her a small smile. "He told me last night that he is home, Isabella. He's made the decision to move back."

Isabella smiled for the first time that day. Happy, her eyes filled with love, she said, "Well, it's about time." They looked together at Alex, who caught their glances and returned his sister's hopeful smile.

"Dad would be very glad to hear that too," Isabella said as she squeezed Charlotte's arm.

The reading of the will took place early that evening after the last of the friends and relatives had departed. Everyone but Marie was surprised when Uncle Ted, the attorney, announced that Anthony had left each of the children $200,000 and the rest of his hard-earned estate to Marie. It was his last gift but not the last of his legacy. That would go on forever.

Saying a goodnight to Marie, Charlotte held her as Marie whispered, "Thank you for taking care of my Alex, Charlotte. Thank you for helping him. I'm very grateful that he has you in his life."

It was Charlotte who felt grateful. The Macchi family was a gift to her, and one she hoped to have forever.

———

Almost a year and a half after the funeral, Charlotte and

Alex were spending a quiet evening in her home. It was Christmastime, and earlier that evening they'd hung their stockings over her fireplace, which, oddly, had rarely been used. Alex decided to remedy that and had received a delivery of wood, now stored in her garden, and had loaded a bin next to the hearth. The two of them lay on the sofa quietly watching the fire burn, relaxed after enjoying the hard day's work and the pleasurable moments of decorating the tree with Petunia, now quietly asleep in her bed on the third floor.

"It's been a good day. Almost perfect really," Alex said as he kissed her. "You've been so good to me and my family, Charlotte. I'll always be thankful to you for that."

"I'm the one who should feel thankful. I'm so lucky to have you in my life, and it was your family who reached out and welcomed me."

"You were easy to love, that's all."

She laid her head on his shoulder and lay back in his arms.

"There is something that I want to talk to you about though. It's pretty important. Come here, you," he said as he maneuvered her to sit up. "Look at me for a second," he said gently.

She looked into his face, his absurdly handsome face, and continued to be astonished that she could love and trust someone so deeply.

He suddenly shifted and got off the sofa. Standing in front of her, he gently dropped to one knee. He smiled at her shocked expression.

"Charlotte. Charlotte Carrows *McGee*, I think I've loved you since the moment we met. Possibly even before. I don't know what I did to deserve you, but my heart, my love, with everything I have, I know that I'll never want to be without you. I was wondering if you would marry me. Will you be my wife?"

Tears sprang to her eyes. Her heart leapt. She didn't say a word but jumped to the floor and into his arms. She kissed him deeply. Pulling away from each other, their foreheads still touching, she said finally, "Of course, I'll marry you, Alex. My God, I love you so much."

Alex released her and sat back, putting his hand in his pocket. His face elated, he gave her a lopsided smile as he pulled out a ring and picked up her hand. As he slid it onto her finger, he said nervously, "I hope it fits. I brought one of your other ones with me to the jewelers."

It did. Perfectly. They looked at it together, the platinum engraved, channel set, three-carat radiant cut ring sparkled. "It's beautiful, Alex." She looked lovingly into his eyes. "I'm so happy."

They held each other, both surrendering, embracing the commitment of a lifetime together, intoxicated by the deep love they had for each other.

A twist of fate had led them to each other, and for that, they would be grateful.

Their engagement would make wonderful news throughout the Carrows and Macchi families. Alex and Charlotte planned to make the announcement to the Macchis at the Sunday family gathering the next day. But first, they asked for Petunia's permission.

"Mom, does that mean he will be my dad? Will I have a dad now?"

This nearly broke Charlotte's heart. She knew that one day she would have to explain the details of what became of her biological father, David.

"Petunia," Alex said, "I will be your father and love you forever, if you'll have me. It's not just your mom and I getting married, it's all three of us coming together as a family."

Petunia looked at them both and smiled. "We'll be a real live happy family," she whispered. "I wished and wished for a family all my whole life. I even asked Santa, Mom. Maybe he was listening!"

Charlotte embraced her young daughter, a tear escaping. "He was, baby," she said.

Alex drove across the Manhattan Bridge toward Brooklyn. Petunia fidgeted with excitement in the back seat. "Will Leonora and Andria be my sisters now?" she said, referring to Alex's nieces, Leonora, age seven, the same age as Petunia, and Andria, age five.

Charlotte turned to look at her daughter's bright face and felt gratitude for Alex's entire family and the way they had welcomed her and Petunia into the fold.

"I'm going to give you the legal answer," said Alex. "No,

they will not be your sisters, they will be your cousins-in-law. However, you can be as close to each other as sisters if you choose to be."

"A whole family," she whispered, accepting another miracle.

The announcement made the Macchi family loudly whoop and cry. The hugging was abundant. Charlotte and Alex watched as Petunia, Leonora, and Andria, all holding hands, jumped up and down and screamed with delight.

Alex and Charlotte had planned ahead and thoughtfully brought in several bottles of champagne. Marie, Alex's mother, raised her glass to Charlotte. "Welcome to the family, Charlotte. Both Anthony and I thought you were right for our Alex. I'll be very proud to call you my daughter."

The planning was on. That morning, Alex and Charlotte had agreed that Alex would ask his older brother Tony to be his best man, and Charlotte would ask Isabella to be her matron of honor. Isabella and Charlotte, almost the same age, found they had a lot in common. Over the course of time, they'd become extremely close.

Champagne in hand, Charlotte asked her.

Isabella smiled joyously at her friend. "Oh, Charlotte, I would love that! Thank you for asking me. But won't your sister get her feelings hurt that you didn't ask her?" she said, tilting her head.

"Isabella, you know that Carey and I are not close. Neither she nor I would want to put a traditional self-imposed ceremony in the way of our mutual dislike. She will most likely attend the wedding, but she definitely won't want to be in it."

As confused as Isabella was by this, she believed Charlotte knew what was best. It was her wedding and her brother's.

"This is such a happy day," said Isabella. "The only thing I wish for is that Dad could be here to celebrate with us."

"I know. That would be my wish too. But as an outsider, I can tell you, as I look around at your family, he is here. Look at the family he grew and left behind. You're all a credit to him," she said as they hugged.

"My God, I get to call you my sister! I couldn't be happier for you guys."

"Alex and I need to make some of the harder decisions about what we want the wedding to look like, and I was hoping we might hang out next weekend at your place and really wrestle it to the ground? I'd love to get away with Alex and Pinky and spend some quiet time with you and Finn."

"That'd be great. Finn's so busy now with the farm, but I know he'll be able to take some time off on Saturday. At least for dinner. Why don't you guys come up on Friday night, and we'll spend the weekend talking and planning."

"That sounds perfect. Thanks for letting me invite myself over. We'll drive up on Friday afternoon."

———————————

It was time to call Henry and Julia.

That night after they returned from the Macchis', they were seated around the kitchen island. Charlotte looked at Alex and Petunia across from her as she placed the call.

"God, I'm so excited," said Charlotte. "It's only eight o'clock in California. Mom texted earlier today. I know they didn't have any plans. They're home."

Julia answered brightly, "Hello there, daughter."

"Hi, Mom," Charlotte said, smiling at Petunia, who had her hand covering her mouth with excitement.

"How was your day with the Macchis? What culinary delights did Marie tempt you with for dinner?"

"Mom. Um, we have some news. I'm in the kitchen with Alex and Petunia. Say hi."

"Oh, hello!" said Julia. "What news? Is everything okay?"

Petunia, smiling, rocked side to side in her chair, squinting her eyes. Alex beamed.

"Yes, everything is okay," said Charlotte, practically bursting. "Hey, is Dad around? Can you bring the phone to him?"

Petunia scrunched her hands into fists and shook them.

"He's right here," Julia said. "Henry, say something. It's Charlotte, Alex, and Pinky."

Henry piped up, "How is my favorite granddaughter today? I got your drawing in the mail. I placed it in the library next to your collection—"

Julia interrupted. "Henry, darling, they said they had news."

"We're engaged!" Charlotte blurted.

Henry and Julia were over the moon. Privately and frequently, they'd brought up how eager they were for the couple to commit. Since Charlotte and Alex were living together, they'd expected an engagement, but the couple's timetable had been different. Since the onset of Charlotte and Alex's relationship over three years ago, Henry and Julia had patiently waited but not without prompting. Henry had specifically told Charlotte that should she and Alex decide to marry, he would wholeheartedly approve. For Henry, that was a very big deal. He'd told her that he felt confident that Alex was a man he could trust, but more importantly, he trusted him with his only grandchild, Petunia.

Petunia had caught the very stoic Henry uncharacteristically off guard. She'd found a pathway directly into his heart and become one of the most important people in his life. He vowed to protect her.

Julia felt the same way about Alex that Henry did. She knew that her daughter would be a happy woman and that Alex would take good care of them. She reminded everyone, often, that it was all her doing that she had brought them together.

"This is kismet, via Julia," Alex interjected in a serious, sarcastic tone, anticipating Julia's upcoming declaration.

"It most certainly is," said Julia, laughing. "My God, a wedding! Charlotte, my first wedding. It *has* to be at

Whispering Cliffs. I know exactly how it should look, oh please let me plan this with you," she practically cried.

"Mom, slow down. We haven't decided on any of the details. The only thing we do know is that we want it to be small. We think. I mean, not a circus. As small as possible."

"Yes, as small as possible would be very tasteful, but please let me help with the planning. We'll be out there in a couple of weeks, and we can go shopping. I'll find a wedding planner here in California. Oh my," she audibly swooned. "It'll be heaven. I know just who to call. Don't worry, I'll take care of everything. Have you spoken with Charles and Carey? I know they'll be as happy as we are."

Charlotte had an inkling of concern about the Carey issue, but nothing could overshadow their day. Charlotte and Alex smiled at one another, greatly enjoying her parents' excitement. They had a lot to discuss but that would be part of the fun as well. Assuming they could contain Julia Carrows.

Chapter 2

Late Friday evening, Alex, Charlotte, and Petunia rolled onto the small farmstead outside of the town of Ithaca, New York, ready for a weekend away from the city. The signage on the driveway announced Isabella and Finn's new business venture, Titan Farms.

The long ride had been fun but tiring. As they got out of the car, Isabella and Finn came outside to greet them.

"Hey! You made it!" said Isabella, hugging Charlotte. "I'm so glad you're here."

"I know! Me too. Thanks so much for having us up."

"When can I see the chickens, Mom?" yelled an excited Petunia, bouncing out of the car.

"Not tonight, kid," said Finn, picking her up and giving her a bear hug. "Ooof," he said, putting her down. "Getting big there, Pink."

"Can I see them tomorrow, Uncle Finn?"

"Hey, I'm not your uncle yet. Gotta get your mom to the altar before she changes her mind and realizes what kind of family she's marrying into."

Petunia looked confused, and Isabella gave her a hug. "He's joking, sweetheart. Come on inside," she said, holding her hand. "I've got sloppy joes and a blueberry pie, which I know is your favorite, and I've got ice cream for it too!"

They got their bags into the small, three-bedroom farmhouse. A fire was going strong in the large comfortable main room off the kitchen.

"Hey," said Alex, as he handed off some items to Finn from the mudroom, "it's looking great. Damn, you've done a lot of work since the last time I was out."

"I know," Finn said. "I can hardly even remember what a disaster it was when we bought it."

"Geez," said Alex, coming into the kitchen and running his hand over a granite-topped island. "It's amazing what you've done. When were we last out here?" he said, turning to Charlotte.

"It's probably been six months," Charlotte said, still in the entry, squatting down to help Petunia take off her boots. Joining them in the kitchen, she said, "Oh, guys, it looks great. You've done so much! It's beautiful."

"Thanks," said Isabella as she grabbed a bag from Finn and walked into the main room. The room, painted a soft mushroom, had warm accents of brown and cream. Large brown leather sofas faced the fire and entertainment center. For the most part fairly uncluttered, an office area piled high with books and papers overlooked the deck.

They followed Isabella as she showed them to the

bedrooms. "You guys are in here, and Petunia, you're across the hall."

"Nice work, Finn," said Alex as he took in the details of the trimming and ran his hand down a wall in a bedroom.

"Yeah, well, I had some time on my hands when the fire department put me back to part-time. It was a trade-off up here. No big city hassles, but no big city job market either. We got some help with the last of the renovations. We're done for now." He walked out of the room, and they followed.

"But hey, you've got the chicken farm now. That's got to keep you busy," Alex said.

"Oh, yeah, it keeps me busy all right." He snorted and walked to the kitchen. "Hey, Alex, you want a beer?" said Finn as he opened the fridge. "Charlotte, can I get you something?"

"Mommmm, I'm hungry," said Petunia, bending over and grabbing her stomach. "Can I have some pie with ice cream? I think I'm going to faint." Petunia crumbled to the floor.

The adults stood, looking down at her. Charlotte shook her head and smiled as Alex said, "She does that. It's her new thing. Just walk over her, you never know how long she's going to be out."

Finn handed Alex a beer, and they stepped over Petunia. "I gotta say, I've never been to a poultry farm before, Finn." Alex made his way to a window, looking out past the deck and over to the various sheds and barns. "How's it going?" He took a long drink of the cold beer.

"Not that great, if you want to know the truth."

Something in the way he said it made Alex give him a second glance.

Isabella interrupted from the kitchen. "Guys, let's get some dinner and save some of the business talk until after we eat, okay? I'm dying to hear the latest about the wedding. How's your mom taking the news that you don't want to have the wedding at Whispering Cliffs?"

Charlotte gave her a half-hearted smile. "She'll get used to the idea. We'll pacify her by letting her take control of it in New York. We've still got a lot of decisions to make. They'll be out next week, and we're going to go shooopppping," Charlotte said, dancing, her happy feet going up and down with excitement. "Can you guys come to the city? We can try on dresses!"

Petunia sat up and stared at them, her hands pressed together as if praying. "Pie, pie, pie, Auntie Isabella? Please, please, please?" she said, sweetly smiling.

Isabella looked at Charlotte, who laughed. "All right. But only if you'll have a sloppy joe for dessert."

"Yeah!" Petunia jumped up and went over to the pie with Isabella.

Charlotte turned and looked at the guys, who had made their way into the kitchen. Finn wasn't smiling. His ball cap was in his hand, the other aggressively pushing back a bunch of hair before shoving it back on his head. Alex communicated a look. Something was off.

There was something in the air troubling them, but the four of them enjoyed a pleasant dinner with Petunia.

Charlotte and Isabella managed to wrangle her into bed after Finn promised she could visit the chickens in the morning. Alex and Finn were watching the weather report on the news as the girls came out of the bedroom.

"Chaaaarlotte," said Isabella with a conspiratorial laugh, "look what I have over here." She picked a tote bag off the floor, and Charlotte looked inside. It was filled with bride magazines.

"Oh, oh, oh! Alex! Look what she's got," she said, running over to him and letting him look inside.

"Oh, is right. What are there, about thirty in there?" he said. "That'll take all night."

Isabella grabbed the bag and, sitting on the carpet, dumped them out, spreading them all around. "I checked out every one they had at the Ithaca Library this afternoon after school. Oh my God, Charlotte, you're going to look so beautiful as a bride."

Charlotte was on the floor too, both of them sorting, flipping pages, fully immersing themselves.

"Finn," said Alex, gesturing with his eyeballs to leave the room. "It looks like the writing is on the wall. Do you wanna stay in here and give them our opinions, or should we take it outside? Pretty nice out there."

Finn got up and went to the fridge and pulled out four more beers. He handed two to Alex and, walking toward the mudroom, said loudly, "Hey, girls! We're going to sit on the deck, in case you're interested."

Alex, zipping up his coat and putting on his hat, chimed in, "We'll be outside, in the freezing cold. Getting out of your way." They got no direct response from the women but heard Isabella say, "Veils," with a reverence usually heard in church. "Charlotte," she continued. "Oh my God, look at these."

"Let's go," Alex said, smiling as they went outside.

"Hey, it's not too bad out here," said Alex as they stood on the deck, his head thrown back, looking at the sky. "Warm for a January night." Alex took a sip of his beer and stuffed the second one in his jacket pocket.

"Yup," said Finn. "Been a warm winter. Don't know what the hell's going on with that."

Alex picked up on the edge in Finn's voice as he looked over and watched him completely drain his first beer. "How's it going? The business? Michael mentioned that there've been some challenges. What's happening?"

Finn's mouth dropped open as he put his head back and groaned. "God, Alex, I don't even know where to begin. It's such a complicated mess. Things aren't going well right now, that's for sure. I'm in a really tight spot. Isabella and I had such high hopes, but now we can't even sleep at night worrying about what's happening. It's bad, man."

Finn deposited himself in one of the deck chairs that was clear of snow and popped the top of the second beer. Alex took a chair next to him.

Alex stared at him. "What happened? Did you talk to Michael?"

"No. Yeah, some. I didn't want anyone to know. I thought maybe it would work out, but now I'm not so sure.

It was our decision, *my* decision to buy into this business, and I didn't want to burden anyone with the problems we're having."

"What problems, man? What's going on?"

"Shit, Alex, this weekend's supposed to be about the wedding. I don't want to bring up this crap and bring everyone down."

"You're not going to bring me down. We're family. Maybe I can help, did you think of that?"

"I thought I could handle it," Finn said, shaking his head, "but it's gotten away from me. If we lose the business? The hell, Alex? It was Isabella's money. Anthony left it to her, and it's gone! I don't know how I'm going to live with that."

"Slow down for a minute," Alex said, holding up his hand. "I know I've been tied up with Michael and the business, but you've got to bring me up to speed here. What happened with Titan? Start at the beginning."

Finn shook his head as he took a long draft off his beer and placed it beside him. He put his hands in his pockets then out again as he whipped his hat off and threw it angrily down beside him and picked up his drink.

"Isabella's really the one getting us by. I don't know what I'd do without her." He gestured around the farm with his beer. "This was all we wanted. Our dream. Living in the country, out of the city. Maybe having a couple of kids. A dog. A place where the family could visit, you know? I'm willing to do the work, you know that. Right? I'll work until my back breaks as long as Isabella is happy, you know? But now I've dragged her down with me."

"Finn, you're a young, smart, educated guy. You've got your degree, you've got skills, you're a fireman, it's gonna work out."

Finn looked at Alex like he was a fool. "Yeah, I got all that. But it ain't doing us any good."

"All right, tell me about Titan Farms. Come on, we got all night."

"I need another beer," said Finn, rising. "I'll be right back."

Alex watched Finn walking away, draining the last of the beer in his hand. Alex got up and walked down the porch and looked inside. He watched Charlotte and his little sister laughing until Finn walked in. He saw Isabella's worried expression and watched as Finn said something as he dug more beer out of the fridge and left the room. She looked like she was going to cry now too. He saw Charlotte grab her hand and say something, and then he turned and walked back along the deck as Finn came back outside.

Finn Laferty had been hanging out at the Macchi home in Bay Ridge for as long as Alex could remember. A scrawny kid from a large family down the street, he was a friend of Michael's until he and Isabella started hanging out in high school. Alex thought of him like another brother.

"Hey," said Finn, ambling down the deck. "Maybe you wanna switch? Maybe a Captain and Coke?"

"Nah," said Alex, drinking the beer. "I'm good." Alex stood at the rail, looking out, and said, "You used a franchise broker in Manhattan, right? He hooked you up with Titan Farms?"

"Yeah. I'd talked to him before. You know, before Anthony died. I just wanted to see if there was something out here, something other than firefighting. Something, a business, we could build on, you know? Isabella's got a good teaching job. She's real happy with that, and we got this place, and it needed a lot of work, but hey, I bring it. I can get it done, you know?"

"No, I know. You've done a great job on the place, Finn. So the broker, what made you guys decide to buy a franchise from Titan Farms?"

Finn, shaking his head, looked emotional as he sat back in his chair and hung his head. Alex continued to prompt him. "I know you said you wanted a business that would get you outside, not a desk job. I get that. You're a hands-on guy. Capable. Farming makes a lot of sense— especially since you had this place."

Finn looked at Alex and nodded. "Yeah. So, when Anthony, God rest his soul, left us, left *Bella*, with the $200K, we thought we should talk to the broker guy again. The first time I did, I found out it required more up-front capital than we had, so I just walked away from it. But then, out of the blue, we had all this money. I told Bella that I didn't want to touch it, that it was hers. I did, Alex," he said, putting his hand on his heart. "But she said she thought that we should use it. You know? Like it was Anthony's final gift to us. We could get a business going, something we could own."

Finn picked his hat up off the deck, placing it on his head backward, and pulled another beer out of his pocket as Alex walked quickly to the window and took a look inside. Charlotte was holding his sister, who was crying.

Enough. Alex was upset now too. He walked back and took a seat next to Finn and said with a somber tone, "So, you talked to the broker, and he gave you Titan Farms."

"No, he gave me a few options. Five, really. That we could maybe do. Titan Farms was the only one, though, that was an outdoor business."

"What happened next?"

"So, Titan Farms was a contract farming opportunity out of New Jersey. It was being sold by a man named Damien Miller. He owned an extremely successful poultry farm in Jersey, and he'd already developed and sold several franchise farms in the tristate area based on his 'model of success,'" Finn said, using air quotes.

"It was exciting, man. The most exciting investment we looked at. The EBITA, you know, earnings before interest, tax, depreciation, and amortization—the operating profit of the model—was capable of a nice earning potential. Not right away, of course, but it would grow, exponentially over the first five years. That's what the numbers said. I'm not afraid of hard work, neither is Isabella. We were going to give any business our full commitment. Hard work, long hours, it was exciting. We'd put our sweat equity into it and build a farm based on the model that Titan presented."

He was off and focused. Alex was glad that the floodgates had opened.

"I'd never run a business or had employees or run administration or payroll," he said, using his fingers to tick off the items, "or taxes or dealt with insurance, licenses, numbers, or so much other stuff that goes into running a business. But my primary worry going into this investment was that I didn't know anything about chickens. I mean, I love the outdoors. Remember when we's went camping? Michael and I made Eagle Scouts. Our folks were busting at that. But that isn't in the ballpark of agricultural farming.

"But, hey, the broker said not to worry! He said it was an 'executive farming model.' He told us to go to the Discovery Day meeting with the company, and they would explain it to us so we could make an informed decision."

"So you went to Jersey and met with this guy. What was his name?"

"Damien Miller. Damien Miller and Walter Wilson, the president of Titan Farms. There were two other couples there too. Older types though, seasoned, successful business guys who wanted out of the corporate world, right? So thems and us, we met in Jersey, and I gotta say, it was provocative. It was really interesting. They brought us around, we visited the flagship farm and Titan Feed store, the whole setup.

"Damien told us that in the last twenty-five years, the US market had doubled its chicken production and now needs to produce one hundred sixty million a week. A week, man," he impressed. "And then there's the whole process. The American people, and the world, for that matter, has only in the last decade really woken up to the fact that what they put into their bodies is important. The type of poultry they're eating is important. They get it now that what the animal eats filters down into them. So, if the chickens were receiving hormones, it would be there. Fatty birds raised in one environment versus a bird who was raised in an organic environment are two different things. They would even taste better. Titan Farms was going to produce that product and capture that niche organic market.

"So, the flagship, model farm for Titan, where Damien established the business, is ideal. It's clean, successful, humane, and it delivers a healthier, safer product to the market. And the beauty is the market finally appreciates the difference. It's a new way of doing business in poultry farming.

"Damien said that in a rough-hewn industry, he had an ideal model because it relied upon using the proven professional standards he'd successfully developed. He stressed that my role would be running the business, not working the day-to-day operations. Initially, there would be a big hands-on element, but that I would hire workers to help with the labor."

Finn put on an accent, which Alex assumed to be Damien, and continued. "Titan is a professional brand; it has marketing consistency, guaranteeing success in building the brand; professional administration; support; training; and streamlined efficiencies, which would take years for you to develop on your own. We'll be partners in the Titan success.

"With the production efficiencies and standardized operation procedures that Titan would bring to the party, the performance of poultry farming would be elevated, and we'd be competitive in an up-and-coming market of organic cage-free chicken farming."

Finn took a sip of his beer and placed it on the ground between them. He put his elbows on his knees and his fists together as he turned his head to Alex and continued.

"The *promise* was that Titan would instruct us every step of the way, building it into a successful business. And, the farms were adaptable on a sliding scale for small, medium, and large farmers to invest in the model. This was something we could do, Alex. We had the capital to go after it in a small way and build it. You can see that, can't you?"

He stopped and looked at Alex, searching to see if he understood, then continued.

"So, after we got home, they kept calling and sending us webinars to look at, numbers of the other farms we could contact. They recapped the financials, which always showed the strength of the Titan model. Titan would bring the systems and procedures that would build a cash business. They would provide training and support to ensure that we would be able to ramp up quickly and get to a positive cash flow within ninety days. They said we would need three months of working capital outside of the investment with Titan and major equipment purchases.

"He said it was a business that could never dry up, that brought in a lot of income, and that was a recession proof, high-ticket/high-profit, year-round business. He pressed on us that each of the existing franchise farms achieved at least a $50,000 profit the first year and grew from there. Damien provided financial model templates, which outlined the yearly potential growth and profitability. It looked like a proven and profitable business model. Damien Miller's model farm and the financial performances were remarkable. Everyone said so!"

Finn sat back in his chair and looked around. He seemed spent.

"Did you have an attorney look at the contract before you signed it?" Alex said.

Finn looked over at Alex. "Yeah. I did. He said it looked clean. Standard. And based on proven profitability, declared it a reasonable investment."

Alex waited and watched Finn's face contort slightly with pain. "But it was all based on a lie."

Chapter 3

Back from their trip to the farm, Charlotte reached out to Julia to give her the bad news. She was righteously disappointed. Charlotte, curled in the corner of a couch, her stocking feet beneath her, stared at her phone as she explained.

"It has to be out here in New York, Mom. We're really sorry it can't be at home. I mean that. I know how excited you were to have it at Whispering Cliffs, but it's just too much for Alex's side of the family. There's too many of them. Friends, neighbors, relatives—"

Julia tersely interrupted, "I thought you said you wanted it to be a small wedding. My goodness, we have a great many friends and acquaintances too, Charlotte. Most of them in California, did you think of that?"

"Mom, I'm mostly talking about the Macchi family. It would be a hardship for some of them to take time off work and travel across the country. The expense for all of them, the travel time. We don't want them to have to deal with a destination wedding. It needs to be in New York."

"My gosh, if it's just a matter of money, we'll take care of Alex's family. We'll get the flights and pay for the hotels. We'll take care of all of that, Charlotte," she said with pressing conviction.

"No, Mom, it just won't work. We've talked about it. The expense is only a part of it. These people have to use vacation time, and it's a big deal for them to use it so they can attend our wedding."

"Well, why wouldn't a vacation in California be a good thing? We have the Pacific Ocean for them at their disposal for goodness' sake. You know I'd take good care of them."

"I know you would, and I, we, appreciate it. Really, we do, Mom. But we just don't want them to feel like this is being shoved at them and out of their control. Also, they have their pride and wouldn't want to accept anything, and then it could just turn complicated, and people's feelings will get hurt. *We* don't want the day to be anything other than one filled with happiness. Please, Mom, no hard feelings. I'll let you help me plan it on this end, okay? Really, if you have any suggestions about something in New York, I'm happy to hear it."

Charlotte could hear Julia's sighs and disappointment, but she also knew her mom would rally. Especially if Charlotte let her have control of the strings in New York.

"Good God, Charlotte. I guess I understand. If it has to be out there, I'll help with the arrangements. And you know, we aren't members of the New York Yacht Club, but I'm sure we could hold the event there, the ceremony and the reception? You could have the ceremony outside by the sea, not the Pacific of course, but the Atlantic, I suppose, would have to do. What do you think about that idea?"

Charlotte listened, amused and relieved as her mom began brainstorming. Julia continued, "I understand you don't want to have the ceremony in a church, but St. Patrick's in the city could be lovely, and I could book the reception at the Carlyle or the Peninsula or the Ritz, which would be wonderful too. What do you think about those ideas?"

"Thanks, Mom. I think they sound good. I want to discuss the ideas with Alex, and then I'll get back to you. We have to decide this month, so that will be a factor. Or available dates. I'm not sure."

"Well, your father and I will be there in a few days, and if we're going to have the wedding out there, I'll need to know immediately so we can start to book things. Get with Alex and get back with me as soon as possible." Julia barely paused for a breath.

"Oh, Charlotte, I just had an amazing idea. What about one of the Gold Coast mansions? My friend just had her daughter's wedding at Oheka Castle in Long Island. I understand it was very tasteful. They have over thirty guestrooms, so we could probably get many of them, but now that I'm thinking of it, why would we share? We wouldn't want your day to be side by side with some awful corporate event. Let me do some checking on the castles in the area."

"Castles? Mom, I don't know, this sounds really big,

and we don't want big."

"It doesn't have to be a big group, but the setting, Charlotte, the setting has to be just right. They have acres and acres of gardens and lawns. We could set something up outside if you'd prefer. Oh, this might work after all. You know we'll pay for everything, father of the bride thing. The Macchis can't complain about holding the wedding on Long Island? Speak with Alex as soon as we get off the phone. I'm going to need some direction to get this started. How many people do you think you'll be inviting?"

"Okay, I got it. I'll get back to you, and when you're in town, we'll spend some time with you guys looking at a couple places. Sound good?"

"Yes, I think this will work. I'll find the best wedding planner in Manhattan. I'm sure they'll be delighted to meet with us next week. Oh, Charlotte, we'll make it a wonderful day," she said with great enthusiasm.

"A mansion? The Gold Coast? The Carlyle, St. Pat's? This is sounding pretty big all of a sudden, honey," Alex said with concern when she told him. Sitting next to each other at her office desk, they were looking on her computer at images of the grand estates built during the Gatsby era, strung along Long Island's famous Gold Coast.

"I know," she said, laughing. "But really, we have to get serious about the guest list. That number alone might force us into a choice. Who do you want to invite?"

He shrugged. "I don't know, my family and friends.

Geez," he said, squinting at the screen. "Look at the Guggenheim Estate. They built four castles. I guess the fifty-thousand-square-footer, Hempstead House, wasn't big enough. I wonder what it costs to heat that place?"

"Alex, we have to get serious. Obviously, we want family and friends, and of course, we want Petunia, Leonora, and Andria to be flower girls. Oh, I can't wait to see them coming down the aisle!" she said, giving his arm a soft punch of enthusiasm.

"So, who else do we want in the wedding party?" he said, sitting back. "I've got Tony, and you've got Isabella. Do you want Charles and Carey to be in the wedding?"

Some of the joy left her face. "No. I don't want Carey to be a part of the wedding. I mean, I know I have to invite her, and I'm sure she'll come. Mom would insist, and I know Carey will be very curious. And Charles, you don't want him to stand up for you, do you?"

"I will if you want me to. He's your brother, so of course, he could be in the wedding. It's up to you," he said, clasping his hands behind his head, rocking back in the chair.

"If we have Charles, then you'll have two groomsmen, and I'll only have one bridesmaid. I could ask Lauren and Abby, and then I'll have three with Isabella. If you ask Tony, Michael, Nick, and Charles, that would be four on your side. God, if you have Charles, then I'll have to ask Carey!" she said, panicking.

"You don't have to ask her. You don't have to do anything you don't want to do," he said, being supportive.

"This is our day. We can do whatever we want."

Charlotte looked down and spun the engagement ring on her hand, still getting used to its feel. "Mom thinks it will be awkward, and a lot of people will ask questions if I don't have them in it. But I don't know. I can't think of anything worse than to be standing beside you on our day, our beautiful day, and looking over and seeing Carey standing beside me. It wouldn't feel authentic. And if she were honest with herself, Carey wouldn't want to be in the wedding either. I don't know what to do," she said miserably.

"Well then, why don't we just have Isabella and Tony? One on each side, keep it small?" he said, grabbing a legal pad, starting to make a list.

"I think we need to do that. I'm sorry if this creates a problem with your family. I hope it doesn't, Alex. I don't want us to start our lives off with anyone feeling left out."

"Hey, don't worry about that. They're not going to feel left out. They only want us to be happy and to be there for the celebration. They'll be fine with whatever we decide."

She felt some relief. "Okay, then just the four of us at the altar. And if we *are* going to have an aisle, what is that going to look like? Outside, inside, morning, noon, night?"

"You know," said Alex, pointing at the screen, "I'm beginning to like Julia's idea about Oheka Castle. I know it's big, but what if we had a private wedding ceremony with just family, the inner circle, in the garden or somewhere, and then after the service we could have a larger reception."

"Yes! We can make the reception as big as we want. That would work. We could have a big dance with all the relatives."

"Great! We did it," he said, writing the word *dance* on the legal pad under the word *wedding* and underlining it. "Done. So, we should plan on having the wedding when it is warmer. How about June? Do you want to be a June bride?"

"A June bride." She smiled. "Marrying the perfect man. I couldn't be happier, Alex." She leaned over and kissed him.

Alex playfully pushed her away from him and said, "Hey, how would your mom feel about hiring Bon Jovi for the dance?"

Charlotte laughed. "Bon Jovi? It's not a rock concert!"

"I just thought since money's no object. You can't blame a guy for trying."

"Well, don't joke. Especially with Mom. If you tell her you want them, she'd probably do it. Despite my objections. She practically worships you."

"I know exactly how to influence Julia Carrows, my dear, and I'm not afraid to become the cavalry when this show gets out of hand." Alex gave her a devilish look. "So... what about Bruce Springsteen?"

Charlotte laughed. "Stop. No. We'll find a band, but how about one a little more practical?"

"Practical? A Carrows wedding practical? Good luck with that."

Henry Carrows was waiting for Julia, Charlotte, and Alex to come downstairs so they could leave for dinner. Sitting at the kitchen table in Charlotte's townhome, he was listening with rapt attention while his seven-year-old granddaughter, Petunia, told him a story.

She held a single finger in the air between them, intently making her point to Henry. "And so, I told her that no, she wasn't really running, she was *galloping*."

She sat back, finished, looking pleased, and gave him a sly smile, the freckles playing across her nose, her long brown hair wild and curly. She looked almost exactly like Charlotte had at the same age. It was like a new beginning again for him.

"And what did she say, your friend? How did it make her feel when you corrected her with such eloquence?"

Petunia scrunched up her face and gave it some consideration. She tilted her head and said, "Well, I expect she was glad that she learned a new word. You know horses usually gallop but people can too," she said, still pressing her point.

"So, you sold her on the idea that a word can have more than one meaning. A different use, a distinction. You showed leadership, Petunia. How did it feel to know that you had such command of the English language?"

She crinkled her forehead, confused. "Grandpa, I don't think I know all your words. You use really big words sometimes."

Henry smiled. "Yes, but you can learn to use them too. As a matter of fact, I think it's time I introduce you to a new game." He raised an eyebrow, enticing her with the word, and continued, "Every day, even if I'm not here, you'll text me your word of the day, or I'll text you. Okay? We'll promise to use that word at least once, properly, that day. What do you think?"

"I guess so," she said, shrugging her small shoulders, uncertain.

"All right then," Henry said, holding out his arms for her to come into them. He pulled her up onto his knee and took his billfold out of his jacket pocket, laying it open in front of them on the table. He reached inside and pulled out a $500 bill.

"This is a $500 bill. A history lesson first, sweet one. That's President William McKinley on the front. They don't make this bill anymore, and what's interesting is that the legal tender, or value of the bill, says $500, but, because it is so rare, it's worth more. Much more than the value shown. Closer to $800 for the right collector."

Petunia picked it up and looked at it closely. Henry continued, "So the word today will be *tender*."

"I thought tender meant like soft, like a kitten's fur. Not that Mom is ever going to let me get one of those," she said, dramatically rolling her eyes.

"Exactly. It has many meanings. But in this case, it means an offer or payment to satisfy an obligation. This $500 bill is yours, Petunia. As my offer of payment for us to proceed with our word game. Will you accept the deal?

Think carefully, now," he said, putting his finger in the air. "Accepting a deal is a very serious matter."

She hopped down, still staring at the money, and said, "I think you got a deal, Grandpa. Thanks!" She looked at him and smiled, delighted.

"My pleasure, angel. I look forward to many more engaging opportunities to further your education." Henry smiled with great satisfaction, certain their game would be priceless.

After the babysitter arrived, the four of them went to dinner to celebrate the engagement at a beautiful Italian restaurant near the High Line in Chelsea. Charlotte and Julia had their heads together while Alex explained to Henry what they were about to experience. "I've never been here, but I've heard great things about it."

They entered the restaurant, the live piano music and European luxury charmingly decorating the room. "We thought it would be a good idea to order the Captain's Menu for the four of us, and let the capable chefs and sommeliers treat us to the five courses. An antipasto, secondo, and two pastas to share. And, of course, the dolce. They have a chocolate *budino*, with blackberries and crème fraîche gelato, which I've heard is very good."

Henry enjoyed Alex's company and couldn't be happier that the discord that had existed between him and his daughter not so long ago had nearly vanished. The news of Charlotte's engagement to Alex had only added another layer of rapport, and his wife's excitement was contagious. Eating his Kobe carpaccio and olives antipasti, Henry was highly amused listening to Julia and Charlotte making plans.

"Charlotte, this is all coming together beautifully," Julia was saying. "We were extremely lucky that Oheka Castle still had a weekend available in June. So the third weekend of June, I've gone ahead and booked about twenty-six rooms. There's another small group in residence at that time." She frowned. "But I don't think they will give us any trouble. A lady's garden club—so about six to ten stray women may be lurking. Hmm, I'll have to give that some thought. The gardens are just beautiful. I'm so glad we'll be having the ceremony outside. I always thought it should be outside, even when I thought we were going to have it at Whispering Cliffs.

"Tomorrow, everyone," she continued, "we have an appointment to tour the grounds and meet with the caterer. The wedding planners we met with today will meet us there. We'll look it over and tour the suites and then, of course, we have to meet with the photographer and the florist and get the invitations done, and Alex, have you decided what kind of music you might like for the dance? Charlotte mentioned that you'd talked about it."

Alex smiled at his beautiful and happy mother-in-law-to-be and winked at Charlotte. "Music, flowers, catering, the *band*—really, I'm just hoping that you'll tell me when and where to show up." He smiled as he reached out to hold Charlotte's hand.

"I can't wait to get out there tomorrow," said Charlotte. "I invited Isabella, but she can't get away," she said with disappointment as she speared an olive. The sommelier filled her glass with a Signorello Proprietary Red. "They're four hours away, and I guess something's come up with their business. She needs to be home this weekend for Finn."

Henry happily ate and watched as his wife and daughter bubbled along. Experiencing real joy in this celebration, he reflected on how right Julia had been about their family being fractured. It had been out of character for her to go behind his back and hire Alex to help solve their personal problems. But now, looking at his daughter and the man she was going to marry, and his wife, all together, he knew she had been very wise.

"I've been really worried about them," Alex was saying. "What I really want to do is just go in there and fix it, but Finn is holding me back." He shook his head and frowned. "He's being stubborn. I think his pride is holding him back from accepting my help."

"What are we talking about here?" said Henry, resurfacing, still halfway chewing on a piece of succulent beef.

"My sister, Isabella, and her husband, Finn, are having some legal difficulties with their business. It's tragic. I'd really like to help them, but I'm not sure how to begin, especially since Finn is resisting."

"They're both resisting," said Charlotte, shaking her head.

Henry picked up his wine glass. "Legal difficulties? Tell me about it."

"Boys!" interrupted Julia. "I don't want a long legal business conversation here tonight! This is a celebration dinner. We have important decisions to make. Specifically, the conversation about the wedding party." Julia raised her eyebrow in Charlotte's direction.

Charlotte didn't parlay but looked to Alex for support and said, "Well, I want to talk about it. Isabella is my best friend, and she's going to be my sister-in-law. Both of them are wonderful, hardworking people who are being screwed over by this guy, this company that they got into business with. Alex and I were up in Ithaca where they live last week and got filled in. It's really awful."

Henry piqued to this. "Really? Well, that doesn't sound good," he said as Julia gave him a discouraging look. He turned to Alex. "Alex, can you fill me in, *briefly,*" he said, acknowledging his wife's subtle warning.

Alex explained. "In a nutshell, they signed a franchise contract and started a poultry farm with Titan Farms out of New Jersey. Finn and Isabella had a small unused farmstead in upstate New York, and they used the inheritance money my father left to each of us as capital. But, unfortunately, they've discovered that the business was based on fraud, and they're staring at the real possibility of losing everything they put into it. All their money, maybe future earnings, possibly bankruptcy. From the looks of it, the brand, the owner, is corrupt, and it was all a scheme to lock them into servitude only for his profitability."

Henry Carrows loved a good scheme and was highly interested whenever one was afoot. Money was not a primary motivator for him. He loved nothing more than a good hunt.

"I'm sorry to hear that, Alex," Henry said with a gleam in his eye as he reached for his glass.

"Yes, that sounds very upsetting," said Julia, giving Henry a knowing, anxious look. He smiled back coyly, the communication between them transparent.

"They're such good people," said Charlotte. "Isabella and I have become so close. I'd trust her with my life. You'd admire them, Dad," she said with confidence. "I know you would. They have this wonderful home that they've renovated all by themselves. They have literally built the home of their dreams. I wish we could help them. If only there were some way." She shook her head and dramatically sighed.

Alex glanced quickly at Charlotte and soberly said, "I've offered them money to tide them over, but Finn just refuses to involve anyone else or their money. I also thought I might be able to look into the guy, Damien Miller, the owner of Titan Farms, a little more closely using Macchi & Macchi, but Finn's refusing that help as well. He says he wants to sort this out himself. But my concern is that he's up against someone who doesn't care about the rules or the law or decency."

Charlotte gave Alex's arm a squeeze and turned to her

father. "Yes, Dad," she said, "just think of it." She leaned over the table. "There is this criminal out there, roping innocent victims into his scheme, hurting good people, *my new family*. You know, Petunia just adores them." Charlotte stared pointedly at him.

Henry sat back and stared at his beautiful daughter and realized with pride where this was going. She was asking for his help. His very special kind of help. For the first time in her life.

He beamed at her as she tilted her head and gave him a sly smile.

"Charlotte?" Julia said softly.

Henry looked at Julia and then at everyone around the table. Finally, he said, "My darling daughter. Using Petunia in your closing argument was fairly transparent but an excellent strategy. My dear, if you or your family is ever in trouble, all you need to do is ask. We're here to help."

Henry noticed Alex staring at Charlotte's profile. He appeared to be somewhat uncomfortable. "Alex, I know this may sound a bit odd and completely out of the blue, but I've just had a remarkable idea. Julia and I have been wondering what we should give you as a wedding gift."

Henry looked at Julia and said, "Julia?"

She knew where he was going and gave him a nod of approval.

Henry continued, "Good. We discussed this, and we agreed we wanted to do something very special for the two of you. We didn't just want to give you a trip or a home or artwork but something you would both value more. What if I were to say that as our wedding gift to you, I would help Finn and Isabella sort out the mess that this businessman has put them in. I would help them as our gift to you both, to ensure that they have their dream of living in their country home with the business they invested in running profitably. It wasn't exactly what I envisioned as our gift, but I believe it's a package made for both of you."

"Dad," said Charlotte as she reached across the table for his hand. "Thank you," she said softly.

Alex, startled, jumped in. "Henry, Julia, thank you for the generous offer," he said as he laid his hands heavily on the table and gave Charlotte an incredulous look. "We should have discussed this, honey. I'm not sure I'm comfortable accepting something on behalf of my sister and her husband. And I'm not really certain what you're proposing here either, Mr. Carrows. Finn and Isabella are devastated for themselves and the situation they're in but also for all the people they've met who're being taken advantage of by this guy. When I offered to help, Finn said that they didn't want to be a part of somehow getting themselves released only to sit back and watch the rest of the farmers left behind to suffer. As of this moment, the farmers want to wage a united front. Finn included. He said he wanted to be a part of the group. To do the right thing together. Wherever that leads."

"Alex, you're not understanding what we're offering," said Henry, waving his hand, dismissing the objections as if they were ridiculous. "I'm not saying that I'll just give them money. I'm saying that I will fix this situation. Permanently. For everyone who has been swindled by this guy." Henry, sporting a wide boyish grin, threw his hands up in the air for emphasis. "It's done."

Henry didn't wait for a response from Alex but signaled over the sommelier, who immediately came to his side. He whispered fairly loudly in his ear to bring them champagne. The sommelier, eyebrows raised, scurried away as Henry said to Alex, "Your sister needs some help, Alex. Let's level the playing field here and see what makes this guy tick. Then, we'll take him to his knees. That simple."

Alex did not look sold on the idea. Henry looked at Julia, signaling her to go in and close the deal.

"Yes." Julia picked up the thread and the heart of the idea. "Alex. This is a gift we can give you. The gift of helping your family, which I know is central to who you both are. Let us help Isabella and Finn. There's no question we'll find a solution."

Charlotte looked at Alex, who appeared flabbergasted. "Honey," she said to him gently, "I saw the pain on Finn's face and Isabella's worry. When I say, when *you* say, that we would do anything to help them to make this better, and if I then turn away an offer to do just that, then I don't think I can live with myself. They're the good guys. Our family. We can help them. We should do this."

Alex sat back, staring at the three Carrowses who were waiting for his response. He shook his head but said, "I'd like that as well. Henry, Julia, we thank you for this gift. As nontraditional as it is. It will mean a great deal to many people and not just my Isabella." He looked at Charlotte. "We're going to have to convince Finn, you know."

"I can't imagine that to be an actual obstacle," said Henry, especially happy. He had himself a hunt.

Chapter 4

Damien Miller loved his sweet baby. He'd had the windows of his customized Audi S8 deeply tinted as he did all of his hot cars. It was his trademark. But this sweet baby, with a vanity plate that read TITAN 1, was the nicest car he'd ever owned. He told himself it was essential that he looked like a successful businessman, and the $129,000 price tag for Titan 1 had been worth every penny.

Foghat was cranking on the nineteen-speaker Bang & Olufsen stereo system. The $14,000 for that upgrade had been more than worth it too. Titan Industries was paying off! Rolling through the city, sunglasses on, he felt like a big badass shark gliding silently along in the deep, dark waters. No one saw him coming. Lost in his image, pleased with himself, he was jolted out of his rapture by the phone.

He turned down the music and pulled up the call.

"Talk to me," said Damien.

"I got another one," said Walter Wilson—his president

of development. "A guy from Illinois. He and his wife want to come in next month."

"That works. So, we got five in the water now?"

"Yeah. I was thinking we make them into two groups, and maybe by next month, we'll have six new interested buyers, and we can split them three and three."

"Sounds good. Hey, I got another call coming in, I gotta go."

"Sure thing," said Walter as Damien ended the call.

He didn't have another call, he just wanted to cruise some more without interruption. Business, even good news, was harshing his buzz. He cranked up the tunes again, "Slow Ride" pounding out as Damien rocked along, shaking his head and smiling at his successful life. It had all been so easy! He thought back to where it all began.

Damien had always been an ambitious, hardworking guy. He'd skipped the college experience because he already had a successful poultry farm, which he had been working at since eighth grade. By the time he was eighteen, he'd purchased his first small home and more importantly, his first hot car.

By that time, he knew all there was to know about the poultry business. Raised on a Christmas tree farm in New Jersey, his father came from a family of farmers. His father, Frank, had a rotation of woody crops and a lumber business on his land, while his older brother raised garden vegetables such as escarole, endive, onions, and squash in a neighboring state. Damien got lucky when his dad's brother unexpectedly dropped dead. A bachelor and childless, the uncle had had a soft spot in his heart for his nephew, Damien, and left him a small parcel of land that was semidetached from the rest of his farm.

Upon receipt of this golden property when Damien was in eighth grade, he quickly put it to good use and started a small chicken farm. With the help of his father, they penned in the land and built a couple of chicken coops, got a brooder, and bought some chicks. Damien cared for and watched over the baby chicks in the heated pen and eventually transferred them into the coop. He purchased some Buff Orpington egg layers, which produced around three hundred fifty eggs a year, and started a small business. Totally dedicated to his birds, he kept a careful eye on their condition, and he and his dad even moved a small rundown trailer onto the property for Damien to live in while tending to his birds. His mom wasn't too jazzed about it, but his father was impressed with his son's dedication and wanted to support his budding entrepreneur. He built a second pen on his property, repeating the process but with dual purpose Rhode Island Reds, some of which were broody and would do the hatching job for him. The others he let be cage free and sold to another local farmer as fryers.

After some time, good luck, and dedication, Damien had a profitable business. He took some classes in business, accounting, and technology and set up an online accounting system, which would easily and beautifully display his profit and loss and balance sheets and other reports, which he gathered up and took to his local bank. Impressed with his budding investment, the bank agreed to help him finance the purchase of a small feed company that had come on the market. Damien grabbed it and branded it Titan Feed, which became the new sister company of the chicken farm he called Titan Farms. He was a bona fide businessman!

He knew the adage that you needed to spend more to make more was true, and that's exactly what he did. For his next small business, he purchased more land and equipment, which was a huge leap forward. His motto had always been Go Big or Go Home, and he would need about $1,000,000 to purchase the land and equipment to open his first large-scale farm. This was no problem. He simply pulled together a false schedule of receivables on Titan Farms and used that as collateral on a loan. The idiots at the bank weren't going to call all his fake customers. They believed in financials, and he was more than happy to provide them with successful ones. He was a self-promoter and used his Barnum and Bailey-esque pitches and boasts, and people just always fucking believed him. Titan Farms was a hit!

He kept Titan Farms lean by working a small staff of illegal immigrants six days a week and paying them cash to avoid payroll taxes. It was a tremendous amount of work capturing the niche market in his community. His birds had access to grass, insects, sunshine, fresh air, and seed supplied by Titan Feed, but Damien made money.

Yup. It was looking good. He was a natural-born salesman and worked hard over the next year to sell his chickens to local farmers and markets. He kept his overhead low and was making some good money and even got himself a boat and married his high school sweetheart, Linda. She was a pistol and loved the excitement of driving his souped-up Camaro with the illegally tinted windows. They were good together and shared the same vision of becoming America's next big success story.

They were doing fine. He and Linda purchased a fixer-upper on a big piece of land, and they had a baby girl and named her MaryLou after his mother. Linda quit her job to be a stay-at-home mom and to begin living and promoting the Miller/Titan brand from the home front. She found great enjoyment in remodeling and decorating their home and establishing relationships with their tony neighbors. She too believed that her life was on an upward trajectory of major proportions.

———————

Damien pulled into the lot of his flagship farm, past a small sign that said Titan Farms, and around to a large trailer parked on the property. He grimaced as he got out of Titan 1 and looked at the piece-of-shit trailer, his company headquarters. Not that many people knew that.

Walking toward him was his foreman, Roland Kylian, who looked like he had something on his mind. Damien pulled out his phone and pretended to take a call, pointing at it and mouthing to the foreman that he had to take it.

He walked up the three wooden steps to the trailer door and was pleased to see his foreman walking back toward the chickens. When he opened the door and put the phone away, his admin was nowhere in sight. Great. He went down the narrow hall to his office and slammed the door.

His feet on the desk, he pulled up his email and scanned it, perturbed by all the mail from his franchisees. It looked like they were group emailing him now. They'd organized. That pissed him off. He got Walter back on the phone.

"Damien," said Walter.

"So, we've still got that office space rented, right? For the days we've got the prospects in town?"

"Of course. Nicest office building in Morristown."

"Stage it better than last time, Walter. I want that place to look like we really live there. You got that? Appearances are everything."

"Got it. I'm bringing the truck over to the place the night before with all that shit I'm storing in the garage. Maps with pins stuck in them, financials, spreadsheets, thick volumes of investment portfolios, office equipment, family pictures, and your stuff."

Damien smiled as he looked over at the nicely framed mock-ups of fake news stories about him through the years. They looked incredibly impressive and legit.

"We gotta land these folks, Walter. I'm getting the feeling that we may have a turnover on our hands."

"The farmer from Ohio called me this morning—"

Damien cut him off, "Sorry, I got another call I gotta take. I'll see you this afternoon at the architects'. The new building design should be ready."

He clicked off and sat back, satisfied, his mind drifting again to his spectacular genesis.

Titan Farms and Titan Feed were running smoothly, and one of the beauties of having a couple of businesses going at the same time was that Damien always had his own labor pool. He could share the employees with whichever company had the jobs that needed covering. He would never suffer from the burden that a lot of his competitors did when their employees didn't show up or called in sick. For some reason, there was a lot of sickness in the chicken and farming industry. A lot of vomiting, pregnant girlfriends vomiting, kids vomiting, they were all vomiting, cars breaking down, grandparents dying, a lot of drama in general. But it didn't concern him; he always had the coverage. In fact, it kept his payroll down, and he worked his crews into believing that he was the best guy in the world to be so understanding and patient with their sporadic work ethic. His flexibility allowed them to overlook the fact that he didn't give them insurance benefits and paid cash salaries.

But it wasn't enough for Damien. He knew his feed and farming business was only the next rung—time to branch out. He'd always been interested in boats, fast boats in particular. But fast boats wouldn't make him money. Fishing boats would. Time to go to the bank!

The bank was only too happy to help him secure a loan to become a part owner of a large fishing trawler. Damien figured managing a fishing boat crew couldn't be any worse than the daily herding of a bunch of farmhands. He would just buy into a currently productive, but struggling, small operation. Maybe a skipper who owned his own boat and who was in need of some major repairs and major capital to complete them. No problem finding that patsy. Damien would come on board, assuring them that he would only be an investor and would schedule his return on investment to come due beginning two years from his initial investment. Over that time, he would learn the business through them and their sweat equity.

One of Damien's greatest assets had been the hiring of Samara Poe. She'd been a hungry, local independent legal eagle. Damien had used her legal prowess to great advantage in the past, and this time would be no different. Samara would write up a contract, making sure it was really big and cumbersome, full of daily late fees, interest rates, clauses that could make the owner fall into default on the loan without even recognizing the legal loophole, etc. The next step would be to default the fishing guys early and force the payment of the loan, which they would be unprepared to pay. Oops, sorry. He would buy them out for a rock bottom, pennies on the dollar price, and it would all work out beautifully for Damien. He would inherit an established fishing crew and business with all the know-how, licenses, and skill. Suddenly, he was a fishing magnate! It was all too easy. Titan Fisheries was born! Bada bing, bada boom.

At least, that was his vision. These things never

work exactly to plan. What happened was that he found Wellington Fisheries, a one-boat father/son ownership, which met his criteria for struggling and needing capital. They'd been in the fishing business for generations, and over the last five years had come into a series of unlucky and tragic events that put them into a hole they were having trouble finding their way out of. They were seasoned, lifelong fisherman and skippers who knew how to use their boat and crew to make a profit, but too many bits of bad luck had put them in the weeds.

After securing the investment loan from Damien, father and son, owners of Wellington Fisheries, would receive about $150,000, which Damien took out of his personal portfolio. Next, Damien went to the bank, secured a loan for a second fishing trawler for about $300,000 after giving them as collateral the note from Wellington Fisheries for their bigger ship, which was worth more than $500,000 after the repairs and upgrades he financed had been made.

About six months into the loan, the note was defaulted on for "illegal practices," which was a large and unwieldy category. Samara threw this one in the contract and then brought it down like a hammer on the Wellingtons, making the note payable immediately—that same day. She used an expired license with the state of New Jersey as evidence. Yes, it had only been expired for two days, and the Wellington boys were in the process of renewing, but it was a gotcha. A minor gotcha, but who cared?

Samara was betting that they didn't have the money to

hire a lawyer to begin the process of obtaining some kind of relief or complaint. She had them in her net. Another nail in the coffin they put in the contract was that Titan Fisheries had first right to the option of securing any future loans, which meant the Wellington boys had to go back to Damien to ask for the money to pay Damien in the first place.

The Wellington boys were pissed, but over the next couple of weeks, Samara went into legal war with threats of immediate evictions and closures, scaring the crap out of them. She also made sure Damien didn't answer his phone. Eventually, when Samara felt the time was right, she instructed Damien it was time for him to go in and rescue them. The option he presented to them was simple. He would buy their boat, and they and their crews could keep their jobs. The father would stay with the old Wellington boat as skipper, and the son would become the new skipper of the newly purchased Titan Fisheries boat with his own crew. This way, Damien wouldn't need to find and hire seasoned fisherman who knew and understood the intricacies of the business and boats. Unfortunately for the Wellingtons, they accepted the deal. They didn't have the time, money, or resources to fight it.

Back at Titan Farms, Damien was also ready to capitalize on his brand. He'd named his brand Titan because he had that vision for himself. Just like fucking Trump, he wanted to plaster his name everywhere.

His next step then, naturally, was to become a national brand. Damien knew that the four big boys in the chicken industry were not remotely threatened by him, but Damien began wondering how he could become number five. He figured he'd just use their business model and replicate their success.

Basically, the big chicken boys had a deal with contract farmers. The big boys would own the chicks and drop them off at their contract farms where the farmer would raise them for roughly six to eight weeks, kinda like daycare. When the fast-growing chickens were grown, the big chicken boys would show up with a truck and take them away. The farmer didn't own the chickens, the big boys did. And that's where all the profit lay. Damien thought this was a splendid idea.

He had the vision of expanding his successful model and bundling it like the big-boy plan. To build his brand, Damien knew it would be easier to penetrate other markets by partnering with people who would work in their own backyards to bring awareness of his Titan brand. If he were to just open more Titan Farms himself, it would take an enormous amount of capital and energy to run them effectively. Instead, he would find other people to put in the capital, let them suffer through the start-up operations, and they would not only be building his Titan brand, but he would make them pay royalties for letting them use it. Making money while he slept. Perfect! After he had built up fifty or a hundred small- to medium-sized farms, the big boys would come calling, and he could flip them, sell them and make millions. It was an awesome plan.

He hired some personnel, a president of development,

Walter Wilson, who would work with his lawyer, Samara Poe. Samara and Walter had worked with each other in the past and would cobble together the development plan and documents to get his party started. His accountant and buddy for the last ten years, Ryan Foster, could be counted on to pull the magical financial funny numbers together that would entice his potential contract farmers.

The four of them, Damien, Walter, Samara, and Ryan went to work and created a three hundred-page contract that the Titan poultry farmers would sign to share in the success and become a partner in Titan Farms. Samara and Walter put together a document that would lock down the farmers in perpetuity.

The biggest selling point, and the one they published on the new Titan Farms franchising website, was the EBITDA number. People were blown away by it. The numbers had pretty significant profit margins, and it began to attract attention. He needed these numbers to attract well-capitalized operators who would be willing to invest in his business. And like chum in the water, they came. It was all so easy!

Chapter 5

You're not still upset with me, are you, Alex?" Charlotte asked as they drove through the north shore of Long Island to meet with Finn and Isabella.

Alex, his hands on the wheel, looked at Charlotte, lovely in a white fur jacket, her eyes locked on his with love and concern. "No," he said, turning his attention back to the road. "How could I stay angry with you?"

"Good," she said, looking out the window, seeing occasional glimpses of grand houses and fortified walls. "They'll go along with it, Alex. This guy is destroying lives. Entire families. Putting Finn and Isabella aside, he needs to be stopped. We both knew we could help them, and you know why." She laid her head back on the headrest and looked at him.

"I was just surprised. I didn't know you'd been considering asking your dad for help."

"Things have changed so much between us. I watch Dad with Petunia, and he's so filled with love for her. Mom too. We've worked really hard to get to where we are today. The last few years, you know how wonderful they've been. We have respect for each other now. I was looking at him that night, and I was thinking about something my mom said about this just being who we are."

She looked down at her engagement ring and considered. "And I thought about how allowing them, us, to wield our power for good shouldn't be a bad thing. Or, at the very least, wield it for the right causes. I think I can live with that."

"I can too. I got a kick out of him giving us advice on how to convince Finn and Isabella."

"My parents had to get back to California. Let's face it, honey, he considers us the B team." She laughed.

Having reached the castle grounds on the highest point on Long Island's Cold Spring Harbor, they made their way up the long drive lined with hundreds of red cedar trees. As Alex and Charlotte entered the French-inspired castle built in the gilded age of the 1920s, they marveled at the wrought iron railing on the foyer's grand staircase, which clearly paid homage to the famous staircase at Chateau Fontainebleau in France.

They met up with Isabella and Finn and toured the grounds, stopping at one of the many reflecting pools. "It's like a dream," said Isabella as the four of them continued to walk on the upper terrace lawn toward the marble gazebo. "We're not that far out of the city—yet look around us. It's so beautiful and peaceful, I can hardly believe it's real. I can only imagine how gorgeous it will be in June."

"I can just imagine the real-life Gatsby parties being held here. There's an eighteen-hole golf course over there too," Charlotte said, pointing.

"Maybe we could get a round in before the wedding," Alex mused.

Charlotte said, "We'll all arrive on Friday. Only the family. My mom had a talk with the ladies of the garden club who'd reserved rooms." She laughed. "I believe they received a very generous donation to walk away. We've got a buyout of the place for the weekend."

"The wedding's at five, and the reception starts around six. We could get in some golf, right?" Alex said.

"I think so," said Charlotte. "There are stables here too. So, the flower girls could get a horse ride around the grounds while the big girls do something?"

"We could do spa treatments or lounge by the pool or picnic," Isabella said. "We could even set up some games, like croquet—or wait! Bride games!"

Charlotte startled, a horrifying image popping into her mind unbidden of Carey dressed as a toilet paper bride. She linked her arm with Isabella and said cautiously, "We'll talk about that. How about we go inside and warm up. Anyone ready for a cocktail?"

The group was more than willing to travel inside. They entered the library with its high bookcases filled with leather books and ordered drinks, which were served to them like they were lords of the manor just back from the hunt. An underlying smell of mustiness lingered, and the room was replete with replica period furniture and paintings.

"To Charlotte and Alex," Finn said as he raised his glass in a small toast. They relaxed into the sofas of a quaint and private seating area near the fire. "Hey," he said after taking a sip of his drink, looking around. "I wonder where that secret passageway is hidden. They said it was in the library, right?"

"Yeah, we'll have to get them to tell us where it is," Alex said, his eyes communicating to Charlotte that it was time. "Listen, guys, we want to thank you again for coming, but we have a special favor to ask. Something you can do for us, for our wedding."

The seriousness of Alex's voice seemed to change the mood. "Alex, of course," said Isabella. "We'd do anything for you."

"All right," said Alex. "Remember you said that because it has to do with you. The thing is, we want to help you with the business, and the favor we ask of you is that you accept our help. Because we *can* help you, we know what to do, and we have the resources to do it."

Alex put his hand up, silencing Finn, who was shaking his head and looked like he was about to jump in. "Before you say no, Finn, we want you to stop and consider if the shoe were on the other foot, if you would want to do the same thing for us."

Finn put his drink on the table in front on him. "Alex, Charlotte...no, we can't accept your money. I told you that. I know you mean well, but it's a losing proposition. We just don't think this business was even designed for success."

"We understand what you're saying," said Alex, "but we aren't offering money to float you over for the next several months." Alex watched as Finn rubbed the back of his neck as if the stress had suddenly caused a cramp. Before Finn could voice more opposition, Alex rushed to complete his offer. "What we are offering is a way for you to have it all. We're offering a way for you and Isabella to take the farm away from the company and take away any future claims they have so that you can run a successful business by yourself, which we know can happen once the contractual obligations and shenanigans go away."

Isabella put her hands over her face and began to cry. Charlotte went to her and wrapped her in her arms. "I love you, Isabella. Don't cry, it's going to be okay."

Isabella, wiping her eyes, said, "What are you saying? You guys do not need to drag yourself into the middle of this mess. Really, we'll be okay. One way or another we'll survive this, and there's always something worse. This is supposed to be a happy time for you."

Alex put his drink down and leaned in, folding his hands between his knees. "Finn, Isabella...you don't yet understand. Let me ask you a question. If we could make the Titan Farms contract go away and make you whole financially, what would you say?"

"I would say you're crazy," said Finn. "The only way any of that is going to happen is if we win in litigation, and litigation would cost a fortune, and they know we don't have a fortune, so they don't give a shit. They want us to sit down and be quiet and take whatever terms they give us even if it destroys our business and us."

"Finn, there is a way, and not through litigation or arbitration. Charlotte and I have a plan, but we're going to need your help to get it done."

Finn's mouth dropped open. He blinked rapidly and looked between Alex, Charlotte, and Isabella and rubbed his hands nervously on his pants. Alex saw him begin to tremble and said, "Take a drink there, Finn, hang on, it's all going to be okay. *We can make it be okay.* All you gotta do is say yes."

Finn took a sip of his drink and placed it on the table. In a low, unsteady voice, he said, "What exactly are you proposing, Alex? I can't imagine."

Isabella, sniffling, came over to Finn and took his hand and looked at her brother. "Alex, Charlotte, thank you. We accept." Finn looked defeated as she stared at him. "We can't do this alone anymore, Finn. And if my brother and Charlotte have a plan, then let's give them a chance to help us."

Finn nodded, searching the eyes of each of the three people staring at him.

Charlotte let out a deep breath and walked over to Isabella and gave her a hug. The first step was complete.

Finn, still confused, looked at them and said, "Ah, okay, but what's the plan?"

———————

They ordered another round of drinks and some appetizers

as Charlotte explained. "So, as you know, my family is very wealthy, and a lot of it my dad inherited, although he continues to be involved and invest himself in a variety of businesses. He likes to stay busy, and work is part of his passion. More than that, it's about making the deal. Basically, it's about winning. He loves to win, and the more difficult the chase, the better he likes it."

Charlotte looked toward the fire, changing her tone as she reflected. "He used to tell me that his father told him that they were descended from pirates and that he had pirate genes. I sort of believe him because my dad, Henry, might be considered by some people to be a pirate. Not a con man, because he raised me to believe that con men were stupid and got caught, but he likens himself more to a grifter, which he finds very satisfying."

"Yes," said Alex. "And Henry and Julia want to help you. As their wedding gift to us."

Finn squinched up his face. "Your *dad* wants to help us? Henry *Carrows* wants to help us, as *your wedding gift* from them?"

"Yes. Now you've got it," said Charlotte. "The Carrows family, and I mean the *entire* Carrows family, will put their full effort and crazy resources into helping you as their gift to Alex and me." Charlotte beamed at them.

"Oh my God! This is insane!" Isabella threw her head back and laughed. "Sorry, Charlotte, I don't mean to offend you or say that your family is insane, it's just that it's a little bit of a crazy situation, you know?"

"I'm not offended. Believe me, I understand what

you're saying, but you're just going to have to take my word for it that this is the way it is in my family."

"I think that's what the Carrows want. They want to see their Charlotte happy and their Petunia surrounded by a happy family here in New York," said Alex.

"They want us happy," said Charlotte, lacing her fingers with her fiancé's, "but let's not forget how much we're giving them in return. We'll give my dad a big, juicy, smelly, and corrupt guy to find, hunt, and destroy. It's a win-win for all of us."

"Well, all right! Thank you, Henry Carrows! What do you need from us to get this party started?" Finn said, now amped up with the belief that there was a miracle solution being handed to them.

"The first thing you need to do is become a very good actor," said Alex.

Finn barked a single laugh at the suggestion.

"I'm not kidding, Finn. You're going to have to be convincing. We need you to stop any legal action you have planned against Damien Miller and Titan and roll over. You become his best buddy and then you invite him and his wife to our wedding."

"What?" Isabella cried. "We're not going to have those assholes here at your wedding and have them ruin your day. That's not going to happen!" she said adamantly.

Charlotte put her hand over Isabella's and smiled at the nearby waitstaff who perked to Isabella's loud exclamation. "Isabella, it's okay. They won't ruin our wedding. Besides, they'll only be invited to the reception.

They *need* to be there for the next part of the plan to get underway. Believe me, every time I see them that evening, I will be smiling, and not faking it either. Get them to the wedding, Finn. The entire Carrows family will be in place, ready to meet them. Win. Win.

"Cheers!" Charlotte said as she raised her glass in celebration. "To a wonderful and *successful* wedding!"

Chapter 6

Henry and Julia once again flew back to New York, ready to begin their work. They took a suite at the Carlyle Hotel on the Upper East Side, pronouncing Charlotte's townhome too small for their purpose. Carey Carrows came with them. Charles Carrows, immersed in his new business venture on the East Coast, would drive in from Atlantic City.

The spacious suite with stunning views overlooking Central Park was replete with luxurious antiques, warm hues, and silk draperies striped in green and brown. The suite was a mix of traditional and modern with an entertainment center, bar, and large coffee table between a green velvet sofa and cream velvet armchairs. A coffee table in the center was filled with food.

Julia sat on the sofa, wearing a soft-cream suede zip-front jacket over white pants and a sweater. "Henry, try a bit less crème fraîche on your blini next time."

Henry ignored her and spooned more of the Golden

Osetra caviar onto the French-style blini and dropped it into his mouth. He picked up a napkin and went to the window and looked out. The warm afternoon sun streamed into the suite.

"He should be here any minute, Daddy," said Carey, sitting next to her mother, staring at her phone.

As if on cue, there came a knock on the door. Henry went to open it. "Charles, come in," Henry said as he turned back and walked toward the table. "You're late. Your mother was worried."

"I was not," said Julia, rising to give her son a hug.

"Hey, Mom," said Charles, lightly kissing her cheek and accepting the warm embrace. Released from Julia's grip, Charles looked to Carey, still seated.

"Hey, come here," he said, gesturing for her to stand. Carey, wearing a black Fendi mink-cuff cashmere sweater and leather pants, gave Charles a hug. She sat back down next to her mother as Charles took a chair across from them.

He leaned over and examined the iced caviar and traditional garnishes. Julia said, "There was more than two ounces of caviar here mere moments ago, Charles. I suggest you get started on it before your father comes back for more."

Charles smiled at his mother and father with adoration and said, "Are Charlotte and Alex joining us?"

"No," said Henry. "Not today. Your mother and I wanted to have a private word with the two of you first."

"I see," said Charles, sitting back. "Then I'm assuming this concerns her."

"Of course it does," Carey mumbled.

Henry regarded his children. He loved them all equally, but they were all very different. Charles was the most like himself—exuberant, high on life, and full of energy. He could be counted on to keep a level head under any situation. An asset and a credit to him, Henry could not have asked for a better son. Charlotte was the most like her mother. She had strength, charisma, charm, and beauty, but her sensitive nature held her back. Even though Charlotte was often speculative and dreamy, as an adult, he'd found an appreciation for her qualities. And thankfully, their relationship was now comfortably on firm ground. Then there was Carey, his youngest. Beautiful, wild, and sly. Julia protected her, often alluding to Henry that there was a deep vulnerability in her nature that Carey protected by pushing people away. He sensed that in her as well. Julia also speculated that it came from a fear of failure, specifically to him.

Henry took the chair next to Charles and began. "We have a campaign to launch. It will be our priority until its completion. We begin planning today on Titan Takedown. We're conducting this campaign for the benefit of a number of victims to a contractual scheme but primarily for a young couple named Isabella and Finn Laferty. Isabella, as you know, is Alex's only sister. Titan Takedown will be our wedding gift to Charlotte and Alex.

"Your mother and I have some ideas, and I've already

gathered a great deal of information. But before we begin, I'd like to say a few words." He sat back and crossed his legs, resting his arms on the chair. He had their full attention.

"Carey, I'm not unaware that you and your brother have had a difficult relationship with Charlotte. No one would ever accuse me of not being observant enough to recognize that. I have been tolerant of your direct and indirect hostilities over the years, but listen to what I am telling you now. That is over. Your blessed mother went to great difficulty to see to it that Charlotte and I were put back on course after that incident with David. Since then, you've had a number of occasions to visit civilly with your sister, but I'm not impressed by your efforts."

Carey opened her mouth to speak, but Henry held up a hand to silence her.

Julia took over. "Titan Takedown will help mend your broken fences. You'll come together in a united front, for a united purpose, and by doing that, we hope that you will begin to appreciate each other. It will make you all realize that families should love one another instead of all this pointless hostility."

"I love Charlotte," said Charles. "I always have. She knows that."

Carey made a face like she had a bad taste in her mouth and glared at Charles. "So, it's all me? Is that what you're saying?"

Henry held up his hand again and said, "This isn't a discussion. You'll do this. For us. For the family. We all learned a hard lesson while we were estranged. My relationship now with Charlotte and Petunia has given me great joy. I want the same thing for the three of you. Charles, we know you love your sister, but it's more than that. You need to spend time with each other, appreciate each other's talents. And of course, I'm sure you'll find the campaign quite entertaining.

"Carey, it's you that I'm worried about. I'll say this one more time. Hostilities end now. The two of you are just different people. You may think of her as easy or dreamy or silly or whatever, but this is your blood, your sister, the only sister you will ever have."

"Daddy," said Carey, examining her nails. "I know you mean well, and I get that she's my sister, but we don't have anything in common. I don't understand the way she thinks, and she doesn't understand me, and just too much time has passed. I think you need to be prepared that there will be *no* reconciliation between us. We'll never be friends."

"My God," said Julia, horrified, slapping the sofa between them. "Listen to what you're saying."

"No," Henry barked, startling them all. "Listen to what I'm saying. This cold war ends now. The two of you will become sisters again." Henry realized that Julia had been right. Over the years she'd told him many times to step in and straighten out their children's priorities. He'd assumed they would work through their differences as they got older, without his interference. Maybe he was getting old, but he wanted this to happen.

"Henry," said Julia softly, "stay calm, darling. Carey hears you. Don't you, Carey?" She looked at her daughter, who was staring wide-eyed at her father.

"Carey," Henry tried again, "make no mistake here, I love you very, very much. And Charles too, and Charlotte, too. You are *all* my children. I'm getting older now, and this is the gift you can give to me. Give it an effort, give it a chance, for my sake. You're both still so young; we have no idea what life will bring our way, and we need to be a family."

Carey stared at him and considered. "Okay, Daddy," she said softly. "I'll try. For you. I promise I'll make an effort. Because I love you too."

Henry walked over, relieved. Carey stood to receive her hug.

Charles, smiling comfortably in his chair, said, "Or just fake it till you make it, sis."

Henry gave him a discouraging look and realized he was going to have to stay on top of this. A reconciliation might take more time than he imagined.

Chapter 7

The next morning, Alex, Charlotte, and Finn Laferty walked through the quiet and sophisticated lobby of the Carlyle Hotel. Black marble floors glistened beneath tasteful apricot sofas. Black laminate doorways, brushed gold-leaf fixtures, and fresh flowers accompanied the group as they caught a glimpse of the timeless Bemelmans Bar as they made their way to the elevators.

"They need to get a feel for the guy," Alex said to Finn as they rode up. "Anything you can tell them about Damien will be helpful."

"I can't believe this is actually happening," Finn said, shaking his head. "I think I slept better last night than I have in a year."

As they came out of the elevator, Alex gave him a quick pat on the back. "It's real, all right. Just remember, you can tell the family anything. Don't hold anything back. You can trust them."

Finn looked at Charlotte. "You've got an amazing

family. For them to be doing this? They must be really good people."

Charlotte raised an eyebrow and smiled. "They are, as long you don't cross them."

"Not helpful, honey," Alex said, giving Finn a reassuring smile and knocking on the door. He whispered, "Give Julia and Carey a compliment. Something personal. They'll like that."

Henry opened the door. "Finn," he said, extending a hand. "Henry Carrows, come in."

As they entered, Henry gave Charlotte a hug. "How's my granddaughter today? Got the dictionary out I hope?"

"Dad." She laughed. "The word of the day is *clandestine*? And she needs to use it in a sentence?"

"It's never too early." He smiled as they walked toward the dining room.

"Everyone," said Henry, "this is Finn Laferty, husband of Isabella, Alex's sister. I'd like you to meet my family. My lovely wife, Julia, my son, Charles, and my youngest daughter, Carey."

Finn, Charlotte, and Alex made their way around the long antique marquetry walnut table, greeting the family.

Carey stood off to the side, her hands in the pockets of her black pants. Her very blond and short hair was tightly curled, framing her face, her makeup accentuating her creamy complexion, peaked brows, and the large freckle near her top lip. She wore a mock-neck long-sleeved orange silk blouse. The tiered, ruffled sleeves and hems had black velvet ties on the forearm and a large keyhole cutout on the chest.

The players in the room watched as the two sisters embraced. Carey whispered, "Thanks for not making me a part of the wedding party, sister. It would have been a bore."

Charlotte stepped back and smiled, having expected nothing less. "You're welcome, Carey. I knew you'd hate it, and I wouldn't want to cause you any distress."

Carey beamed at her. Charlotte, noticing an impressive orange citrine and orange sapphire ring in eighteen-carat gold on Carey's hand, said, "Nice ring. You're looking well."

Carey put out her hand and admired it. "Harley will be flying in this afternoon. *Le cinq à sept.*" She winked at Charlotte, referring to the French expression linking afternoon and evening. "I thought we'd make it an early night."

Alex, having met Carey on only a few occasions, took Carey's hand in both of his and kissed her cheek. "Carey, you look beautiful. Charlotte and I will forever be in your debt. You're doing a very important service for many families. I'm sure they'd be incredibly appreciative of you if they knew."

Carey nodded slightly. "You're welcome, Alex. Daddy means the world to me. I'll do whatever I can to help him on his campaigns. But I'm glad to hear this will help so many people. Congratulations, by the way, you two," she said, giving Charlotte a head-to-toe examination of her wardrobe and coming back with a dubious look on her face. "The wedding is going to be lovely I'm sure. Mom can hardly contain herself from speaking about anything else."

Carey walked past them and over to Finn. "Mr. Laferty," she said as she gently grasped him by the shoulders and gave him a kiss on each cheek. She pulled back and stared warmly into his eyes. "Finn. It's so nice to meet you."

The family watched Finn; his face actually reddened. He shot a quick look at Alex for assistance and then to Carey said, "It's nice to meet you, too. You look very pretty in orange."

Charlotte saw Alex's face break into a wide grin.

"Do I?" said Carey. "Thank you for the compliment. Your wife, Isabella, won't she be joining us today?"

"Ah, no," Finn said. "She works. She's a teacher. Elementary school. She couldn't afford the day off."

Carey put her hands in her pockets and gave Charlotte an inquisitive look. "I see," Carey said, "and I was so looking forward to meeting her. My sister, Charlotte, practically thinks of her as family." Carey looked at Henry. "And we all know how important family is. Isn't that right, Daddy?"

Henry pursed his lips and gestured to the table. "Let's get started," he said. "Take a seat, everyone." They did so, Carey next to her father, who sat across from Julia, each at the heads of the table.

Henry continued. "Finn. I'll open by saying that we're very sorry to hear that you've had a difficult time with your business venture at Titan Farms. It wasn't necessary.

"After this was brought to my attention, I had my close associates uncover what they could about Damien Miller and his business. We've reviewed the situation, and I can confidently come to several conclusions. Damien Miller is a short-sighted misanthrope. He may have a master plan, but it's foolish. That said, he's done a very nice job bamboozling his bankers and associates. Had we not been informed and intervened, he may have gotten away with it for some time. If he were lucky. But it might have caught up with him in other ways."

Henry shrugged. "Either way, he's done. Right now, time is of the essence. Charlotte and Alex's wedding is a perfect opportunity to meet Mr. Miller, and that date is fast approaching. We'll also need to discuss the legal proceedings, the financial health of your business and that of the other farmers, and the role you will need to play so Damien Miller can be logically invited to attend my daughter's wedding reception. Let's begin with you telling us everything you know from the very beginning."

Charlotte grabbed a legal pad and pen from the middle of the table, as did the others. Finn, looking uncomfortable and unsure of how to start, looked around, everyone waiting on him.

Carey, playing with her pen, looked across the table to Finn and said, "Jump in anywhere, Finn baby. I spent the night going over your life last night with my family. We already know this guy is a prick. No need to watch your language or be careful with your words. Come on, tell us everything. Why don't you start with telling me what you know about his little wife, Linda."

They spent the next several hours revisiting the Titan contractual scheme, Damien Miller, and his "army of skanks," a term Carey borrowed from the movie *Mean Girls*. They had lunch brought in and moved around the suite, each of the Carrowses taking a turn with Finn, giving him advice on how to manage Damien going forward. They spent time role-playing and writing scripts, warming Finn up to the art of lying. Finn enjoyed it immensely, especially with Carey, who had him laughing with discomfort and pleasure by her obscene and absurd responses. Carey, playing the role of Damien to Finn's conversations, at one point interjected an admission that a particularly inadequate appendage was at the root cause of his desire to screw over the world.

Everyone again at the war room table, Henry said, "Finn, my boy, you're up first. You have my numbers, and I expect a full report after every conversation you have with Damien. Anything else about the operation, you'll report to Charles. Do you have any questions?"

"Yeah, I still don't know what you're going to do to him or how this is going to work."

Henry stood and reached out, indicating for Finn to stand. "I'm afraid that's for us to know, Finn. Not because we don't trust you, but because the less you know, the better. And you need deniability. You do your part, play buddy-buddy with Damien Miller, act the fool, suck up to his apparently huge ego, amuse him, flatter him, everything that we've told you. Then leave the rest to us.

The most important piece to remember is that Damien cannot know that we're coming for him. Can you do that?"

"I can, sir," Finn said.

Alex and Charlotte rose. "We'll take you to your car, Finn, so you can get back," Alex said.

Finn looked around the table, uncertain again of what to say as he turned to leave. Finally, choked up a little, he managed, "Thanks."

––––––––

Finn, back at his home office in Ithaca, was staring at a legal pad with scripts by Carey Carrows full of foul words and belittling profanity written all over it. He was on the phone with Damien. Again. He'd made a couple calls to him since his meeting with the Carrowses, getting Damien to relax with innocuous and playful conversations. Everyone knew Damien screened his calls. Now that he had the man answering, he needed to move it to the next step.

Nervously chewing his nails, he said to Damien, "That's hilarious. The whole time, he never noticed his barn door was open?"

"I'm telling you, Finn, bankers are idiots. When are you going to start believing me? You guys are all crying, worrying about cash, just go get some. It's paperwork. They love paperwork. They love spreadsheets. Make the shit up! Just get your ass over to the bank and do it."

Finn's mouth hung open, mouthing the words "Oh my God" as he wrote the words *BANK FRAUD* on the legal pad and underlined them. He couldn't wait to call Henry Carrows.

"Yeah," said Finn like he was considering, "maybe. You know my brother-in-law, Alex Macchi, said he'd float me, I could just do that. Hey! I had a thought. This weekend, Isabella and I are going to be in the city. We're having dinner with Alex and Charlotte Carrows, his fiancée? Isabella is the matron of honor for their wedding. You and Linda want to join us? Maybe we'll make a night of it?"

There was a moment of silence on the other end until Damien said, "Yeah? I don't know. In Manhattan?"

"Yup. Some swanky French food place. The Carlyle Restaurant? Isabella's been shopping, trying to find the right outfit. Charlotte and Alex, they're cool. They're up for a good time. How about it? Do you want to see if Linda's interested?"

"Sure, I'll ask her. Let me know what time, and I'll run it past the GM. Sound good?"

"Yup, I'll text you. Thanks for all the advice on the labor problems."

"You need to start listening to me, Finn. Fuck 'em. Just keep hiring new guys who don't know shit. There's plenty of people who need work and will do it for chump change. Like I said, just pay them cash, keep it off the books, and you'll have a profitable day."

Finn called Henry in California and reported the call. "Well done, Finn," Henry said. "He's a sneaky bastard. He never responds to your emails, never puts things in writing, but you get him to talk, and he's got all kinds of slippery solutions. He thinks he's smart not to leave a paper trail." Henry chuckled. "It's coming together. Since we know the Titan team has access to your banking records—it's frankly remarkable that he got that in the contract—we've set up a private account for you. Alex has it."

"He gave it to me. I've got access. I don't know what to say, Mr. Carrows, it's so much money. I'll never be able to pay you back."

Henry, in a quiet, serious tone, said, "Finn, son, it's nothing for you to worry about. I don't expect repayment, ever, so stop thinking about it. Relax. Get some sleep, keep doing what you're doing. And you let Charlotte help pretty Isabella with her outfit for the dinner. She'll know what to do."

Finn disconnected and stared out into the yard toward the outbuildings.

There was a light now at the end of the tunnel. It gave him great comfort that the Takedown would also save his employees and his fellow Titan contract farmers and their families, but it pained him that he couldn't share that hope with any of them.

While he and his fellow farmers were sucking wind and finding no profitability to the business that was sold to them, coercive blackmail efforts to remain silent or face massive fines for disparagement had begun in earnest from Titan's lawyer, Samara Poe. Damien and Titan couldn't be slandered because Damien needed to sell more franchise farms. If you slandered them, they'd make you pay.

Damien and his "army of skanks" continued to sell farms, but the newest farms were not given the names or contact information of the original nine in order to isolate the newbies from the veterans.

The legal fees were crushing the farmers. The original nine were heavily leveraged and on the verge of business and personal bankruptcy. Times were bleak and painful for all of them.

He opened the latest private email sent from Russ Rhode, the farmer Finn had always felt closest to in Ohio.

"...organic, free-range officially out the window. Blackout curtains installed per Samara's demand letter. Birds in the dark; they can't breathe or fly, no room to roam. It's sick out there. Can't make the numbers. Samara's latest threatened to reduce my rate if I didn't comply and produce more. She fucking gave me a 'gentle reminder' that if I didn't produce, I'd receive a poor score. God help us. So worried about Cindy. Her heart tests come back next week. I gotta keep producing, 'cause I gotta keep my health insurance paid. Don't know where I'm going to come up with the cash to pay the lawyer..."

It made Finn sick. He didn't know how he'd explain to any of them that he was now a company guy.

Chapter 8

Charles Carrows loved his sister. Both his sisters. He thought they knew that, but Pop had told him otherwise. He'd be happy to step it up. Maybe he'd spend more time in New York with Charlotte, Alex, and Petunia. The wedding was certainly an opportunity, and he really liked spending time with Alex. He fit into the family perfectly.

Driving his Lexus SUV down the Garden State Parkway toward Barnegat Light, Charles was excited by the Takedown. It would be his pleasure to drag down this particular scumbag. The timing was difficult but interesting. Involved in a million details opening his first of what he hoped were many casinos, he and his family had brainstormed how to use it to trap Damien Miller.

After Finn left, it was Carey who brought up the horror movie *Buried Alive* with Tim Matheson. Tim's wife, played by Jennifer Jason Leigh, believes she has successfully murdered him. But he comes back from the dead, and through a series of events, physically traps her, offering her only one way out of each area, eventually leading to a small hatch she crawls through. Once inside, she realizes too late that it dead-ends, allowing Tim Matheson to box her up. It becomes her coffin. Hence the title. Charles laughed, recalling his mother's horrified reaction.

It was a thought but not really their style. They hoped to use a similar trap, however, one from which Damien couldn't escape. Charles's first task was to meet with the father-and-son skippers of Titan Fisheries.

Barnegat Light, population roughly six hundred, was a small borough at the tip of Long Beach Island, which had for decades suffered through the effects of ill-fated storms and erosion. The weather was beautiful today as Charles pulled in front of Poppy's Ice Cream. Zipping up his jacket against the cold breeze, he nevertheless felt the salty ocean air to be invigorating.

He ordered a selection of pints, returned to his car, and traveled a short distance down narrow streets to the small home of Earl Wellington. The father and previous owner of the fishing trawler now sadly known as Titan 1.

Charles grabbed the sack of ice cream and walked to the door. A large man, craggy faced from his years outdoors, greeted him with suspicion.

"Help you?"

Charles stuck out his hand. "Mr. Wellington, we spoke on the phone? I'm Charles Carrows."

Earl looked him over and eyed the package. "What you got there?"

Charles held it up in front of him. "Ice cream! From Poppy's. I didn't know what you'd like, but I got some chocolate peanut butter, peppermint chip, cherry chocolate, and a pint of butter brickle."

"Huh," said Earl as he turned around and headed inside.

Such a small town, Charles figured an ice-cream store down the road would know exactly what kind of ice cream Earl Wellington liked. People tended toward their favorites. Earl's was butter brickle, his wife was not as particular.

Charles followed Earl inside, immediately inhaling years of secondhand smoke. Charles's eyes adjusted to the light as he watched Earl look into the kitchen and say, "He's here."

A woman, one of the tallest, largest-boned women Charles had ever seen, came into view. With long, wild red hair, she had on a bright pink T-shirt and a pair of jeans. Sporting generous amounts of makeup and long, pointy, pink painted nails, she was smoking a cigarette.

"This here's Squirrel," said Earl by way of introduction.

Charles, smiling, ran forward, his hand extended. "Charles Carrows. Thank you for seeing me on such short notice." He handed her the bag.

"Thank ya," she said, looking inside and turning to put it in the icebox.

Earl sat at a small laminate kitchen table and stared at him. "What's you doing here?"

Charles gestured toward another chair, and Earl

raised an eyebrow as Charles pulled it out and sat, facing the kitchen. Squirrel, staring at him, squinted at him as she inhaled.

"Let me ask you something before we begin," said Charles. "Do you happen to know who I am?"

"Name *Carrows* rings a bell," Earl said. "A rich bell, like Rockerfeller."

Charles nodded. "That's me. From California, originally. I have family in New York. I'm opening a casino soon in Atlantic City too." He beamed at Squirrel and noticed her attempts at fashion, long dangling silver earrings and pink Chinese slippers.

He pointed to them. "My sister Carey has slippers almost identical to those. I've been looking at versions of them my entire life." He laughed. "They're practically her trademark. She tells me they're timeless."

The three of them stared at her slippers for a bit, and Charles saw a slight upward tilt of the mouth from the impressive Squirrel.

"Why you here?" said Earl. "You said somethin' about wantin' to go fishing and needin' some advice?"

Charles tapped his finger on the laminate table, then smoothed his hand over the finish. "That's right. I'm fishing right now, as a matter of fact. Looking to hook me a Damien Miller."

If there had been any oxygen in the room left to suck out, it would have gone right then.

Earl glared at him. The Squirrel looked menacing. Earl pointed to a row of religious saint candles on a shelf above him. "We light those when that man's name comes up in this house. Squirrel?"

Squirrel walked past them and picked up a lighter and lit three of the candles. She turned to Charles and said, "We gonna need to get some more for you?"

Charles smiled at them. "No, I don't think you will. I'm not here to hurt you, I'm here to help you. The fact is, Damien Miller, through an odd twist of fate, has come onto our radar. My family and I, if you'll forgive the metaphor, might be considered killer whales. Damien Miller is swimming in our pond. We'd like to permanently remove him, but we're going to need your help."

Squirrel walked past him to the kitchen and lit another cigarette. Charles continued. "We've found a trail of victims attached to Damien's wake. You and your family are some of them. If you help us, I promise I can help you. If you're uncomfortable helping us, I completely understand. I'll leave, and there will be no hard feelings. Either way, however, Damien Miller is going down. And, either way, I'm hoping I can rely on you for your discretion. We don't want him to see us coming."

Earl smiled for the first time, revealing several missing teeth. "What you going to use as bait there, Mr. Carrows?"

Charles smiled. "I'd be happy to tell you all about it, Earl. But first, as a gesture of our goodwill, I was wondering if there was something special I could do for you. Today."

Earl looked confused. Charles elaborated. "Like a signing bonus. I'm asking you for help. I will compensate you for that help. That's only fair."

"You got lots of money, right?" said Squirrel from the kitchen.

Charles beamed at her and bowed his head. "I do."

She smiled back and said, "How 'bout some ice cream, Mr. Carrows?"

"I'd be delighted."

Chapter 9

Damien opened the front door of his home and noticed a box containing a new light fixture for the front entry sitting by the door. He and Linda had shopped together online and ordered it from Home Depot. He frowned, thinking about the effort it would take to wire it up. Maybe he should get someone who didn't make as much as he did an hour to do it. His time was valuable. Puddin', Linda's white Yorkie, greeted him with a few yaps, and Damien growled back at her. He laughed as the stupid mutt gave him a frightened look and scurried away.

Whistling, he walked into the kitchen. Newly remodeled, it was the centerpiece of their home. The white granite on the island, counters, and backsplash, the gray and black cabinets—he loved it. They'd argued about the design, but he was gratified when he finally got his way. Score one for Big D.

Linda stood by the stove, stirring a pot of macaroni. She turned, a glass of wine in her hand, a look of boredom on her face. He walked over and gave her a kiss on the cheek. She smelled like smoke. He frowned. At least she didn't smoke in the house anymore. She resented bundling up and smoking in the garage, but he didn't give a shit. His home wasn't going to smell like an ashtray.

"How you doing? How was your day," said Damien as he took a seat at the island and folded his hands.

She took a sip of her wine, placed the glass on the counter, and folded her arms across her chest, facing him. "Fine. How was yours?"

"I had an interesting conversation today with Finn Laferty."

Linda snorted. "Right. Interesting is not the word I would apply to Finn. What's he want now? Did you remind him how much he owes us at Titan Feed? The balance is ridiculous. I was looking at our receivables today, and you're letting all these asshole farmers just jack up the balance."

She turned around angrily and stirred the pasta. "I can't believe that stupid Finn Laferty is going to be related to Charlotte Carrows." She shook her head and placed the spoon in a trivet that looked like a chicken and walked to the fridge. She pulled out a crock of butter and placed it on the counter. "She's like a dream, like a goddess. Have you seen her pictures in the paper? Unbelievably beautiful. I wonder if she's had any work done. Probably, with all that stinking money." She turned back to the stove and grabbed her glass.

"Well, Linda, I have some news," Damien said proudly.

"Finn invited us to join him and his wife and Charlotte Carrows and her fiancé for dinner in the city next week."

"What?" She spun around and splashed the remaining wine out of her glass onto the floor. "Noooo. We're going to dinner with Charlotte Carrows?" she screamed.

Geez. Damien knew she would be excited but wished she didn't have to scream so loud all the time. "Yup. I know! Can you believe it? That's just the kind of guy I am, Linda, rubbing shoulders with all the right people."

"Shut up! I can't believe this is happening to me!" she shrieked.

"Next week, in Manhattan, the six of us."

"Oh my God!" she shrieked again as she ran past him to her phone. "You finish dinner for MaryLou, I've got to call Betsy, and I've got to go shopping! Oh my God! Oh, D! Feed Puddin' too! What am I going to wear? Thank God I have a hair appointment tomorrow!" she screamed as she grabbed a bottle of wine out of the fridge and ran out of the room.

Damien went over to the stove to check on the mac and cheese. It looked good; maybe he'd have some too. Damien smiled, feeling satisfied and thinking about how he might leverage a relationship with Ms. Carrows. He turned on the Bluetooth speakers, pulled up his Spotify playlist, and scrolled through for something big to play, just like him.

Linda Miller went into overdrive that night telling

everyone who would listen about her dinner plans the next week with Charlotte Carrows. "It's better than even a regular celebrity, I mean, she's like California *royalty* or American royalty or really, she's the Big Apple's royalty. Oh my God! I just had a thought. What if we're photographed together out at dinner, and I get into the tabloids with her listed like, 'Charlotte Carrows at Le Cirque with unknown friend,' and she'll be like gazing into my eyes and speaking really sincerely, and I'll be listening and looking great too, and it will look like she's confiding in me, 'cause I am her good friend. God, this is going to be amazing. I wonder if there's some way I can tip off the paparazzi that she's going to be at dinner somewhere so they can take our picture. How do you even get ahold of paparazzi? Do you know anyone who knows someone? Oh shit, I know! How about you just make sure you're in the area or walk into the bar and grab some shots with your phone and then we'll shop them around for publication? Oh my God! I'm going to be a celebrity with Charlotte Carrows!"

Damien listened to versions of this all night as he put MaryLou to bed. And while he got annoyed with Linda sometimes, especially when she got sloppy drunk and really loud, he had to admit that this was an awesome event. Who knew what it could lead to?

Late that night, Damien came downstairs for a snack. Linda was at the kitchen island, her laptop open, her wineglass still full. She was smoking.

"The fuck, Linda? Put that out!" said Damien, looking in the pantry.

"Damien, baby, come over here and look at dis," Linda said, pointing to the screen.

Damien was too tired to argue about the smoking. He walked over, stuffing his hand in a box of Cheez-Its. His mouth full, he leaned over and peered at the screen. It was a picture of something called a "band-aid dress with studs."

"Jesus," he said, "it's see-through. Is she wearing a bra?" He put his face closer to the screen.

She smiled at him and ran her hand down his chest. "Silly. You don't wear a bra with that."

"Holy crap, Linda," he said. "The fuck. It's twenty-three hundred dollars! For a dress?" He pulled back, recoiling as if there was a bad smell in the room.

Still sitting, she swiveled her bar stool and hugged him by the waist. "Wouldn't I look gorgeous in it?" she asked, standing up. "It's couture."

"It's twenty-three hundred dollars, Linda. For a dress!" he said, gesturing at the screen with his box of Cheez-Its.

Linda had been kissing his neck. She pulled back and looked at him. "Baby, wait till you see the shoes."

"The shoes? How much are those gonna cost?"

"Come on," she said, turning to grab her wine. She pushed back the chair and walked out of the kitchen. "I'm going to bed. I'll be waiting for you." She left, smiling.

Damien put his finger on the pad and pulled up another tab that said Jimmy Choo. Some kind of boot covered in crystals was listed for twelve hundred.

"What?" Damien squinted at the screen. "For shoes? Is she kidding me?"

He put the Cheez-Its down and closed the laptop. He considered the dress as he walked toward the bedroom. He'd worry about it tomorrow.

———

The night of the dinner, Damien had his Audi S8, his sweet baby with the vanity plate TITAN 1, washed and gleaming for a night in the city. He was extremely pleased with himself that he'd purchased the luxury automobile, and tonight, it would pay off when the valet brought *this* car to the curb for him in front of Charlotte Carrows. That would feel great.

He and Linda had argued about the clothes, but eventually, she bought a black dress that fit toga-style. She told him it was called a Band-Aid dress with ruching. Whatever the fuck that was. She bought the sparkly Jimmy Choo boots, too. She shopped all week for the other accessories. He didn't even want to know how much she spent on those items. She looked good, though. He was looking forward to an amazing night.

"I'm so nervous, D," Linda said as they cruised along into Manhattan.

"You'll be fine, you look great."

"You look great too. But, damn, I'm nervous. I didn't think I'd be this nervous. I can't wait to get a drink. I wanted to grab a roadie, but your mom was following me around," she said, looking into the vanity mirror, dabbing at corners.

Damien glanced over at his wife. He was a little worried Linda would get drunk and loud, but he didn't dare say a word. He didn't want her to walk in angry at him and then belt down a couple of martinis in retaliation. That was a surefire recipe for disaster.

———

Charlotte, Alex, Finn, and Isabella were in the bar of the Carlyle Restaurant, waiting for Damien and Linda to arrive.

Charlotte wore a black Tom Ford sleeveless turtleneck cocktail dress. The open back was knotted, and she wore her dark hair in a high pony, poofed on top with large dangling emerald earrings. She ran her arm down Isabella's conservative long-sleeved red velvet dress. "You look beautiful in that dress, Isabella. Remember that, okay? I'll manage Linda, you just go along with anything I say. Got that?"

"Got it," said Isabella, admiring the large Fred Leighton ruby and diamond cocktail ring Charlotte had lent her. "Oh God," said Isabella, turning her back to the door. She mumbled out of the side of her mouth, "I see them. They're here."

Charlotte smiled at Isabella as she looked across her toward Damien and Linda. "It's perfect. Come on, Isabella. Let's have some fun."

First greetings aside, the group followed as the maître

d' led them to their table. White tablecloths, decorated with white tulips and small warm lamps, accompanied the delicate bone china place settings. After getting comfortable, they ordered their first drink, most of them martinis. Charlotte had made certain the table was not round and insisted that the ladies all sit on the same side, across from their husbands. Charlotte, taking the chair at the end and placing Isabella beside her, leaned across to Linda and said, "I just love your sparkly necklace, Linda. It's so festive, matching those Jimmy Choos."

"Thank you," said Linda, placing her hand over the obnoxiously large silver accessory and giving Damien a knowing look.

"Such fun," Charlotte said as she took a sip of her water.

Damien said, "I hear congratulations are in order. Alex, Charlotte, you're getting married."

"Thank you, Damien," Charlotte said, reaching across the table and taking Alex's hand. "We're very happy."

Alex, smiling across at Linda, said, "Wedding talk, don't get us started."

As the drinks were placed on the table, Linda said, "Oh, I don't mind. I love weddings. Are you getting married at Whispering Cliffs?"

Charlotte reached for her martini. "I'm afraid not. Mommy and Dad were righteously disappointed, but Alex's family lives out here." She patted Isabella's hand and smiled at her as she took a large sip of her drink.

Linda followed suit, practically finishing the first one.

She glanced at Damien. Alex followed, putting his entire glass back quickly. "Ahhh," he said as he took an olive off his spear and chewed it, giving Linda a big grin.

Alex picked up his menu. "Would anyone object if I were to order a Pouilly-Fuissé with the Caspian Sea caviar?"

"Oh, I adore caviar," Linda said in eye-rolling ecstasy.

"It's up to you, Alex," said Finn, shrugging. "I don't think I've ever had it."

"That's settled then." Alex smiled as he signaled for the waiter and placed the order for the white wine. Continuing with the waiter, he said, "If you would let the sommelier know that we'd also like a couple bottles of the Chapelle-Chambertin Pinot Noir decanted before dinner?"

As the waiter left, Alex said to the table, "Finn and I were thinking steak for dinner. Have you been here before, Damien? Linda?"

Damien said, "No. I haven't been to many French food establishments. I'm looking forward to the meal though."

Linda leaned across Isabella and smiled at Charlotte. "I'm wild about French food."

They talked about the restaurant and that it was a favorite of the Carrowses when they were in town. Charlotte suggested that after dinner they head into the famous jazz bar, Bemelmans. "There's a jazz trio performing tonight. I hear they're amazing."

Linda finished her martini and handed it to the waiter as the white wine arrived at the table. "I simply love jazz," she said.

Charlotte gave Alex a quick smile as she saw Damien openly give Linda a look of disbelief. The caviar and wine were served. Alex winked at Linda as he raised his glass to her and took a large swallow. She followed suit as Finn and Isabella peered at the caviar and the assortment of sides with confusion. The waiters placed a small mother-of-pearl spoon and chilled plates before each of them.

"Linda?" said Alex, drinking more. "Do you prefer the crème fraîche or a less fat sour cream with your caviar?"

Charlotte saw Damien raise his eyebrow in Linda's direction as Linda reached over and picked up a crispbread. Linda shrugged. "Listen, either way, it's delicious."

Alex finished his short glass of wine and gave the waiter a circular motion with his finger, indicating for him to refill the glasses.

Linda, crispbread in hand, hesitated over the selections and finally put a large dollop of crème fraîche, some caviar, and a scattering of red onions on top. She toasted the table with the treat and popped it into her mouth.

Isabella turned to watch her chew. She appeared to be enjoying it but swallowed quickly and made a grab for her wine. Charlotte, reaching for one of the small gold edible nasturtium flowers, pulled off a small leaf and put it into her mouth. "So good," she said. "When I was little, Mommy and Dad used to let us eat the caviar with Wonder Bread. We'd squish up a piece, put the caviar inside, and then squish up the sides. It was really good."

The conversation turned to family backgrounds, and Alex and Charlotte encouraged Damien and Linda to share. As more food came and the wine flowed, Charlotte kept a breezy chatter of girl talk going on her side of the table as Alex listened intently to Damien speak about his business. According to the plan, Finn and Isabella said very little. Damien and Linda didn't seem concerned, or even aware.

At one point, Charlotte excused herself to go to the ladies' room. Linda threw her napkin down and announced she'd join her. Isabella as well. In the ladies', Charlotte continued her bantering with Linda through the stall. Linda came out laughing and ran into Charlotte, who gave her a large smile. After washing up, the two stood in front of a full-length mirror checking their makeup. Charlotte put an arm around Linda and, leaning close, gave a quick squeeze. There was a distinct odor in Linda's hair.

Charlotte said, "You're so much fun, Linda. I'm so glad you could join us."

"Oh golly." Linda shrugged, powdering her nose. "This is great. Thanks for inviting us!"

Charlotte fussed while they waited for Isabella. She said, "Poor Alex is probably dying for a smoke right about now. I wish he'd quit." She shrugged. "But I understand. Daddy and practically everyone in my family smokes except for me."

"I smoke," said Linda, her eyes wide, warming greatly to the subject.

"You do?" said Charlotte. "Does Damien?"

"No. I've been trying to quit. It's so hard." She pouted.

Isabella joined them at the mirror but remained silent

as she applied some lip gloss. Charlotte put a gentle hand on her back and said to the trio in the mirror, "You look so pretty tonight, Isabella."

Linda glanced at Isabella and noticed the large ring. A questioning look on her face, she said, "That's a beautiful ring."

Isabella pursed her lips as she put the gloss in her purse and said, "Charlotte loaned it to me."

"Oh," Linda said as she picked up Isabella's hand to examine it. "It's soo pretty."

Charlotte said, "Hey, you guys walk back to the table alone. I'm going to step into the lounge and give a quick call to the babysitter. I don't want to be rude and do it at the table."

"Sure," Isabella said.

Linda gave Charlotte's arm a quick squeeze and giggled. Charlotte left the restroom with them and peeled off to the bar. She purchased several cigars and stuffed them into her purse. Poor Alex.

Arriving back at the table, she sat, noticing Alex and Damien involved in a heavy conversation while Finn sat back looking miserable between them.

Alex disengaged as more wine was brought to the table, and they ordered dessert. Linda, her glass in hand, thrust it out to the waiter for more and said, "Alex. Do you smoke?"

Alex looked quickly at Charlotte, who gestured her nonchalance. He said, "I do."

Charlotte shrugged. "I've been trying to get him to quit,

but I don't want to be one of those wives who nitpick their spouses. Isn't that right, darling?" she said as she reached over and patted Alex's hand. "I put a few in my purse on the way out." She gave him a large smile.

"Thank you, my love," Alex said, returning the smile and looking to Linda and Damien. "I don't suppose either one of you would care to join me after dinner before we head to the club?"

"I'd love to," Linda breathed, relieved. Damien gave her a challenging look.

Later, at the club, Charlotte and Linda sat next to each other, their heads together, and talked animatedly about their children. Charlotte peppered her for motherly advice since Linda's daughter was two years older than Petunia. The waitstaff at the bar had been privately informed that the drinks for everyone at the table but Damien and Linda's should appear to, but not contain alcohol. Poor Alex would have enough of a headache the next morning after smoking the cigars outside all night, yukking it up with Linda.

The jazz music kept the evening lively, and Charlotte flirted shamelessly with Damien each time Alex and Linda were away. But there came a moment toward the end of the evening where Charlotte was sorely tempted to let loose on Linda. She kept her head, however, as the clearly drunk Linda spilled part of her drink onto Isabella and said loudly over the music, "Oh, who cares. I'm sure it's off the rack."

Charlotte grabbed Isabella's hand under the table

and gave it a firm squeeze. Not long after that Charlotte pronounced the evening over.

In the Carlyle lobby, Linda swayed and grabbed Alex's arm as she dug her cigarettes out of her purse. She thrust out her bottom lip and said, "Please, one more."

Alex, his hands in his pockets, put out an elbow and a smile to escort her. The two of them laughed as they made their way outside.

Charlotte put her hand on Damien's arm and said with concern, "You're going to stay here, aren't you? Have you got a room? No way you can drive, sweetie." She shook her head.

Damien, his hands in his trousers, looked around the sophisticated lobby and said, "No, yeah. We can stay. My folks have MaryLou. We're cool."

Charlotte gave him a wide smile of approval and guided him toward reception. She kept up the small talk as he paid for his suite. The Lafertys stood to the side.

Alex and Linda stumbled back inside, Alex making a "shhhhh" sound with his finger as Linda put her hand over her mouth. They walked over to Damien, finishing up at reception. Charlotte turned and gave Damien a lingering hug.

"You guys are great," she said and repeated the performance for Linda, giving her a kiss on each side of her face. "We'll see you later," said Charlotte as she linked her arm with Isabella and walked toward the door. Alex and Finn said their goodbyes, and the four of them left Linda and Damien, sloshy and happy in the lobby.

Outside, as the valet ran for a house car to drive the four of them back to Charlotte's townhome, Finn said, "So what did you think?"

"I think I got a new girlfriend. And a headache," Alex said.

Isabella, unhappy, said, "Don't joke, Alex. That was terrible."

Charlotte put her arm around her. "It was terrible, Isabella. I'm sorry you had to be a part of it, but both of you did a great job playing the role of scenery. The family will be very proud when I tell them."

Isabella went over to Finn, who put his arm around her. She rested her head against his chest. Their car pulled up, and as they walked toward it, Charlotte felt awful for what she had put Isabella through. She realized they understood what was happening, but it was another thing entirely to be a woman and ignored all evening, spilt on, and insulted while watching her family turn a blind eye. Charlotte grabbed Alex's hand. She said, "God, Alex, that Miller woman was horrible to Isabella all night. I wanted to kick the shit out of her."

Alex gave her a tender kiss on her cheek and said, "The Millers have their big toe in the web, honey. We've got a much better idea of who they are. Come on, let's get home."

———————

Damien sat in his crappy trailer, his feet on his desk, as he scrolled through his phone. Linda yammered at him from her small desk across the room. She worked on the books at home but from time to time came by to help him with the business.

"Jesus," said Linda, her back to him, looking at the computer screen. "Did you see this email from Russ Rhode?"

Damien didn't look up. He had, but he also had no intention of replying to the whiney farmer from Ohio.

"Yup."

"He's not paying Titan Feed again?"

"He'll pay. Eventually. Got to. No way around it. One way or another, Linda. It's all in the contract. Samara will take care of it."

"God, he just drones on," she said, shaking her head. "Blah, blah, blah, health insurance, blah, blah, blah, listing all his *personal* problems."

The trailer rocked as the door slammed shut. Damien looked down the hall and saw his foreman, Roland, standing in the doorway. He yelled at him, "Take it outside. I'll be at the barn in twenty minutes."

Roland left the trailer.

Linda plugged her nose and looked at Damien. "Why does he always smell so bad? God, we've got to get a better office..."

Damien's phone rang. "It's Laferty," he said to Linda as he pulled it up and put it on speaker.

"Hey, D," said Finn. "Got a minute?"

"Got all the time in the world for you, buddy."

The two of them talked trade for a few minutes until Finn said, "So anyway, Isabella and I wanted to ask if you guys wanted to join us at Alex and Charlotte's wedding reception?"

Linda spun around in her chair, her eyes wide, her mouth hanging open.

Finn continued. "They had a great time when we went out, and Alex said that the family could invite guests out to Oheka for the big celebration. So, naturally, I thought about you and Linda."

Linda slapped her hand on her leg, mouthing a silent, "Oh my God!"

"Dude, right," said Damien casually. "At Oheka. Thanks, man. I think I can speak for Linda. We'd love to go to the reception. Thanks for the invite."

They went over a few more details, Damien smiling broadly at Linda for the duration. The two of them were thrilled to be going to a Carrows wedding. He could use the bragging rights on that one for miles.

Chapter 10

———

The third weekend of June arrived quickly, and the weather promised to be warm, sunny, and glorious. The week had been filled with last-minute errands and decisions, but Julia had no trouble delegating the details, leaving Charlotte the luxury of relaxing before her big day.

Friday morning found the Carrows and Macchi families traveling east on the north shore of Long Island toward Oheka Castle. The Gold Coast was dotted with some of the wealthiest old homes in the country. A bygone world of Gatsby-esque leisure, sadly fewer than half of the five hundred Gold Coast mansions had survived.

By early afternoon, all twenty family members had arrived, and wedding preparations were in full swing. The excited flower girls, Petunia, Leonora, and Andria, pretty much ran wild through the home. Charlotte's babysitter followed them around, and with the caveat that they were respectful to the staff and security, they were tolerated and encouraged to wander.

Charlotte took the largest and most impressive Olmsted Suite, which she would have to herself on Friday evening but would share with Alex as their bridal suite after the wedding. The two families spent the afternoon in small groups as staff assisted them through the organized events. Most of the activities were attended by all, and the croquet and tea on the terrace lawn made a breezy and easy gathering for the two families to get to know one another.

On Friday evening, the wedding party and the flower girls were guided through the ceremony rehearsal, after which they all gathered for a casual dinner in the Oheka Bar and Restaurant. Isabella took over the event with a slide show presentation and the video interviews she had conducted with Charlotte and Alex separately in which she asked them the same set of questions. The presentation wasn't obnoxiously long and was peppered with expressive reactive pictures of Petunia's face in response to their answers. It was a PG event and tastefully done.

After dinner, the families went into the library for more drinks and conversations, and Isabella took over again, insisting that they play an easy game of charades with clues based upon Alex and Charlotte's life. Alex's mom, Marie, and Julia got along very well, and except for the toast made in honor of Anthony, the evening was mostly filled with smiles and happiness.

Saturday dawned with the castle abuzz, filled with caterers

and decorators all intent on making the couple's stylized dreams come true. After breakfast, the men decided to golf as Oheka staff led the little girls on pony rides around the grounds. The babysitter also brought kites, and everyone enjoyed watching the children run over the grounds making them fly. The women took advantage of the spa services both from the castle staff and from the aestheticians and massage therapists who were brought in for the day. Manicurists, makeup artists, and hair stylists ran around as the time got closer and prepared everyone for the wedding.

Chandeliers, bistro lights, sofas, tables, and heaters were set up outside for the guests if they chose to enjoy dancing and socializing on the veranda and lawns. The indoor reception area was set for dinner for over three hundred guests and was resplendent with ambient lighting and flowers with a gold and white theme.

Charlotte had selected Isabella's dress. The full-length black Armani gown had a surplice neckline, a fitted bodice with an A-line skirt, and cascading ruffles falling from a natural waist. Sleeveless with minimal shoulder coverage, it was classic and elegant and suited both Isabella's beautiful figure and Charlotte's color theme of black, cream, and white.

At five that evening, the Macchi and Carrows families were seated outdoors by the garden surrounded by white and gold gauze curtains slightly flowing in the warm breeze. The weather at eighty degrees was ideal. Alex and Tony, both dressed in classic black ties with black waistcoats, looked handsome and expectant as they stood at the altar next to the priest.

All eyes turned as the music began.

Inspired by the French castle, they had chosen a nontraditional processional of Andrea Bocelli and Edith Piaf singing "La Vie En Rose." As the full orchestra of violins began the sweet, emotional song, Isabella opened the procession looking lovely carrying a small bouquet of white and cream ranunculus and avalanche roses. The tenor's lyrical voice floated around them as Leonora, Andria, and lastly Petunia made their way toward the altar. Scattering pink rose petals from baskets trimmed with flowers and ribbons, like fairies, they wore floor-length cream-colored princess dresses with black sashes and crystal headbands adorned with pink flowers. As Petunia, her beatific face filled with innocence and joy, passed Julia, their eyes met, and Julia's filled with tears.

Henry and Charlotte left the castle and stepped onto the lawn where he paused and kissed her cheek. "I couldn't be happier for you today, Charlotte. I'm such a lucky man to have you for my daughter. You know I love you very much."

Her smile reflected her deep happiness as she squeezed his arm, and they made their entrance. "I love you too, Dad," she whispered. "Thank you for everything."

Charlotte's eyes sparkled as she floated down the aisle in a strapless ball gown of soft cream and rose. Draped tulle with three-dimensional beading and embroidery through the bodice and skirt filled the aisle as the dress flowed around her. She carried a small bouquet of cream roses, and her dark hair was pulled back with a few very small antique diamond clips accentuating her only other accessory of ten-carat drop diamond earrings.

The family stood as they watched Charlotte and Henry move past them. As she and Alex's eyes locked on to each other, Charlotte recalled the first time she'd seen him, standing on her doorstep. The stirring moment was so vivid, their first kiss in the same spot as well. In what seemed like slow motion, her eyes pooled looking at him, waiting for her, their love so powerful, it was surely felt by everyone. With the paradise surrounding them and the soulful stirring of the music, looking at Alex, she knew, and would always know, that he loved her as she loved him.

The ceremony was conducted by the Macchi family's Catholic priest, who had agreed to officiate in a nontraditional Catholic wedding outside the church. The ceremony, prayers, blessings, and vows were kept relatively short as the couple spoke of their love and their commitment to each other.

In what seemed like only a moment, the priest joyfully pronounced, "You may now kiss the bride," and Alex and Charlotte proceeded to do just that as the family stood and cheered. The music launched into a joyful and upbeat Harry Connick Jr. singing "It Had to Be You" as Alex and Charlotte each reached down and gave Petunia a hug and kiss.

The two of them smiled at each other and held hands

as they walked down their path together, for the first time, as husband and wife. It was time for the sparkly and exultant celebration to begin.

———————

The guests arrived, the champagne flowed, and spirits were high. Charles and Carey sat together and watched as their sister and her new husband began their first dance, accompanied by the sixteen-piece band.

"They look awfully happy," Carey said as she watched Alex whispering something into Charlotte's ear, their faces pressed against each other.

"They certainly do." Charles turned to her and smiled. "You're not jealous, are you, Carey?"

She shot him a quick glance. "Of course not."

Charles mused, uncertain. "Last night I heard them saying goodnight to each other. Charlotte called him her hero. She told him that she had his wedding ring engraved with the words 'The world except for you is filled with little men.'" Charles smiled, watching as Alex moved his hand behind Charlotte's head and kissed her. "Something about Cleopatra saying it to Caesar, I'm not sure. I moved off after that. Thought I'd give them some privacy."

Carey shrugged. "He's a nice guy."

"High praise, indeed, there, sister."

At that moment Petunia ran over to Carey and grabbed her hand, breathless. "Oh my gosh, we just heard that they are going to play the "Hokey Pokey" later! Will you dance with me, Aunt Carey?"

Carey smiled and gently plucked Petunia's headband off her wild head of curls. "Of course, I will," she said as she smoothed Petunia's hair and placed the band back in place as Petunia played with Carey's necklace.

"This is so pretty," said Petunia. "You look pretty in gold, Aunt Carey."

Carey hugged her young niece and said, "I relish the compliment, darling. Thank you."

Petunia gave her a smile, some of her teeth missing, and took off.

Charles and Carey stared after her as she ran up to Isabella and pushed her way onto her lap.

"That kid is a charmer. I'm glad she's so close with Alex's family," said Charles. "Almost makes you want to have some of your own, doesn't it?"

"Harley and I are nowhere near that," Carey said, glancing across the room at Damien and Linda Miller. The siblings had been keeping close tabs on them during the dinner and watched as Henry's friend and family banker spoke intently with Damien. John Wallace, indebted to Henry Carrows, was happy to play the role of family friend and friendly financier. He and his wife had been seated next to the Millers for dinner.

"Little Linda looks bored. Or drunk. I can't tell which," said Carey, returning her gaze to the dance floor.

Charles gave a quick glance. "Not bored, but it may be nearly time for you to reel them in."

"She's trying hard to look interested in what John's wife is saying, but all I see is a hungry wannabe. My God," said Carey, scornfully shaking her head. "What the hell is she wearing. Versace? Some knockoff? She has incredibly bad taste."

"Use it. You know what to do. Where's Harley?"

Carey pointed with her head as Harley walked toward them smiling. If there had been a wind machine, he would have fit perfectly on any cover of Latin GQ. Lean, tall, olive complexioned—his bone structure made women swoon. More than one head did a double take as he walked by and sat down next to them.

"Harley," said Carey. "It's almost time. Are you ready to meet the enemy, sweetie?"

Harley grabbed a chocolate mint off the table and popped it into his mouth. "I'm ready for a drink. Been cleansing all week to get my liver in shape." He patted his pocket and pulled out an elegant cigarette case and gave her a wicked and alluring smile. "Nearly all my vices at the ready."

"They're at least one or two ahead of us," said Carey as she took a mint as well. "No way am I going to smoke with that bitch. It will absolutely ruin my skin. Come on." She stood and grabbed a small bag. She smiled at Charles. "Get over to the table and get them outside, brother. Linda's probably dying for a smoke. We'll be waiting."

Charles watched them leave and looked around the elegantly decorated room. The Macchis were an impeccably mannered group and looked to be having a nice time. The evening before, he'd been touched by how close they were as a family. He stood and popped another mint. Maybe after he was done with his evening duty to the Takedown he'd dance with Marie. He wanted to make sure they knew that they were now each a part of the Carrows inner circle. He was pleased that Charlotte had chosen so well.

———

Carey and Harley waited until they saw Linda and Damien emerge on the upper terrace lawn. Linda had pulled out a cigarette, and she and Damien appeared to be arguing as they walked toward the bar.

"I'll go over alone," Carey said to Harley. "Give me a few minutes with them before you walk up and take her fucking smoke-filled breath away." She smiled at Harley as she slid a hand under his jacket and reached down to pinch his ass.

Carey walked toward her prey, dressed in the full Carrows package. Wearing a one-shoulder gold sequined sheath dress, which came elegantly to her knees, it was just the right side of conservative, expensive, and deadly. Not trying to upstage her sister on her day, she nevertheless had on extremely large and important gold and diamond earrings, necklace, bracelets, and the sixty-five-carat fancy yellow replica of the diamond ring known as the Tsarina's Fancy. There had been some discussion about the appropriateness of Carey wearing the ring, but in the end, Julia had declared it a good choice.

"It may only be a replica of the original, but no one will know that. Peter Carl Fabergé did a very nice job. Secreted out of Russia on orders from the Tsarina, we have a responsibility to take it out from time to time and let it sparkle. It may have been David's undoing, but let's not forget that it was also the reason Charlotte and Alex met."

———————

Damien spoke in hushed tones to Linda. "We should get back inside. John Wallace and I were making some real headway before Charles Carrows took him away."

"His wife is unbelievably old and boring, Damien. I wasn't going to miss my chance to come outside and get away from her. Give me a minute here to finish my cigarette and then we'll..."

A voice from behind interrupted. "Hi! Ya'll having fun tonight?" Carey said brightly.

Damien and Linda turned toward Carey and were both brought up short by the blond and gold stranger. Linda jerked her cigarette to her side, making Damien jump slightly out of the way.

Linda glanced down quickly and then tried recovering her cool. "We sure are," she said, matching Carey's brightness. "Hi there. My name's Linda Miller, and this is my husband, Damien." Damien stuck out his hand to the gold lady with the electric presence.

"Hello," Carey said politely as she shook Damien's hand. "I'm Carey. So nice to meet you. Are you a friend of Alex or my sister?"

Damien glanced briefly at Linda, who seemed to be preoccupied staring at Carey's hand. "We're friends of Finn and Isabella Macchi *and* Charlotte and Alex," he said. "We've recently gotten to know one another. Finn and I work together."

"Oh, Finn and Isabella! Wow, they are just really lovely people, aren't they? Salt of the earth. I know Charlotte thinks the world of Isabella, and I've got to say, I totally get it. The two of them are so kind and sweet. I've been lucky enough to get to know the whole Macchi gang over the weekend. Lovely, lovely people."

"Oh, they are," Linda suddenly gushed. "Damien and Finn have a *great* relationship, and I totally get what you're saying about Isabella. Sweet, sweet girl."

"How long did you say you've known my sister and Alex?" Carey tilted her head.

"Not long really. Finn and I go back a couple of years now I guess. What a great party," Damien said, changing the subject, not wanting to dwell on the fact that they'd only met Charlotte once. "It was really nice of them to give us an invitation. Great day for it too." He stared pointedly at Linda as she dropped her cigarette butt into the grass. "Do you live in Manhattan?" he continued.

"Oh, I live everywhere really. Daddy has homes and businesses all over the world, but I spend most of my time in California, you know, to be near them and all. What are you all drinking tonight? God knows it's been a great day, and I'm so happy for my sister and Alex, but I was looking around for some people who might be more my speed and really want to party?" Her eyebrow peaked suggestively.

"Oh, look." Carey pointed. "Here comes Harley, my boyfriend. Kind of." She glanced at Linda and mouthed the words, "You know how it is." Carey gently took Linda's arm and turned her toward Harley as he drew near. "Not bad, though, huh," Carey said as the three of them watched Harley walking toward them smiling. His shoulder-length hair flowed as his dark, brooding eyes assessed them, too. He approached the group and extended his hand toward Damien.

"Harley, I want you to meet my new best friends. This is Damien and Linda Miller. Guys, this is Harley, my beloved boy."

"Hello, Damien. It's a pleasure to meet you." He smiled at Linda, who slightly lost her footing when Harley touched her. "Linda, nice to meet you too." He boyishly tucked his hands into his pockets and said, "So what are we talking about over here? Carey, did you order something from the bar?"

"Not yet, baby, I was just about to, but I ran into these guys. They're close friends of Finn and Isabella." Carey dropped Linda's arm. "Guys, what are you drinking? Are you up for something adventurous—how about some tequila?" Carey reached out for Harley's hand, and the two of them wandered toward the bar. Carey looked over her shoulder and gave them an enticing smile.

Linda grabbed Damien's arm in a vise grip and whispered, "Oh my God! This just gets better and better and better! Did you see what she is wearing? That's probably a million bucks of jewelry on her. At least. Shit, that ring? Probably more. And they want us to party with them." Her voice dropped like she might faint. "Mother of

God, let's go!" She pulled Damien along.

Damien was impressed with Carey and Harley as well and always knew when to take advantage of an opportunity. Drinking tequila with Carey Carrows, of all people, had just been handed to him. He hadn't expected that but figured that he and Linda probably looked like a fun couple compared with some of the older folks. He hated to admit it, but Linda was right about John Wallace's wife.

He'd been furious with Linda for having spent so much goddamned money on her outfit tonight. If he'd thought she'd gone overboard for the dinner with Charlotte, that was nothing compared to the nut he was shelling out for this ensemble. But maybe she was onto something. They did attract these two creatures.

Damien was slightly stunned when Carey ordered an entire bottle of 1800 Colección and limes at the bar and instructed it to be brought to them. The four of them wandered away and settled into deep red velvet sofas overhung by a crystal chandelier sitting smack dab in the middle of the terraced lawn.

Damien looked around, wondering how much a setup like this would cost.

"So, guys, tell us more about yourselves. Do you live in Manhattan?" Carey asked as she reclined, her arms stretched out on both sides on the back of the sofa. Harley sat back, crossing his legs and pulling out a cigarette case.

Damien could practically feel Linda swoon with relief. He knew she'd just been given the social green light to smoke with them. Linda smiled at Harley and grabbed her bag as Damien answered.

"No, we don't live in the city, we have a place in the country, in Jersey."

Carey gave him a curious look. Damien looked at the sky. "Man, what a night. Look at the stars. We're in the city often enough for the nightlife and the shopping, but at the end of the day, we like our peace and quiet." He smiled at Carey.

The tequila came and was poured for each of them. Carey didn't hesitate but picked up her glass promptly and held it high, waiting for them to follow her lead. "To the bride and groom!" she said as she put back her drink and slammed it on the table. She glowed at them.

"To the bride and groom," they said as they followed suit. Neither Linda nor Damien was unfamiliar with tequila, but this was a particularly delicious and buttery bottle of extremely expensive liquor. It went down very smoothly. Damien realized that the entire Carrows family knew how to party.

Carey nodded to Harley, indicating for him to do a refill.

"God, you're so right, Damien, it is a beautiful night," Carey said as she leaned back, arching and stretching her back like a cat, looking at the stars. She looked back at them and continued. "So you have a place in the country? You get to enjoy the stars all the time from your place, too. When I'm at Mommy and Daddy's in California, I could just lie on the beach all night and stare at them.

In fact, Charlotte and I used to camp out there with our telescopes, and we'd make up all kinds of stories about the constellations. We were so close," she sighed. "I couldn't be happier that she finally found the right man. Alex is a dream, at least for her," she purred and kissed Harley lightly, placing her hand on his thigh.

Harley picked up the next shot of tequila and raised it in the air. "To our new friends, Damien and Linda. And to the stars," he said as he gestured toward the heavens.

The rest of them followed suit. Damien was slightly worried that Linda would get sloppy. That made four drinks for the night, and she'd hardly eaten her dinner, worried about the tightness of her dress.

"How long have you all been married?" Carey asked Linda.

Linda, still sucking on her lime, was looking down, her hand cupped below the fruit so it wouldn't squirt on her new dress. "Oh," she said, wiping her chin and placing the lime on the table. "We've been married forever. I mean, we've been *together* forever, since high school. We got married right after graduation." She hurriedly continued with a big smile plastered on her face. "I mean, we couldn't help it. Daaammmien and I were in love. Couldn't get enough of each other, had to get married, well, I mean, we didn't *have* to get married, but we wanted to. Big fat love story, you know?"

"High school sweethearts? How cute!" Carey exclaimed.

Damien worried that this was going badly. He

was particularly worried that they'd judge him for not attending college and about what Linda might say next. It was time to reassure them that he was a big deal too. He crossed his legs and stretched his arms across the back of his sofa, mimicking Carey. "Yeah, we were able to marry so young because I was already financially stable. My dad and I actually started a business when I was in high school, and over the years, I leveraged that into several other companies. It's been a lot of work, but if things go as planned, we'll probably retire by the time I'm forty," he said, feeling confident.

Harley was busy pouring another round and said, "Really, Damien, that sounds interesting. Admirable, too. Do you and your dad still work closely together?"

Damien had a quick flash of his father, who was probably at home drunk right now, snoring in his recliner with a soup stain on his shirt.

"No, not really, Dad's semiretired. He has his own successful lumber business, so it's mostly me and the officers in my companies that run the day-to-day."

Carey leaned in. "I'm really glad we had some time to get to know you guys tonight." She tilted her head slightly. "It seems like we have a lot in common. Harley and I have known each other since high school too, although we're not married, yet," she said as she winked at him. "It's so nice to have someone you can lean on who knows you so well. Someone who's known you almost from the very beginning. Harley and I are best friends too."

Linda smiled, looking gratified, as she grabbed another

tequila shot off the table. Loudly, she toasted, "To best friends!" and drank.

Carey and Harley followed suit, but Damien demurred. "I don't think I should. It looks like I'm the designated driver tonight."

Linda shot him a look.

"Oh, that's all right, Damien," Carey said. "Last I heard there were a few open rooms here tonight. I can arrange one, so you don't have to worry about having too much fun. What do you think?" she said enthusiastically as she signaled a waitstaff over to them. "That way we can party all night and *really* become best friends."

Carey spoke to the waiter. "Would you please see if there are any rooms available tonight at the castle and if so, would you please let them know that Damien and Linda Miller will be staying." She spoke with authority, and the waiter nodded soberly and left to do her bidding.

They had no idea how to say no. Linda giggled as she called the babysitter.

Carey was pleased. They'd kept the drinks flowing and danced with the Millers all night. She'd gossiped with Linda about the women in the room and shared confidences like they were long lost friends. She'd convinced Linda that they were kindred spirits. By the end of the evening, Linda, quite drunk, had built up her "country home" into a smaller version of Oheka and insisted that Carey and Harley come out and stay with them. Carey promptly accepted and then disengaged from the slobbering fool as coolly and quickly as she could. The evening was over.

———————

My God, Damien thought as he woke the next morning. He recognized nothing, not the bed, the wall, the windows. Where the fuck am I? And then he heard Linda puking in the bathroom. That brought it all back in a hurry. Why in the world had they drunk so much last night? And as so many drunken stories go, he lay there while the room spun, trying desperately to remember everything that had happened. Had they embarrassed themselves? Had Linda embarrassed him? What the fuck time had they even gotten to bed? Shit, he remembered hugging Henry Carrows and Mrs. Carrows and telling them thanks for having such great kids. He shouldn't have hugged the man. Regrets, they were starting to surface.

Linda looked like hell as she crawled slowly back into bed and stared at the ceiling. "Damien, I'm so sick. What time do you think checkout is? I can't believe I have to do the walk of shame out of here in my evening clothes. We should have left last night."

"Left? How were we going to get home? I couldn't drive, and you sure as shit couldn't drive. Do you know how much a taxi would cost to get back to Jersey? And what about my car? Ohhh, my head," he groaned.

"Well, don't yell at me. You're the one who said it was a great business opportunity to meet and greet and press the flesh," she mocked him.

"Christ, Linda," he said, suddenly remembering, and whispered, "you invited Carey and Harley to spend next Saturday night with us at our *country estate*," he said, imitating her.

That popped Linda's eyes open. Damien cringed, remembering Linda's bragging, talking up their place like they were in a similar league with the Carrows. When he got a chance, he'd whispered to her that she should dial it down, but as usual, that backfired. He remembered she'd hissed at him, that she was becoming girlfriends with Carey Carrows, and said that he could suck it. "Well, maybe they won't remember," he said hopefully. Even he was aware that their place wasn't grand enough for Carey and Harley. But damn, he sure did want to continue the friendship. He was certain there would be leverage or opportunity in the relationship.

"Maybe they won't." Linda sweated, laying her arm over her head.

No such luck. They managed to get out of the castle without running into anyone they knew, but just as they drove off the grounds, Linda's phone rang. She groaned as she noted the caller ID: BFF. It was Carey.

"Good morning, sunshine! Did you all want to meet for breakfast in the dining room? I'm so hungover I need to eat something right away," Carey commiserated.

"Carey! Hi!" Linda said brightly. "No, Damien and I left over an hour ago. We had to get back home to MaryLou. We have some plans today. Sorry, we would have loved to!" Her hand flew over her mouth as Damien sped around a corner.

"Of course. Give me a call tomorrow, and let's get our plans together for the weekend. I can't wait to see your place. It sounds like heaven. Thanks for inviting us. We have so much business in the city this week, it'll be the perfect getaway. Give me a call, okay, sweetie?"

"Oh, Carey, I sure will. Thanks again for the fun time last night. Say hi to Harley for me! Bye!"

She hung up and said, "Pull over, I need to puke."

Chapter 11

"D amien!" Linda shrieked, recovered from the reception. "They're coming to our place next weekend! What are we going to do? I can't let them see the place as it is! There is so much we need to do and so fucking much that needs to be *decorated!* I can't let them come over. They'll know I lied to them," she wailed.

This had been going on all day Sunday after they got home from the wedding. Linda was miserable as she slammed around their house pointing out the zillion things that were inadequate and wrong with it.

"Linda! Stop! I get it! I know what you're saying, but what do you want me to do? We planned to take the projects one at a time. We just finished the kitchen, and it looks great. I need to invest money in the business right now, you know that."

"I know that, but, Damien, I cannot have them come to this place and see that I was exaggerating about it. You know that!"

"Then why did you have to brag about the place so much? Why couldn't you be vague and talk about other shit? Why did you have to go on and on about our *country estate* for God's sake? I love this place, but it's going to take time to make it really great, you know that. We have a plan."

"I don't give a shit about your plan! We need to do something about this house. Now. They are coming over here, for God's sake! Look at the floors! And the furniture!" she yelled as she gestured around. "It's all so common.

"You know, Damien," she continued, "*you* said it was a really great thing to have friends that were so fucking rich because they could lead us to better connections and business deals. Did you mean that? Do you want to have them as friends? 'Cause if you do, then you know as well as I do that you have to spend money to make money, and we need to spend some money on this *goddamned house* if we don't want them to think we are fucking hillbillies. You saw her diamonds. *Those were real*, Damien! They are millionaires! Real ones, not paper ones like you, who is always looking at tiny spreadsheets with projections. They are already rich. Super rich and always have been. This is our opportunity to be in league with the really super rich. I don't see this coming our way again anytime soon. You always say you should jump at any opportunity that smells good. Well, dear, it's right in front of us. Literally, almost ringing the goddamned doorbell."

He knew she was right, but he didn't really want to spend money on the house. For all his braggadocio, he was cheap. Other than cars and boats, he didn't really care about fixing up the house. The kitchen was nice, and they had a great property, which looked out over the river, but they had yet to invest in the serious landscaping it would require. He knew it would take a small fortune to bring it up to speed quickly, and God knew what Linda would require to make it acceptable for the Carey Carrows visit.

"Okay," he said, "how about this. You see if they can come over in two weeks instead of this coming weekend, and we'll pull it together. At least some of it. We'll need to make a list and agree on a budget, but there is no way we can pull it together in one week. How's that?"

Linda almost swooned with relief. Their humiliation was put off. They could do it. But they had to do it fast.

———————

Carey disconnected the call and looked at Charles and Harley. "They wanted to know if we could delay our visit another week." She smiled. The Carrowses had done some discreet surveillance of Damien's home through a real estate broker, and they knew it needed lots of work. The night of the wedding, Carey didn't have to work hard at all to get the horribly put together Versace tragedy to brag about her *country home*. As the night grew longer, she'd encouraged Linda to share more and more about their *little cottage by the river*.

"That's just fine," said Charles, smiling. "Let them do a little remodeling. Well done, Carey."

The next two weeks were a whirlwind of spending and work. The landscape company Damien hired was owned by a friend from high school. The guy had big plans, but since time was an issue, they agreed to an easy layout. Damien pulled in favors from everyone he knew to help pitch in and tackle the work, getting a fairly decent porch, patio, and some gardens laid around the property. The $50,000 budget horrified Damien, but he gave the green light under the condition that it could all be accomplished by the Friday before Carey and Harley would arrive.

Linda went wild on the inside. Again, they pulled in favors from every contractor they knew and arranged to have the flooring replaced throughout, the walls painted and papered, new, beautiful and exotic light fixtures installed, and furniture purchased for many of the rooms. They had a knock-down-drag-out fight over Linda's insistence that they redecorate every room in the house because Carey would see them on their tour, but in the end, Damien convinced her to leave the basement semifinished and concentrate on the two upper floors. Linda didn't have time to quibble. She hired a decorator, and while the contractors installed the flooring and redid the walls and lighting, she and the decorator shopped for furniture. Even Linda did some hand-wringing over the amount of money she was spending on the house, but she reminded herself that it would be worth it, and after all, this was their dream home, and they had been planning to do it eventually. Damien would just have to push back a project or two. It would be fine.

Damien secured the home improvement loans from the obliging bank and, when all was said and done, in two weeks they had spent nearly $150,000.

The last items on the list were new clothes for Linda, catering for delicious foods and flowers, expensive wine and liquor, new porcelain and silver, and upgraded stereo speakers. They dropped MaryLou off at Linda's parents' for the weekend. It was perfect. Or as perfect as it could be in two weeks.

———

Carey and Harley drove up to the Millers' home on the appointed Saturday in their Ferrari, greatly satisfied with their progress. They noted the freshly dug flower beds and newly laid sod in the yard. They'd received reports of round-the-clock workmen, yard laborers, and furniture delivery persons. Yes. It was all very satisfying. They walked up to the front door and rang the bell.

"Ding dong, little Linda, the Trojan horse is here," said Carey under her breath, beaming at Harley.

The Millers were in high spirits, and Linda was obviously thrilled to pieces about the workmanship that had gone into their home. She gave them the grand tour filled with tiny apologies about this and that being future projects, and this and that being incomplete, and this and that not quite what she envisioned, but she would just have to find an interior designer that was more in tune with their point of view.

Carey was very complimentary and gave her the name of the best interior designer on the East Coast. "Just give her a call," Carey said as she watched Linda program the number into her phone. "She's exclusive, but tell her you're a friend of mine. She'll really help you with all the finishing touches, Linda. Really, she has the most wonderful taste. The area over the mantel? What you choose for that—trust me, it's everything."

Damien didn't like the sound of that and steered them on to the newly completed porch where he had set up a bar. "So, guys, I thought we'd just hang here tonight. Enjoy the stars. I got some steaks for the grill. We can relax, maybe play some pool?"

Carey made a face and looked at Harley. "I'm sooo bad at pool. Harley enjoys it, but the last time I played, I ripped up Daddy's billiard felt with my cue. Not my finest hour." She shrugged. "Maybe we'll try it."

Damien cringed, thinking of the felt on his pool table being ripped up.

"We could play some cards or games, whatever strikes our mood. What can I get you to drink?" he said as they sat down on the new all-weather wicker porch furniture surrounded by wildly excessive floral arrangements.

Carey had to lean forward in her chair to see Damien around a massive spray of gladiolas and eye-poking birds of paradise. Linda made a leap to move it out of the way. "Whatcha got over there?" said Carey.

Harley stepped up to the bar and began lifting some of the bottles, showing them to Carey for inspection.

"Whatever you want," said Damien, confident that the wine and liquor were more than adequate, even though he was still smarting over the several-thousand-dollar tab he'd spent setting it up.

Harley walked back over to Carey and said, "I think some red wine would be nice."

"That sounds good. Maybe we could make a sangria?" Carey said hopefully, looking at Linda.

"Ooooh, that does sound yummy!" Linda said enthusiastically.

"Do you have a pitcher and some sugar, and limes and champagne?" said Carey. "You have some really nice reds over there. Damien, did you want to try some sangria?"

Damien fidgeted in his seat. What were they talking about? Were they going to take the hundred-dollar bottles of red wine that the liquor store said would be a perfect complement for steak and mix them up with sugar and champagne? He had only bought four bottles of red! How many were they going to use?

Linda ran to the bar and grabbed a couple bottles of red. Carey, behind her, snagged the remaining two. "Let's go in the kitchen and mix them up," said Linda, giggling. "Naturally we keep the champagne in the fridge. There are more limes inside as well."

Damien stared at the door and wondered what the heck just happened to his plan. Harley walked the length of the porch as he languidly ran his hand along the rail and inspected the view of the river. "Sangria is nice, but one glass is plenty for me. It's so sweet, I'll probably switch to a cab with dinner if we're having steak."

Damien felt sick, knowing there would be no "cab" to be had when dinner was ready.

"This is a beautiful view, Damien, you're a lucky man! How long have you been in this place did you say?"

"Oh, a few years," said Damien, grateful for the change of subject. "We bought several lots and plan to have a garden over there. Linda wants to plant vegetables, have a few chickens, maybe even get a goat and a horse or two."

"Chickens and goats? You mean you're building a Petit Trianon? That sounds very charming. Will you have other animals as well?"

Petit what did he say? "Yeah, I don't know, I'm not sure I'm on board with the horse thing. We'd have to build a barn for it, and frankly, it seems like a lot of work for Linda. I really won't have any time for any of it with my businesses, but MaryLou and Linda have been spending a lot of time talking about it recently."

"Where is MaryLou? I was hoping we could meet her. Will she be home soon?"

"No, she's staying with Linda's parents this weekend." He took out his phone and pulled up a picture of MaryLou and handed it to Harley. "That's her a few months ago. Father of a good-looking girl. Guys will be lining up in a few short years. That'll be interesting." He smiled with pride as Harley nodded and handed it back.

"You're lucky to have a daughter, man, and to have her

while you're still so young. My dad was really old when he had me, and we didn't spend nearly enough time together growing up." He shrugged. "But now that he's older and I'm older, we have a more mature understanding. He's not just a dad, you know? He is that, but my business adviser now, too. Kinda different I guess."

At that point, the giggly girls emerged from the kitchen with a huge pitcher of red wine filled with oranges, lemons, and limes.

"Damien! You're gonna love this!" shrieked Linda. "Carey gave me the recipe that they use at Whispering Cliffs when they celebrate Cinco de Mayo! It is sooooo yummy," she said while pouring out large glasses for everyone.

"Let's take a walk by the river," said Harley. "Damien was just telling me about your plans to recreate Marie Antoinette's Petit Trianon! Carey, you would love it. You've always talked about how you wanted a *leetle farm,*" he said as he kissed her.

The next afternoon...

It was an awesome evening, thought Linda. *I can't believe I'm best friends with Carey Carrows! God, I think I'm half in love with Harley too. Oh my God, they are sooo sexy together. My stupid Jersey friends can suck it. Remodeling the house soooo paid off, and Carey was so complimentary. I love my new and wonderful life!*

It was a productive evening, thought Carey. *I got a lot of details about their schedule, their home, and their family, which will be useful. Her decorator was God-awful. Crap contemporary in the house with weird, uncomfortable furniture juxtaposed with rocking chairs and crocheted afghans on their porch. I'll have to remember that broad's name, she might be useful in some twisted way in the future.*

She smiled, trying to envision her parents, Henry and Julia, actually celebrating Cinco de Mayo with sangria. Maybe they would have a piñata too. It was clear Linda and Damien were trying awfully hard to impress her, and that's exactly where she wanted them to be. Time for the next step.

Yeah, it was a fun night, thought Damien, but damn, it was expensive. The investment on the outside of the property was never going to be a waste, but he couldn't write off the interior decorating as home improvements. He'd been really uncertain about the stuff Linda and that snooty decorator bought, but Harley and Carey seemed to like it, so what did he know? Linda and Carey seemed to really connect, and it sounded like she was going to be around the East Coast for some time. Damien was going to have to put on his thinking cap and try to figure out how and when the Carrows slot machine would start to pay off.

Chapter 12

Henry and Julia went back to California while the rest of the family stayed on the East Coast to continue their work against Titan. In daily contact, they each knew their roles and when to play them. After Charlotte and Alex got back from a brief honeymoon at a secluded beach house in Nantucket, Charles used their guest room as his Manhattan base. The four of them with Petunia were making up for the past few years apart and having a wonderful time.

Charlotte, Alex, Charles, Isabella, and Finn sat together in Charlotte's kitchen at a long antique butcher block table of light pine that matched the hardwood floors. The open cabinetry, crockery, and copper pots gave the country French kitchen a soft, warm feel. Clusters of ornately framed landscape oil paintings by noteworthy impressionists decorated the walls.

Charlotte reached into the oven and pulled out a tray of chocolate popovers. She turned them over on a wire rack and immediately poked a small hole in the side of each to let the steam escape.

Finn said, "The farmers started organizing a few months ago. Every one of us signed a letter from our group lawyer asking for a meeting with Damien, and it was a complete failure. He just shut down and told us he would no longer speak to us without Samara Poe being in on the calls. Now everyone is paranoid about calling the company about anything for fear of being recorded."

Charlotte placed a dish with honey butter and another with fresh whipped cream on the table. She gave Isabella's arm a short squeeze as she turned to the stove and began plating the steaming popovers.

Finn continued. "About a month ago, six of the original nine hired a litigation lawyer and started to get serious about getting Damien to the mediation table. I would have made that number seven, but as you know, I dropped out and became best friends with Damien." Finn made a disgusted face.

"The other three farmers don't know what to do. Everyone has been hammering at Titan with questions about the model, and they have no answers. The lawyer for the six farmers standing sent Samara and Damien a letter demanding mediation, and yesterday they got a response. Samara sent each one of them default and termination letters. One of the terminations was immediate for the farmer in Pennsylvania. And listen to what they terminated him for. Last winter, we all came together for an annual operations conference. We were all complaining that we were really sucking wind because we didn't have any money, and this farmer says he can save money by purchasing feed locally rather than through Titan Feed. So, Damien, in front of all the other farmers, told this guy to go ahead but only because it made sense for his territory. Now that this guy is asking for mediation, Samara and Damien sent him an immediate termination notice for failure to use Titan Feed as outlined in the contract."

"Ah, hell." Alex grimaced. "He lied to the man, and you were all witnesses to it, and he used that as grounds for termination? Immediate termination? You realize they are doing this to keep the fraud under wraps."

"Yup, as of yesterday, this guy can no longer even sell his birds or raise birds or even answer his phone as Titan Farms unless he wants to break federal law and suffer a possible Lanham fine, which is legitimately serious. The lawyer told him that reversing a termination would be really difficult since courts usually only look to the contract, but that he could sue for wrongful termination. But the problem is, what is this guy going to do in the meantime? We all signed noncompetes in our contract, so it's not like he can remove the marks and the signs and do business as Bolten Farms or something. He's totally screwed. He's dead."

Charlotte jumped as the water kettle whistled. "Sorry, Finn, go on," she said as she removed the kettle from the stove and poured it into the French press with freshly ground coffee waiting on the table.

Finn continued. "The rest of the group were defaulted for nonpayment of various loans they got from Titan so they could purchase the latest mandated equipment, but none of us are making regular payments to them so we can keep production going. We all had a choice to make. Feed the birds, make payroll, or pay on the loans. But now three of them have ten days to cure, and Titan even added a $50,000 penalty for failure to cure, and if they don't pay it all, they will be looking at the same thing as the Pennsylvania guy."

Charlotte stirred the brew while Charles reached over, put a popover on his plate, pulled it apart, and added the honey butter. He licked some melted chocolate off his fingers and reached for his napkin. "So, Damien Miller is going scorched earth and terminating. He'll probably explain to new interested parties that the first group of farmers were deadbeats and didn't pay him, and he didn't have a choice. He could still sell more farms, and if nothing is filed in court, he doesn't have to disclose any litigation claims."

"You want to know something else that's sick?" said Finn. "Samara signed the default and termination letters with 'Have a lovely day.'"

"She's a sick twist." Charles ripped off a part of the pastry and popped it into his mouth. "Okay." He chewed. "So, we have a problem that needs immediate resolution. We have to get a legal defense fund together for the remaining guys to string this out until we're done with the Takedown. Lawyers have a way of responding to money.

Research, huge, weighty briefs filled with cumbersome legalese will slow things down. We'll finance it, but the money needs to purportedly come from someone's wife or family member and not from you, Finn. Damien may be an ass, but it wouldn't be hard for him to figure out where the money came from since you're so associated with us. But then, it's not like anyone has to disclose to Damien or Samara how they're funding their legal fees."

"Well, I'm no longer in the group," Finn said as he jammed a butter knife into his roll. "Some of them won't even talk to me."

The coffee went around the table as each of them poured a small cup and dug in to the spread of food.

"The thing is, the group can't say a word about sudden legal financing. Maybe we could approach the lawyers directly and make an—" Alex air quoted. "'Anonymous' donation to the cause. The lawyer could present it—tell them he got the money on the condition that it not be revealed who did it." He paused here to watch Charles chew over the words. Getting no response, he added, "They'll scratch their heads, but my guess is that they won't turn the help away."

"I'm worried about some of them too," Isabella said, her eyes downcast as she picked at her popover. "They're really nice people with families and mortgages. The farmer in Ohio, his wife has heart problems. All this is causing terrible stress on her. We heard he cried on the conference call yesterday and was so embarrassed he hung up. I can't believe Titan would just burn them all and not want to help build the business."

"He doesn't have to, honey," said Finn. "He'll get his money or the business through the liens on the foreclosures or the bankruptcies, assuming they don't settle. And he can keep selling more. Once it's over, he'll be there to pick through the bones."

"Not anymore," said Charlotte as she reached over and took Isabella's hand. "Dad's going to take Titan away from Damien and support all of the farmers until they're profitable. I don't know if he wants to expand the model, but he told me he would see to it that either they became profitable, or he would structure a deal to make them whole again so they could walk away relatively unhurt."

Alex lowered his voice and said with gravity, "Damien Miller came into the farmers' homes, ruining them to line his pockets. Now it's our turn to go into his house and do the same."

Charles nodded and said, "Correct. Time to ramp this up." Smiling, he looked down at his hand and twisted a gold ring on his finger. "Finn, I'll let you in on a little something. I know we're keeping you in the dark, but for something to savor, Damien's foreman, Roland Kylian, the guy running Damien's model farm, was just made an offer he couldn't refuse. Damien's about to have a difficult day."

Charles stood and grabbed his cup off the table. "Finn, Isabella, enjoy the rolls. Alex, let's take this in the other room. We've got some calls to make. Carey needs to get on the phone with the simpering Linda Miller, and unfortunately, we have to have another dinner with her and her husband." Charles looked amongst them, almost gleeful, and whispered, "And the two of them will receive a very special delivery while we dine."

Chapter 13

The perpetually smelly Roland Kylian stood in front of Damien. Practically spitting out his words, he said, "I've been with you for four years, man. You talked and talked about giving me more money, a 401K, health benefits, more help, but they were just words to you. You never came through!"

Damien was completely stunned that Roland was leaving him. He'd talked to the guy about the money, but he couldn't believe one of his competitors had actually come through with such a great offer.

"Heritage is offering you $50K more a year?" Damien said, still trying to wrap his head around it. Roland had been his best and most reliable foreman. He was critical to Damien's model farm and affiliate companies.

"And benefits. Health insurance, man. It's bullshit that you never gave that to me."

"We've been ramping up, Roland. I told you that! Once the numbers hit a certain level, then I can offer benefits to everyone. I told you I couldn't just make the offer to you. If I gave benefits to you, then I'd have to do it for everyone. It's some bullshit law. It's not my fault. *I* appreciated you. Come on, you know that. You've got to stay. How 'bout I give you some cash, something off the books, right? Heritage sure as shit isn't going to offer you that. You're going to pay taxes out your ass over there, buddy."

"Even with taxes, I'm coming out way ahead. You had your chance. I'm out of here." Roland left the trailer and slammed the door.

"Shit!" Damien said as he kicked a wad of actual chicken excrement with the tip of his boot. He opened the trailer door, pushed it outside with his foot, and yelled, "Roland!"

Roland turned around and glared at him.

Damien pointed at him. "One word. You say one fucking word to the rest of the crew about your offer at Heritage, and I swear to God I'll have Samara take it out of your ass." Damien slammed the door and made his way toward his office, fuming. He knew Heritage Farms was doing well, he just didn't know they were investing so much in their labor.

"Fuck!" He was going to have to find another foreman fast. Who could he promote? Jose? Yeah, he could handle it for a while. Maybe. He'd tell him he fired Roland. Gotta find someone more capable though. He picked up his phone and jumped when it rang.

It was Linda—screaming. He held the phone away from his ear but could still hear the shrill words.

"Damien! You'll never believe what happened. Carey just called and invited us to go to Atlantic City with them over the weekend! And, they want us to fly down there in *their plane!* They said they have the presidential suite at the Atlantic Hotel, and there are four bedrooms, so we could share that with them too. Oh my God! Isn't this great? D? Say something!"

"What? Yeah, that sounds good. I'm just having a shitty day," he said as he smashed his hand on his half-eaten tuna fish sandwich and threw it hard into the trash. "When did you say we needed to leave? Did we need to catch the plane in Manhattan?"

"No! They said they would have the plane fly to our local airport, and they would pick us up on Friday afternoon."

"Really? They're gonna pick us up at the Morristown Airport?" He sat down behind his desk and hit a familiar link on his computer to Craigslist.

"Yup, on Friday. I already called Mom, and she can take MaryLou and Puddin' for the weekend, although MaryLou didn't seem all that thrilled to spend another weekend with them."

His brows creased with irritation. "Why doesn't she stay with my parents this weekend? It's their turn anyway."

"I don't know, D. You know I worry about your dad. He just drinks way too much around her. I'd rather have her stay at my mom's."

Damien bit his tongue about his own concerns over Linda being the one drinking too much around MaryLou. What was the difference? "Look, it's their turn. Give them a call, and check and see if they want her, will ya? They know your folks had her last weekend."

"Okaaayyy. I'll make it work, sweetie. I'm so excited! We're gonna have a ball. But, Damien, you do realize that I'm going to need to do some shopping for the weekend?"

Whatever. *Yeah,* he thought, *I deserve a weekend away from all the petty shit of the business.* Fuck his foreman, he'd find another one. What a bunch of fucking whiners.

———

That Friday evening as Carey, Harley, Linda, and Damien landed in Atlantic City, a man in a yard maintenance vehicle pulled into the Millers' driveway. With the closest neighbor being a half mile away and yard maintenance trucks regularly coming and going, it was no big deal when this one arrived. The man got out of his truck and filled his lawn spreader with buckthorn seeds and proceeded to spread them all over the Millers' yard. After he took some time to water the yard, he pulled out several crates and placed them into the brand-new flower beds and spread a nice variety of flavorful seeds all over the area. He then carefully opened each of the crates and released about fifty mature and infant voles. He reloaded his truck and drove away.

———

"So anyway, I hope you don't mind," Carey said to them as the limo from the airport drove them to the Atlantic Hotel, "tomorrow night we're having dinner with Charlotte, Alex, Charles, and John Wallace, who's a good friend of Charles's. Did you meet him at the wedding?"

Damien remembered the man. He'd been pleasantly surprised that he and Linda had been seated next to him at Charlotte's reception. The man was a major Manhattan banker, and Damien had been thrilled to have the chance to fill the guy's ear. He was always in need of good and obliging bankers. Damien recalled that they had gotten along incredibly well. This was perfect.

"Yeah, I remember him. He was seated at our table. Nice guy."

"Oooohhh, he *was* a nice guy," said Linda. "His wife was really nice too. She had on some beautiful jewelry, but I wasn't sure if it was real or not," she said, wrinkling up her nose.

"Oh, it was probably real," said Carey. "The Wallaces would have wanted to impress Daddy. They go back a long way, and John is our personal banker. For almost all of my friends too. Very generous, if you know what I mean," she said and winked at Damien. "He's a lot of fun, but his wife can be pretty boring. Thank God she won't be there."

"I completely agree. She really iced me out that night at dinner. Pretentious bitch." Linda gulped the champagne.

By the time the limo dropped them at the hotel door, they were already half in the bag, but the hotel staff went out of their way to make sure the Carrows party were treated like royalty. Or at least half of them were. From the moment they arrived, staff were respectfully accommodating and thoughtful to Carey Carrows and Harley's every desire.

The four of them left the hotel that night after a few appetizers in the bar and pub-crawled along the boardwalk. They stopped in a few places and danced. Regardless of where they went, the night was paved with solicitous courtesy. Damien saw Harley doling out cash left and right. There was something about Harley and Carey that people made room for. Their posture, their beauty, Carey's jewelry, Harley's cash—the blend kept them above the fray. The red carpet followed them wherever they went.

Back at the Atlantic Hotel at the end of the night, they finally hit the casino tables. Carey brought them to a room cordoned off from the rest by security. A heavy cross-stitch needlepoint carpet in golds and reds blanketed the floors. Draperies in similar shades framed the doorway, and a nautical theme graced the walls, depicting great ships and Revolutionary War–era portraits. Carey walked directly over to her brother, Charles, who was seated at a blackjack table under a portrait of Blackbeard's famous ship, *Queen Anne's Revenge.*

Charles suspended his play and stood briefly to greet the group. "Hey, guys, having fun? Damien, Linda, good to see you," he said, shaking Damien's hand and giving Linda a hug. "Carey texted me. I got in after you left, otherwise, I would have joined you. Glad I didn't though, I'm on a roll here. You want to join me?" he said, indicating the two open comfortable chairs next to him as he sat. There was only one other player at the table, a quiet man, but he didn't have quite as many chips in front of him as Charles.

Carey said, "I don't want to play, but Harley does. How 'bout you, Damien?" She smiled at him and grabbed Linda's arm. She whispered loudly in Linda's ear, "Come on, I've got to pee."

The girls giggled off as Harley and Damien took a seat. Damien saw the load of chips in front of Charles and figured the guy had about a quarter million dollars in front of him. He blinked in astonishment but tried to retain his cool.

An impeccably dressed pit boss approached the table and said, "Gentlemen, this is a no-limit table. Minimum bet is $500. Have you established your credit limits with us?"

"They're with me," Charles said. "I'll back 'em. Give them what they want. I'll settle up with them later."

The pit boss nodded. Harley said, "I'll start with a hundred."

Damien was slightly sickened when he realized that meant he'd asked for $100,000.

The dealer turned to him. "Sir?"

"Yeah, ah, I'll start with twenty," Damien said.

"Yes, sir," the dealer said as he counted out the chips.

The girls were gone for an extraordinarily long time. Drunk but emboldened, Damien played the high-stakes game with Charles, Harley, and the quiet man. A very expensive brandy was offered to the table. Several beautiful women appeared, standing near him, encouraging him and flirting with the table. But other than those perks, it did not go well.

———————

Damien and Linda woke up the next morning in their sumptuous bedroom in the California king bed, each with a set of personal regrets, which they didn't immediately share with the other. Linda was horrified that she had puked in Carey's bathroom while Carey held her hair and Damien that he had lost about $30K at the blackjack table. Charles told him to mail him a check.

Damien knew he had it, but he sure as hell didn't want to use it. It was too late now. No way could he welch on that IOU. But more than that, he didn't want to tell Linda. Besides, she looked ill. Again. Maybe he'd find a time to tell her about it later.

Damien left the bedroom in search of coffee. He was surprised by a stranger. Harley and Carey were not in the room. "Good morning, sir. My name is Cadell. I'm your butler. I've taken the liberty of setting up a small buffet. Coffee and tea, a selection of juices. If you'd prefer, I can have something else off the menu brought to you."

Damien looked over his shoulder as Linda walked into the room and stared at Cadell. "Good morning, ma'am." Cadell nodded in her direction and continued. "Naturally, if something you require is not on the menu, we'd be happy to prepare it." He looked at Linda and said, "Or if you'd like, I could provide service for you in bed?"

Linda gathered her robe around her and sat open-mouthed on a sofa as Damien said, "No, this is fine. Are the others up?"

"No, sir. But I've been instructed to arrange for a masseuse either in your room or on the balcony. It's quite nice today. You may enjoy it. Are you ready for that? May I call them?"

Damien turned to Linda, who nodded slightly and lay back.

"Thank you. That would be nice," Damien said.

"Anything else I can prepare for you?" the butler said, indicating the food and beverage.

"No. This is fine. I'll let you know."

"Very good, sir," he said, nodding his head and extending a card. "Call me anytime. I'm here to be of service." Cadell left the suite.

Damien looked back at Linda, who had a small smile on her face. "Call him back. I think I'd like a cheeseburger, fries, a Coke, and Advil. In bed." She got up. "Medium well, Damien," she said as she left the room.

Damien did as instructed.

———————

The morning proceeded, and they received tender loving care by the solicitous staff. After a long nap that afternoon by the pool, they were feeling better as the four of them came back into the suite to prepare for dinner. It was a lifestyle the Millers could become accustomed to. They had no idea until that weekend what truly little lives they'd lived and how incredibly different the very rich were treated.

Cadell appeared as they entered the suite. Carey kicked off her shoes and said, "We're going to jump in the shower. Have the makeup artists here in thirty minutes."

"Very good, madam," said Cadell. "The stylist is here with the racks in your room. I believe she is preparing."

Carey put her arm around Linda and said, "Sweetie, you're going to look gorgeous. I've got the perfect dress for you. You will try it on, won't you?" Carey pouted.

As they lay by the pool that afternoon, Carey had shared that one of her favorite things in the world was fashion. "Wherever I go, I always have loads of clothes. It's so much fun. Please play dress-up with me tonight, Linda. It would make me so happy."

Linda was happy to oblige. "Of course, Carey."

"Yay." Carey clapped her hands and ran toward her room. "Wear your robe. Meet me in my room in thirty minutes." She stopped at the doorway and said, "Oh, and, Cadell, we'd better have a couple bottles of Cristal handy, just in case."

The fawning staff helped transform the women. Cadell served the champagne as the makeup artists went to work. The stylist had laid out several options, and eventually, they made their decisions.

The men waiting, Carey walked into the main room in a sequined mini cocktail dress that plunged into unadorned, voluptuous cleavage. The metal tips of her lace-up suede sandals caught the light and elongated her legs, and she wore impressive yellow diamonds on her ears and hand. The long sleeves of the dress were the only modest part of her head-to-toe Balmain attire.

Linda emerged behind her and floated into the room wearing a floor-length, strapless printed trapeze gown with a banded neckline, in colors of blue and white. But the touch that really brought the dress together was the Cartier choker of eighteen-carat white gold set with diamonds and lapis from their Panthere Collection. She also wore the Cartier earrings of white gold and diamond panthers made with sapphire, onyx, and diamonds, which cascaded in beaded drops.

"Doesn't she look great?" Carey said, approaching Damien, his eyes wide staring at his wife. Carey gave him a couple of air kisses and a head-to-toe appraisal. "You look very handsome yourself, Damien. I'm glad Linda told you to pack a suit."

Carey went over to Harley, kissed him softly on the lips, and steered him toward the front door.

Linda smiled and searched Damien's eyes as she put her hand to her throat and to the diamond choker. Damien walked over and gave her a kiss on the cheek and said, "You look very pretty."

Linda blushed and whispered to Damien, "My God, Damien. She told me the jewelry is from Cartier. It's worth about a quarter million dollars. Can you believe it?" she enthused, all lit up.

"Just don't lose that shit," he mumbled as they walked toward the door.

Linda shot him a look filled with hate. Just like that, the fantasy bubble she was luxuriating in burst. She was *royally* pissed off.

Linda shook off Damien's hand after they got off the elevator. The four of them walked through the hotel to meet up with the rest of the group in the lobby of the Atlantic Art Gallery.

"Mommy and Dad are big supporters of their favorite artists," Carey explained. "They're major collectors. Art has been an important part of my life for as long as I can remember. Mom and Dad couldn't be here tonight for the opening, so the rest of the family is representing them. I'm sure you'll enjoy it. You know Charlotte is a bit of an artist herself. I don't know where she got it, but my sister has so many wonderful talents."

They entered the gallery. "Ah, here we are. Charlotte!" Carey gushed, greeting her sister and embracing her in a huge and lingering hug. "I missed you! How was the honeymoon? You look amazing!" she said, pulling back and examining her.

Charlotte had on a black Alexis embroidered hi-lo dress with structured pleats, a halter neckline, and V-back, with considerable emerald jewelry. Carey turned to bring Linda into their circle. "Look at my sister, Linda, don't emeralds match her beautiful eyes perfectly?"

"Thank you for the compliment, Carey." Charlotte blinked. Turning her attention, she said, "Linda, you look great. That dress was absolutely handmade for your figure."

"Didn't I tell you, Linda?" Carey smiled. "The three of us are certainly doing the Carrowses' image justice tonight," she said in a whisper.

The couples glided through the exhibition, and Linda ignored her stupid husband. Carey and Charlotte led her over to a particular painting and stopped to admire it.

"Linda, look at that," said Carey. "It's extraordinary. And you know what? It would be perfect for that spot above your mantel in your great room where you were looking for an important piece. Don't you think?"

"This particular artist," said Charlotte, "is a favorite of Mom's. She must have three or four of his pieces at Whispering Cliffs. It's the reason we're here supporting him this evening. Mommy told me to keep an eye out for something new that she might love. God knows she'd love this."

Linda was overwhelmed standing between the Carrows women, swaying in a beautiful gown, wearing extravagant jewelry. *This must be what it feels like to be them*, she thought, swept away. Overcome, Linda heard herself say, "I'll buy it." The Carrows girls turned to look at her and, as fortune would have it, the gallery owner happened to be standing next to them.

"Yes ma'am," he said. "I'll have it delivered to your suite this evening, and you can pay for it at checkout. I hope you have many happy years enjoying this wonderful work of art." He bowed and disappeared.

And later...

At dinner that evening, Linda realized that John Wallace was indeed a lot more fun without his wife in attendance. Once again, it turned into a raucous party, albeit one set with exquisite wines and five-star dining. Linda noticed that Carey seemed to be a lot more fun than Charlotte, and she dressed a lot more funner than Charlotte too. Charlotte was sooo conservative! Why the press was always interested in Charlotte and not Carey was now a mystery to Linda. She only hoped that they would all finally have their picture taken and be seen in the tabloids. Especially in this dress!

At dinner that evening, Damien took advantage of his time with John Wallace and Charles Carrows and worked his best to impress them and to project his image as a man who was going places. Charles sure seemed interested in his vision. Damien was proud of the way he'd instinctively kept his cool the night before when he'd lost $30K at the blackjack table. He was pretty confident now that it had impressed Charles. Except for his gambling loss and Linda's incredibly stupid purchase at the gallery—without even fucking asking him—Damien thought the weekend had gone very well. The fact that he'd secured a meeting with John and Charles the following week was the maraschino cherry on top.

At dinner that evening, Charlotte grabbed and squeezed Alex's hand under the table when she saw Damien whispering furiously into Linda's ear after she loudly ordered more wine from a passing waiter. Charlotte was also impressed with, and appreciated more fully, the vital role Carey was playing with these two losers. She reminded herself to sincerely thank Carey for doing the dirty job of hanging out with the slime.

On Sunday evening after Carey Carrows's private plane once again touched down at the Morristown Airport, the pilot taxied over to the hangar where Damien had left his car. While the girls and Harley were hugging it out next to the plane, the copilot and Damien retrieved the bags. Damien wheeled Linda's new soft-sided suitcase across the hangar to his car, and as he got closer, he noticed that something was terribly wrong. The entire driver's side of the car was crumpled inward as though it had been T-boned.

"What the fuck?" he screamed, rushing over to caress the battered door of his $128,000 Audi. The group came running over, their faces drawn.

"How the fuck did something like this happen at a private airport hangar? Who did this?" Damien yelled.

"Damn," Harley said, inspecting the car. "Man, did a truck do that? Maybe something backed into it?"

"Goddamn it! Who did this? Isn't there any security around here or fucking cameras?" Damien gestured wildly around the extremely small and quiet airstrip, his voice echoing in the dark night.

There was no one on duty that evening next to the hangar, and they all realized that Damien wouldn't be able to drive the car home. Carey got out her phone, trying to be helpful, but came up saying, "I wonder if they have a limousine service in Morristown."

"I got this," Harley said as he jumped to order the transportation. "I'll call a cab."

"Someone should be here in a few minutes, Damien," Carey said, walking over to comfort him, stroking his arm. "I'm so sorry this happened, and after such a fun weekend too. Listen, I know it sucks, but cars can be fixed, right?" she trailed off, looking at heads for support of her statement. She mumbled something supportive and walked back to Harley.

Damien tried to recover himself and be cool about it too, but he was beyond furious. He squatted next to his sweet baby and ran his hand over the crushed wheel rims, staring at it. He fucking *loved* his car.

Sitting back on his heels he said, "No, you're right, it can be fixed." He got up and looked at Harley, his arm supportive around Carey, still scrolling through his phone. "Linda and I will take a cab home and have it towed to a body shop tomorrow. Sorry I lost my cool there, it's just that I love that car so damn much."

"No sweat, bro," Harley said, smiling as he closed his

phone, the call to the taxi service forgotten. He pointed back toward the airplane with his thumb. "We gotta take off and get back to Manhattan. Sorry to leave you like this. You're okay, right?"

"Yeah, of course, no problem. We'll be fine. Hey, give me a call, we'll hang out."

"You guys are so great. We'll see you soon!" Carey said as she and Harley walked back to the plane. As they climbed the stairs of the Learjet, they turned to wave one last time before they disappeared inside.

Damien stared over at Linda, looking hungover as hell, grasping the bubble-wrapped painting she'd bought at the gallery, and fumed. Damien pulled up his phone and called a cab. They waited for it in silence as they watched Carey and Harley's jet fly off toward the stars and into the night.

Carey relaxed into the plane's velvety-soft leather seats and smiled. She called Charles. "It was perfect. The car was undrivable."

"How did he react?" said Charles.

"He nearly came undone," Carey said, looking at Harley, who had his head thrown back and his eyes closed. He looked exhausted.

"What else did you get?"

"MaryLou's big dance recital is on Wednesday at 7:00 p.m. I think we should impede Damien's attendance."

"I'm on it. I know who to call. By my calculations,

wading through all the information we've obtained on Damien's financial picture, we made a very big dent in his personal portfolio this weekend."

"His marriage is certainly not solid either. I can tell you that. He's constantly giving her the stink eye but not when she's looking. Linda was acting like a total prima donna last night. Did you hear her bad-mouthing the taste of some of the other guests? This coming from her?"

Charles sighed. "Well, now it's my turn to step it up with Damien. I can't wait to spend more time with him."

"We'll be at the Carlyle. Call me if you need me."

"We're going to need you back in AC soon," said Charles.

"Not tonight you won't. Talk to you later."

Chapter 14

Damien couldn't believe the weekend they'd had. It was both awesome and awful at the same time. The only really good news was that he'd had a chance to steal some quiet time with Charles and John Wallace, and they agreed to meet with him to discuss some mutual business opportunities. Damien had *plans*. He was sick of all the petty shit he had to deal with and all the peons in life. It was time for him to become a real Titan.

The rest of the week didn't get any better. He was driving a piece-of-shit rental while his car was being overhauled, and the insurance company was bellyaching over the cost. It wasn't his fault that replacement doors and siding would cost almost as much as half the cost of the car. He didn't care; he just wanted his baby back. The dealer wouldn't commit to the length of the repair job. So for now, it was Chevy city. He felt like a dope. No cameras at the airport either, and the stupid Morristown cops just shrugged and filed a report. Nothing else to do, just one of those things.

Then, midweek, as he left the office to attend MaryLou's year-end dance recital, he ran over some kind of spike in the parking lot and got a flat tire. The timing couldn't have been worse. He called roadside assistance, but they would take about an hour to get to him. He tried calling some of his crew to ask for help or a ride, but oddly, they didn't seem inspired to come help the boss. He growled, pretty confident that Roland Kylian had told everyone about his big break at Heritage.

He ended up missing the recital, and he knew Linda was never going to let it go, MaryLou either. So many tears and so much drama. It wore him out. He didn't want to listen to Linda's whining. Or *anyone's* whining for that matter. He finally got them to quiet down by greenlighting their new project of creating a Petit Trianon.

Carey had put this brainchild into Linda's head, and Linda wouldn't let it go. It was all she could talk about now. They were going to be just like Marie Antoinette. It looked like they would be constructing an outbuilding and buying some sheep. What the hell.

At the end of the week, he couldn't wait to get back to Atlantic City to meet with Charles and John Wallace. He couldn't believe how great it felt to know that he'd soon be back in the company of rich and powerful men. He needed to get away from all the crappy little drama. Linda didn't bitch at all about his leaving to meet with them. She fully supported the idea and reassured him that he was destined to be a great man and that she was positive *Johnny and Charlie* would help him get there. On the way out of the house, he crossed paths with the architect who would be planning their new "leetle village."

Oh, man. Whatever.

———————

On the drive down to Atlantic City, Damien reflected on his life and explored his feelings of uncharacteristic angst. Maybe it was just growing pains. He reminded himself that he'd always been successful, and he could get whatever he wanted if he just had enough guts to take it.

And he had the guts. Look what he and Samara were doing to those stupid farmers who thought they could take him down! They shot off some termination letters and told the farmers to sit down and keep quiet, and that's exactly what they did. Intimidation, power, and a damn good contract—it worked every time. Samara was on top of that one, and he frankly couldn't care less what happened to them. There were always more people who would invest in his plan, and he would just keep raking in the cash. That part of the business was working out just fine. He was annoyed that they were incurring some impressive legal fees since Samara had to hire a private lawyer to protect their rights since they were being named personally liable for making the asshole farmers go bankrupt. Let them rot. They wanted to pierce the fucking corporate veil and come after him personally? Let 'em rot. He could always sell more.

He'd worked himself into a small lather vacillating between self-pity for his problems and pumping himself up as Damien-fucking-Miller, a guy on the way to meet Charles-fucking-Carrows and *John Wallace* of Atlantic Banks. He'd be just fine. Tiny setbacks and worrying were for small men, losers. And he was no loser.

That said, he was a little worried about the amount of cash that was going out the door at his businesses and the cash that also seemed to be flying out of his home keeping up with the Carrowses. But he reminded himself that they were all investments that only enhanced his portfolio, image, and professional relationships. Gotta spend money to make money.

Charles had instructed Damien to meet them at his nearly completed casino, simply named "Carrows." According to Charles, the hotel and casino had been a principal project for him and his family, establishing themselves on the Eastern Seaboard and capitalizing on the brand that was theirs. People responded to the Carrows name, associating it with elegance and sophistication. The Carrows family and Whispering Cliffs were like the Hearst family, but without the crazy abductions and bank robberies. They were legend, and they chose Atlantic City to profit on it.

Damien drove through the wrought iron gates that separated the dramatic high-rise from the rest of the world. The exterior had been completed, but the area still bustled with contractors and landscapers, and a construction trailer sat parked in the circle. As Damien pulled around, his wide eyes drank in all the signs of opulent wealth. Twin, twenty-foot doorways rose in a graceful arch, the doors themselves being intricately filigreed wrought iron with the letter *C* worked into the top center. The top of the arch was crafted of faceted glass, giving a peek into the grand foyer, with its massive domed ceiling. A simple gold and black sign hung just beyond the outer iron doors bearing the name "Carrows" in clean, bold print.

As Damien pulled up, a liveried footman came down the red-carpeted steps to greet him.

"Hello, sir. I'm afraid we're not yet open. Do you have an appointment?"

"I'm here to meet Charles Carrows," Damien said, quite proud that he knew the owner.

"Very good, sir. As you can see, we're still under construction, but we have valet." He opened the door for Damien.

"Your name, sir?"

"Damien Miller."

"Mr. Miller, please see reception inside."

"Thank you," Damien said. As the footman got into the car, Damien said, "No ticket?"

"No need, Mr. Miller."

Damien walked up the stairs. The domed ceiling in the reception area was illuminated. Elaborately carved mahogany paneling adorned the walls, the floors a black and white checked marble with the letter *C* framed in the middle. Workmen filled the lobby, all of them assembling what looked to be a massive crystal chandelier. Damien walked past what appeared to be a large wood-burning fireplace and toward a reception area.

He was greeted by a man in a suit. "Hello," said Damien. "I have an appointment with Charles Carrows."

"Yes," the man said. "Mr. Miller?"

"Yes," Damien said, pleased that he was expected.

"Mr. Miller, we apologize for the state of the construction. Mr. Carrows asked me to escort you to his office when you arrived. If you would follow me," he said, coming 'round the space and gesturing down the hall.

Damien followed him. Everywhere, people were working. The receptionist brought him to a closed door. He knocked. Charles's voice from inside said, "Come in."

The receptionist opened the door and revealed a room that resembled an exquisite home space, not like an office at all. Charles stood next to a small dining table with another man wearing jeans and a sports coat. Charles looked over, waving Damien in, and said, "Thank you, Harry." The receptionist left, closing the door behind him.

"Damien," said Charles, "I'll be a moment." He turned back to his guest and spoke quietly.

Damien nodded and walked toward the elegantly draped back windows and looked out at a formal finished garden. Beyond that, he could see an infinity pool, ponds, and pathways. The private exterior of Carrows was peaceful and elegant. No neon in sight. He turned around and examined the tasteful furniture, the leather chairs next to an unlit fireplace, the large ornate desk. The wallpaper was some mix of modern and traditional but in a colorful and peaceful way. Framed art hung on the wall. Damien had a brief flash of his trailer. Disgusted, he shook it off.

Damien looked to Charles as his voice became louder. "As usual, then, my regards to your family." He shook the man's hand, then Charles put his hand on the black duffle bag between them and gestured for the man to take it.

The man picked up the bag, apparently heavy by the way it dropped to his side, and nodded at Charles. "And you to yours," he said. The man looked sharply at Damien, who tried to look innocuous, and left the room, shutting the door behind him.

Charles, at last, addressed him, extending his hand. "Damien, so glad you could make it. Have a seat," he said, indicating a sitting area with two large leather sofas, a coffee table in between.

"This place is amazing," Damien said as he sat. "I had no idea. When do you open?"

"Thank you. We're very close. The upper floors of the hotel are some ways out, but we're on schedule. Or as much as you can be for a project like this. I'm looking forward to the day I can move in." Charles smiled, playing with a gold ring on his finger. "Can I get you something to drink?" he said.

"No, I'm good. Thanks," Damien said, looking around.

"John will be joining us shortly," Charles said, smiling.

There was a long pause. Charles continued to stare at Damien while spinning his ring. Damien had been used to Charles and his high energy. He thought Charles might have something further to say, but when he didn't,

Damien, oddly uncomfortable, said, "Great, can't wait to get started. Hell of a time last weekend, wasn't it?" He smiled back with confidence.

"I heard your car was damaged. That's unfortunate."

"Yeah, the cops don't have a lead. No cameras. I don't know if someone did it by accident or what. Must have been a hell of a hit though."

Charles shook his head. "I'm sorry to hear that. Will you have it back soon?"

"Hope so. Had to drop off a crappy Chevy outside with the valet." He laughed. "You probably don't get too many of them here, huh?"

"Nothing wrong with a Chevy." Charles smiled again. "Nothing wrong with anything really. It all depends on how you look at it." Charles leaned back into the sofa and crossed his legs, his hands clasped in his lap. "Damien," he began slowly, after a long pause, "let me ask you a question. We've been spending some time together. My sisters are certainly fond of Linda. What do you think of us? The Carrows family."

Damien had no idea how to respond to that. "I think you've been great. All of you. We've really enjoyed getting to know you." He wasn't sure why, but he felt himself begin to sweat.

Charles nodded his thanks. "But the Carrows image, the Carrows name, our background, I'm curious. Do you have any thoughts on that?"

"I know you're successful. I mean, obviously. The image? Well, it's an image of luxury, of wealth, I guess."

"Mmmmm," Charles said, looking off, taking some time to consider the response. He looked back. "Do you think my hotel and casino will represent that image well?" Charles questioned, raising an eyebrow.

"God, yeah. It's amazing. I didn't see the casino. I didn't see much actually. Came from just down the hall." He pointed with his thumb. When Charles looked confused, he added. "From reception?"

Charles nodded. He seemed distracted as he removed the ring from his finger, looked at the inside, then slid it back on. "My grandfather's ring. His encryption," Charles said quietly. "It all began with him."

Charles uncrossed his legs and scooted forward, clasping his hands between his knees. Smiling again, he said, "I'd be happy to give you the guided tour a bit later. After we meet with John. Carrows is—" Charles made a small gesture with his hand. "Well, we almost see it as a private club. People off the street will be vetted, and some will get access to the casino, but they will have to pay a large entrance fee to get in. Undesirables will be dissuaded." Charles nodded to himself and stared off as if he was thinking deeply, then resumed. "We want to be an exclusive destination and not a place where people with socks and sandals can just walk in. The accommodations will be five-star, of course. That will attract the moneyed crowd. The hotel will be open to the public as an almost stand-alone with some smaller gaming rooms, a sports bar, and restaurants. But the real money action will be in the clubby, privileged, and luxury atmosphere we will create in the private rooms and casino." Charles stared at him, nodding.

"That sounds cool. Like James Bond time, right?" Damien said.

Charles smiled. "Yes, indeed." He slapped his hand on his leg and rose. He pointed at Damien as he walked to his desk. "I like you, Damien. I've been listening to you carefully. So has John. Speaking of—" He pushed a button on his office telephone and said, "Has Mr. Wallace arrived?"

"Yes, sir. He appears to be in conference with your last appointment. I'll let him know you're ready for him."

"Thank you, Harry," said Charles. He walked toward Damien and picked some architectural drawings of the building off the coffee table. He sat next to him and said, "Let me show you what we're building here, Damien. Let me show you the first step of my dream."

As Charles flipped through the beautiful, colorful renditions, he said, "There will be tiered membership levels in the private casino. Each level will marry differently with hotel accommodations, gratuitous dining, maître d' service, private planes, strippers..." He grinned impishly. "Just kidding on the strippers. But just about everything. We want our members, specifically our investors, to be happy. This is my namesake property. My family and I have already begun planning our next hotel and casino in Las Vegas. After that success, we'll go to Europe."

A knock on the door interrupted them, and John Wallace walked in carrying a briefcase. John, an older man with gray hair, wore a three-piece suit. Damien and Charles stood.

John walked over and greeted them, then went behind Charles's desk and opened his case. "What have you been discussing, then?" asked John, reaching up and adjusting the brightness of a desk lamp.

Charles took a chair in front of the desk, Damien followed suit. Charles said, "I've shown him a few of the plans; we were just getting started."

Damien wasn't sure what was going on as he watched John Wallace continue to unload documents from his case and then, appearing satisfied, clasp his hands on the stack before him. He said, "I see."

John pulled a pair of reading glasses out of his pocket and said, "Damien. What do you think of Carrows?"

"Of the hotel? It's really impressive. I haven't had a chance to see the casinos, but it's different from the other places on the Strip. And in Vegas too. They're all so much bigger."

"True," said John. "Carrows is actually very big, it's just not sprawling in the traditional manner. It has an interesting design. Did he get a chance to look at the drawings?"

"Not really," Charles said. "Some of them. I'll take him around when we're finished."

Damien looked confused. "Excuse me," he said, "I thought we were going to talk about your interest in investing in one of my businesses? Titan Farms, Titan Feed, Titan Fisheries?"

John waved his glasses through the air. "No. That's not going to happen. At least not today. However, Charles wanted to make you an offer. It would certainly lend to your portfolio, and I'd be happy to take a look at your business needs at a later date."

"Damien, Carrows will be owned by my family," Charles said. "Myself, my father and mother, my sisters, and by our shareholders. Even though the project is nearly complete, we are still welcoming partial investors who would support the vision and participate in the profits by purchasing shares in the casino and becoming minor owners. I'd like to extend an invitation for you to invest in my dream. To become a minor shareholder. The absolute minimum shareholder investment is $1,000,000 and would guarantee a percentage of the profits after debt service on construction is satisfied. As I mentioned earlier, all shareholders will receive access to a set number of comp weekends in one of the high-rollers suites and a number of other perks that will not be available to anyone but shareholders. The structure allows for a small, finite number of minor owners. Again, only by invitation, and I am offering that to you."

Charles stopped speaking, and the two men looked at him.

"Really?" Damien sat back in his chair, surprised. "Thank you." His heart raced. He hadn't seen this coming. Charles smiled at him. Damien's wheels turned, considering the offer. He could not see a downside. Henry Carrows, Charles Carrows, Carey, and Charlotte were all investors, and they were family. In addition, Damien had never heard of a scandal or business failure attached to any of them. It was a legitimate business opportunity that would have immense potential and future income guaranteed as the casino business in Atlantic City thrived.

Charles interjected, "I can't give you a list of all the shareholders, but there are a few that you might have met if you've attended a concert or two at Madison Square Garden."

Damien tingled with excitement.

Charles whispered, "Bruce, Bruce, Bruce," and smiled.

Damien quickly did some math. He threw his head back in exasperation and pounded the arms of his chair. "Guys, I would love to become a shareholder of the casino. That's a no-brainer and, really, thank you for the opportunity. It's like a gift, and I get that you are offering it. It means a lot to me. But I just don't know if I can swing it right now. I'm spread out with investments and loans for the companies, and I'm not sure my bankers will see me clear for a million right now. I mean, sure, maybe next year after the boats are paid down, but I'm not seeing it right now," he said with great disappointment, shaking his head.

John Wallace folded his hands on the desk as Charles turned his head and gazed out the window. John said, "Damien, I understand that you have a very loose association with the Carrows family, with a business partnership through Charlotte's marriage, am I right?"

"Yes, Isabella's husband, Finn, and I are business partners in Titan Farms. He's more of a straight farmer, but I consider all my farmers to be partners. It's really important for the health of the organization and for building a successful brand."

John picked up some papers and glanced at them. "I've gotten to know you a little over the last month, and I don't mind saying I've been very impressed with you and what you've accomplished for such a young man starting out on his own."

"Thank you. I appreciate the compliment. Hard work, a commitment to excellence, dedication to the right organizations, and business plans with generous and gutsy capital investments have gotten me where I am today."

"Yes. Prior to meeting with you here today, I hope you don't mind, we took the liberty of doing a criminal background check and a financial background check on the health of your businesses and investments."

Damien was surprised, but he assumed this must be how proactive, high-level-thinking financial guys worked. He glanced at Charles, who looked inquisitive. "I don't mind. I appreciate you taking an interest. I hope you like what you see?"

"I do. The poultry and feed business has been very successful for you. I applaud you for taking the leap in expanding the brand. Your numbers are extremely impressive, and it looks like you're on target to continue growing over the next several years. If you can successfully accomplish that, I believe you will be flying your own plane to and from AC very soon," John said as he smiled at Charles.

"Damien," Charles resumed. "We looked into your background before I made the offer because I couldn't do that if I didn't think you would be a good fit. John and I have been talking, and we think you would be the type of investor we're looking for to help complete our shareholder portfolio at Carrows. You have the guts, the vision, and I think I could see you becoming a larger partner over the next few years as we take our success in AC and extend into Vegas."

"I think you're right in having that confidence in me, and once again, I appreciate it. I'm just not sure how I can swing the million cash right now. It's killing me to say no." Sweat actually ran down his sides as he said this.

"After going over your books, again, only at a high level, John and I agreed that we would be willing to help you finance that loan. We'd need to see a few deeper personal and business financials, but from what we see so far, I don't think there would be an impediment for us to help you get that loan."

Damien felt a lurch in his stomach, as if he was on a rollercoaster. Bingo! he thought. He just leveraged his way into the big boys' club. "Wow, John, Charles, that's great," he said as he put his hand on his heart. "I don't think anyone can lose on this deal. I'll have my attorney send over the financials today."

"All right then, Damien," John said, putting on his glasses and writing something on a card, which he handed to him. "Have your attorney send them over, and I'll send him a draft of the contract outlining the proposal. Do you think he can take a look at it over the weekend so we can sign early next week? I see no reason for delay."

Man, this was moving fast. "Absolutely. She. Samara Poe. We can do that."

Charles stood and helped Damien up with a handshake. "All right, we have a deal...well, almost. How about you call your attorney, and she and John will swap documents, and we'll all meet for dinner tonight to celebrate?"

"I'm sorry," said John as he picked up some papers and glanced at them. "I can't make dinner tonight. I have plans with Trudy." He looked up. "You men enjoy yourself. I'm sure you'll want to spend the rest of the day looking around Carrows and going over the plans and the health of our financials as well. Charles will go over those with you. I'll send the loan and shareholder agreements to your attorney."

John stood and walked them to the door. "Charles," he said, shaking his hand. "Damien," he said, doing the same with him. "Let's shoot to close this down early next week."

"Sounds good, John," Damien said, holding the hand of John Wallace, banker to the stars, and now his new cash cow and best friend. "Just great. Thanks again for the opportunity."

"Charles," he said, "I'll be here for about another hour before I head out."

"Take your time, John," Charles said as he slapped Damien on the back and headed into the hall. "Let's begin the tour with the private casino, shall we?"

John Wallace closed the door on the two of them, walked back to the desk, and placed a call. "Henry! I thought you should know that I just met with Charles and Damien about the million-dollar deal. So, I've done my part, and one more phone call means I've repaid my debt to you. And next time, don't send me these little penny-ante million buck deals. I don't meet anyone who needs funding for under ten and you know that." All bluster, he was having a great time.

Chapter 15

My God, thought Damien, *I'm going to be part owner of a casino.* Not in his wildest imagination would he have believed that this could be happening. If someone had suggested to him only two months ago that he would be in this position, he would have thought they were crazy. It was a dream come true for him. Not just a next step up but a trajectory to the very top. He could just see himself in his casino in a James Bond-like tux playing blackjack next to Mick Jagger. *That could happen.* He pinched himself.

He went into his bedroom of Charles's suite at the Atlantic Hotel before dinner and got on the phone with Samara. "Did you get the company P&Ls over to John Wallace? Did you receive the contract from him about the loan?"

"Okay, settle down now. Yes, I sent Mr. Wallace the P&Ls of Titan Farms, Feed, and Fisheries. I also sent him a copy of your latest personal tax return and your personal loans, contracts, and spreadsheets with our two banks."

"Did you speak with him? Did you get the shareholder contract? Have you looked it over?"

"I'll answer your questions one at a time. Number one, no, I did not speak with him. We have been exchanging emails and documents. Number two, yes, I did get a boilerplate-type contract from him. Number three, I have given it a cursory overview."

"Okay, so what did you think about it overall?" he said, pacing the room.

"Well, like I said, it's boilerplate and a pretty typical bank contract, but where it varies is where it ties directly into the Carrowses' shareholder plan. It is not a stand-alone from him, John Wallace, and his bank. It is a direct agreement for your purchase of shares for $1,000,000, which would be supplied initially by John Wallace and his bank. They must be handling all the shareholders' buy-ins this way, is what I'm thinking. It's boilerplate right now because he hasn't had a chance to review your documents and attach your equities and assets as collateral, and I don't know exactly how that is going to look. I would assume he would need attachments, any bank would."

"Well, when can we expect the final document? Did he say?"

"You both seem to be in a bit of a rush here because he said he would have it back to me today, which is really, really fast. He must not have a lot of higher-ups to deal with if he's just going to write it up himself and send it over."

"I wouldn't imagine he would need those, Samara. It's

John Wallace, remember? We're speaking with the top."

"Again, you seem to be in a hurry here, and I'm not exactly sure why. Have you had a chance to look at Carrows Casino's numbers and shareholder investment disclosures?"

"I've looked at them, but that's your job. That's what I'm paying you to do. I'm the high-level strategy guy, you figure out how to make it happen. That's our arrangement, and let's be clear on this one. I want this deal to happen. It needs to happen. This is the big one for me, the leap I've been waiting my whole life for. The other stuff is small potatoes. So, after you get the documents from John, and after you have a chance to review them, give me a call. I'm in AC with Charlie Carrows right now. I'll be at dinner with him and then we're going out, so hopefully, we can go over this stuff by breakfast tomorrow? Does that sound reasonable?"

"It sounds reasonable. I'll burn the midnight oil and give you a call in the morning."

He hung up. Samara was good. She'd make this happen for him, even if they had to play hardball with John Wallace. God, his head was going to explode if he didn't calm down. Maybe he should take her advice and ease off the pedal and slow this thing down.

––––––––––––––

That evening Charles and Damien walked into Fat Tony's, an upscale steakhouse on the Strip where Charles had asked Damien to make them a reservation. Unfortunately, when the two of them arrived at the restaurant, there was no reservation under Damien's name, and they weren't going to let them in. At that point, Charles stepped forward and had a private word with the maître d'. Damien fumed, embarrassed, as a table suddenly opened up for them. Damien felt like a stupid kid. He was sick of being the little man.

After dinner, they went back to the Atlantic Hotel and hit the casino floor. They spent some time playing a few slots, but Charles begged off early and said he had somewhere to be in the morning. Damien decided that was cool and called it an early night as well. Worldly men, making business come first. Righteous.

The next morning Damien woke up to the sound of his phone. It was Samara. "Hey, D, I'm not waking you up, am I? I thought you wanted to talk after breakfast?"

"No, you didn't wake me up," he lied. "I'm just moving slow. I had a long night with Charles Carrows at the blackjack table."

"Yeah, so I got the final contract from John Wallace, and it has quite a few attachments of your assets. You're stretched pretty tight right now; a few false steps and you wouldn't have much room to move."

Damien threw back the butter-soft, six-hundred-thread-count sheets and slid out of bed. He wasn't going to listen to any crap that could mess up this deal. "Samara, you don't seem to understand what is happening here. John Wallace wants to make a deal with me. He has confidence in me and my success, and I'm sure it's just a starting point—I can always go back for more. He's our new silver tuna."

"I'm not sure about that. How bankers work sometimes baffles me. I know you have two really solid bankers here locally, and that's one of the reasons it works, because they're local. The boys in AC and Manhattan, I don't know how they work."

"Well, what about the rest of the agreement? Does it seem pretty straightforward?" he asked, pacing the room.

"For the most part. It's a solid document. They have a lot of protections, but then I would expect that. You're not unfamiliar with most of them. This is the first time you would be in the back seat so to speak, however. It's a document that protects them from you, not the other way around. Do you understand?"

"Yeah. I got it. I also don't need to tell you not to say anything to Linda, right?"

"Of course not."

"Everything's titled in my name, even the house. That, and the power of attorney I have from her, I don't need to bring her in on this up front. Got it?"

"Of course. May I change the subject now to the farmers? We need to talk about Titan Farms. Those default and termination letters are shaking loose some responses from the farmers and lawyers. I need you to make some decisions, and you need to give me some direction."

"I don't give a shit about the Titan farmers. We'll talk about that later. I'll look over the Carrowses' document as soon as I get home. I should be there this afternoon. Mark it up for my signature, and courier it over to the house, and let's talk tonight. I gotta go." He hung up.

Damn. He wanted this bad, but he cautioned himself again to slow down. He grabbed the complimentary robe from the bathroom and walked out into the main room. It was empty. No Charles, and no Cadell. No coffee service either. Charles hadn't offered for him to spend the weekend, but Damien had packed for it. Just in case.

Disappointed, he walked back into his room and closed the door to get dressed. Part of him had hoped that Charles would extend an invitation for him to stay, but the other part of him was anxious to get home and look over the contracts.

Damien stopped packing; he had a sinking thought. Charles hadn't mentioned Saturday being a no-go until they were at dinner last night. And not until after Damien had mentioned some anxiety over the contracts. Damien looked around the extraordinary suite that he almost considered a second home. Was Charles angry with him for lacking confidence? Did Charles think he was ungrateful? Whoa. Would he take the offer back?

Shit. Gotta think hard about this one.

Chapter 16

Charles Carrows was at the Carlyle Hotel in Manhattan, in what was now officially called the Titan war room. Carey and Harley had encamped in the suite, the two of them lounging on a nearby sofa, Carey's bare feet propped in Harley's lap. The three of them were listening to Henry Carrows on speaker from California.

Henry said, "Your mother and I will be in Manhattan next week. This has got to happen by the time the farmers begin mediation."

"We know, Dad," said Charles. "The timing is really tight on this one. We've got no wiggle room on this. Not with Plan A."

"And if Plan A doesn't work? If Damien doesn't take the bait?" Henry said.

"There's always a Plan B, Daddy," Carey said, her head lolling to the side of the green velvet sofa. "Has anyone looked at his life insurance? What happens to Titan if

Damien accidentally comes to harm? Maybe he drowns in a pile of manure."

Charles gave his sister a discouraging look and said, "We're working on Plan B, we always are. We're just hoping we won't have to use it. We've got players all over Atlantic City."

"How is Mr. Ronnie Bianchi?" Carey said. "Did he enjoy his bag of cash?"

Charles said, "Yeah. Damien walked in right as I handed it over. He didn't know it was a real bag of cash, but he saw the bag exchange. He was interested." Mr. Ronnie Bianchi was the owner of the Atlantic Hotel.

Henry said, "Bianchi's going out on a limb, letting us have that high-rollers room and controlling the outcome on his premises. The man is entitled to a little money. It's a small price to pay."

"Small price?" Carey said, sitting up. "Daddy, we gave him two hundred grand in cash!"

"He's taking a risk," said Henry. "Fixed gaming is illegal. Even if it is against only one customer. Besides, we're making a home now in Atlantic City. Mr. Ronnie Bianchi is now securely our friend. I'm sure I don't have to tell you how important it is to have friends you can count on. You never know when you'll need them."

Charles said, "He knows we're going to need the setup again. He said he'll have it available to us on a moment's notice. He's been very gracious with all of us while we've stayed at his hotel. I'm looking forward to a friendly relationship with my new neighbor."

"How long do you intend to give Damien to sign before we move to Plan B?" said Henry.

Charles looked at Carey, who had gone to the buffet and was making a cup of tea. "A day. Or two. That's all the time we've got. Carey, you need to call Linda today and find out what's going on at the Millers'. If she's holding Damien back, if he's reconsidering, maybe you should invite her to the Bahamas or Vegas for a girls' trip."

Carey threw her head back in exasperation. "Ahh. I don't want to play with her anymore. She's exhausting. I swear to God if we get photographed together I'm going to be ill. She even suggested that she could get a friend to follow us around in Manhattan, and they could take our picture and then she could send it to the papers."

Charles smirked. "What did you say?"

Carey sat next to Harley and placed her cup on the table. "Nothing. I doubt she even remembers."

"Give her a call, Carey," said Henry. "This evening. The farmers' lawyer is working overtime. Maybe he'll get them an extension and force Titan to pause the terminations. We should know this week."

Carey shook her head and took a sip of her tea as Henry continued. "Your mother and I will be staying at Charlotte's. She has got to find a larger home so she can accommodate all of us when we're in the city. Charles, have you spoken with her about that?"

Carey rolled her eyes as Charles said, "They're discussing it. It'll happen."

"What about a townhome for me, Daddy?" Carey said.

"I'm stuck at the Carlyle while you give all your time to Charlotte."

"You chose Las Vegas, Carey," said Henry. "Are you saying you're unhappy with your new condo?"

"No, of course not," she mumbled.

Charles smiled at his sister. "Nice try. Carey, you're up. You know what to do. We've got to move this thing along fast."

"Let me know how it goes," said Henry. "And, Carey, I expect to see you at Charlotte's townhome next week for dinner. Harley, naturally you're welcome too."

Carey smiled sweetly at the phone and batted her eyes. "I can't think of anything I'd rather do more."

"Good girl."

Damien raced home and found the document stuck in the front door. He noticed that the girls weren't home. What was that mound in the yard over there? He didn't have time to investigate, he'd do that later.

He fast-scanned the documents and slow-read through the section that outlined that the minority owners were guaranteed a working relationship with the major shareholders and a share of profits immediately after the construction debt was paid. His pulse quickened. He called Samara.

"Okay, Samara, here's the deal. I saw where you crossed off using the house and property as collateral, and

I suppose that makes sense, but I don't want to mess this up."

"Damien, he's also attaching the businesses. If something goes wrong, he gets them too."

"What the hell is going to go wrong? Everything is fine! The business is making money! I just sold five more franchise farms, and we're keeping the overhead low like we always do."

"Well, like I mentioned to you yesterday, the original farmers are up in arms and are pressing for injunctions and mediation. If my secret grapevine is accurate, I think they're threatening arbitration and talking about group litigation. It could get costly."

"I thought you had this all figured out," he said, pacing the room, staring heatedly into the phone in his hand. "We separate them, and we break them. We give verbal promises that are worth shit, and then we pull out the rug. It's scorch and burn the bastards, cut our losses, recoup every fucking dollar we can from their hides, and move on. We'll still be standing without them, it's just a setback. I sell, we milk them. If they fold, they fold. Just as long as I can sell more. We've got to keep them out of arbitration."

"I got it! I just wanted to make sure that that's the avenue you want to take. I support it 100 percent, just wanted to double-check. It's my job to ensure you understand the ramifications of everything. And remember, we will incur some extra legal fees with this, but they should be manageable."

"Just do it. Float the homestead strike past Wallace

and see if we can get that off, and let me know. Did he say if he'll be around tomorrow?"

"He said he would be available all weekend. I can email him now if you'd like. If he says no to the homestead exclusion, what do you want my response to be?"

"Don't respond to him, just call me."

Damien threw himself on their new uncomfortable sofa, let out a sigh, and waited. He thought it would be a short wait, but Samara didn't get back with him until late that evening. Damien's stomach had been in knots all day.

"What took you so long? What happened?" Damien whispered finally that evening as he walked into a quiet room in the house. He peeked around the corner for Linda.

"Nothing, he just took a long time getting back to me. It is the weekend, you know."

"Right, I get that. Well, what happened?"

"He said no to deleting the homestead attachment. What do you want to do?"

Damien had been asking himself that same question all day. "Let me call you back."

"Shit," he said under his breath as he walked into the kitchen pantry and grabbed a box of cherry Pop-Tarts. He walked over to the toaster, ripped open the foil pack, and put them in to bake. He could hear Linda on the phone in the other room. He knew she was talking to Carey.

He stared at the toaster and chewed on his nail, waiting. What in the world would Linda say if she knew what he was considering? Should he ask her opinion? He heard her laugh loudly as the Pop-Tarts finished. No, he did not want her opinion. She wasn't capable of thinking rationally on this high level of business. He needed to make the decision alone.

He put the hot pastries on the counter and got some milk out of the fridge. Contracts. That's what this was about. He'd spent the day examining them, and he felt good that they were pretty straightforward. How could he lose on this deal? The Carrowses, the *entire Carrows family* was backing this thing. They wouldn't want it to fail. No way. Not with their name on it.

He dunked a tart into a glass of milk and thought about what it would be like to sit at a blackjack table next to famous celebrities. If he thought the Carrows were big stuff, that was nothing compared to the names Charles had dropped last night at dinner.

He considered them—the Carrows family. It was interesting that everyone knew about them, but really, nobody knew about them. They were a nice family. Easy to be around, and damn—they sure could party. It had been a blast hanging out with them.

Damien licked some milk dripping down the side of his hand. If he didn't sign the contracts, if he rejected the offer, the invitation to invest in Carrows Casino, then how would they feel about that? Would the Carrowses' door close? Would they still remain friends?

Linda walked into the kitchen. "What you eatin' there, D?"

"Was that Carey?"

"Yeah," Linda giggled. "She was just telling me about

this show in Vegas. She's got a place there. You know that, right?" she said as she pulled up a chair next to him and stroked his back.

"Yeah."

"We could afford a trip to Vegas next month, couldn't we?"

He turned and gave her a look of exasperation. "We can't go on vacation. Not now. We've got jobs, Linda."

She removed her hand and nodded. "No. I know. We've got to stay focused. We're a team, right, baby?"

"Yeah," he said as he got up and put the milk back in the fridge.

"So, is that a hard no to Vegas?" she whimpered.

"That's a hard no. It's time to tighten the belt. Got that?"

"I got it." She put up her hands in surrender.

Damien left the room. Damn.

———

From the Titan war room, Carey called Charles at Charlotte's. "She doesn't know."

"He hasn't told her?" Charles said, surprised.

"Believe me, if she knew, she'd be talking about it."

"Hmmm. Damn. I just spoke with John. Last he heard they had all the documents and confirmed that there would be no modifications."

"So, we're waiting."

"Yes."

"Charles, I swear to God, don't make me take her to

Vegas. I cannot have that baggage around me in that town. Did you see her snap her fingers at Cadell? I've never met someone who felt so entitled so quickly. If she ever does come into real money, she'll be a nightmare."

"Two days, then the offer is off the table, and we move to Plan B."

"I hate Plan B," Carey groaned.

Chapter 17

They didn't have to wait for two days. Henry called Charles the next day. "John Wallace just called and told me that our fish is in the net. Damien signed the documents this morning."

Charles put his head back, relieved. "Thank God."

"What's interesting," said Henry, "is that Damien signed the documents alone. He has a power of attorney from Linda."

"That is interesting. We'll be sure to use that nugget when the next shoe drops. Speaking of, did John call his fellow banker?"

"As we speak. John's personal friend, he'll do whatever John asks. Apparently, they play poker together, too. John believes his debt to me is now officially paid." Henry laughed.

"This is going to be a very big week for the Miller family, and we need for them to agree to come to Atlantic City this weekend," said Charles.

"Good. Have you spoken with Earl Wellington?"

"Next call I make," Charles said, smiling.

Squirrel answered the phone.

"Hello, Mrs. Wellington. Charles Carrows. How are you today?"

"Real good, Mr. Carrows," she rasped.

"I'm happy to hear that. I wanted to let you know that the plan goes into effect today. My men will be out to take your car and bring you a loaner. They'll deliver your car back to you later today. Of course, not in the same condition as it was left in."

Charles could hear Squirrel inhaling. Ice was tinkling in a glass near the phone too. "We'll be ready. What kind of loaner did you say that was going to be?"

"A midsize sedan," Charles said. "It will have an Enterprise sticker on it. The permanent replacement will come later."

"And what will that be?"

Charles smiled. "Anything you'd like, Mrs. Wellington."

Damien felt like he could breathe again after he'd signed the documents. Which was a good sign. His instinct in taking the leap was the right decision. More than anything, he didn't want to lose this deal. He realized that an opportunity like this might never come his way again. He was unafraid. It was going to be awesome. It was going to be great! Titan Casinos was born!

Damien dreaded the conversation, but he made the announcement to Linda that Monday evening after work.

"You did what? You didn't even ask me or tell me about it, Damien! What do you mean you got a loan for a million dollars to go into the casino business?"

"God, Linda, I just told you." He rubbed his head and gave her an incredulous look. "I was given an opportunity to invest as a shareholder of Carrows Casinos. You've heard about it. They discussed it over dinner. This was *an invitation* to invest. It's not like they have brokers out there looking for people. It's handled differently with really big players, and it's an investment in a business that has their name on it. They want it to succeed. They need it to succeed, and they all invested in it to succeed, and now we are invested too. It's going to be great. I thought you would be happy that we were going to be business partners with your new pals from the Carrows family?"

"I am, I am! It's just that a *million dollars*, Damien! That's a shit load of money! I thought we were belt-tightening around here." Linda slammed her hand on the white kitchen counter.

"We are," he said as he sat on an island stool, trying to stay calm. "This is exactly what I'm talking about. If we keep our personal and business expenses on a tight leash, then we can afford to take advantage of opportunities like this when they come up."

"Where did you get the million dollars? Did you have to sign something?" She threw her hands in the air.

"Of course, I had to sign something. Samara looked over the contract, and I trust her. It looks good. I have to make monthly note payments to them as an investor/shareholder, but we can swing it. The businesses are doing great. The pissant farmers who are grumbling will either get back in line or lose everything; that's being handled. I need to sell some more franchises, but I can do that in my sleep. I just sold five more."

He thought she appeared calmer, but she had kind of a vacant look on her face. He plowed on. "Would you be willing to trade off the pet farm for a few weekends in Atlantic City at *our* casino? Hobnob with a few celebrities?"

Linda stared at him, her mouth hanging open. She shook herself loose. "It's one thing to invest a million dollars in equipment and a business with customers, and it's another to invest a million in a casino to be a shareholder. I don't even know what that means. Are we going to get our money back? What the hell are we buying?"

"We get our money back in the long-term, probably five years out. Once the building loans are paid, and we've paid our note, we'll start taking a cut from the profits. In the meantime, we have access to the casino and free weekends and some other stuff. It's all in the contract."

"I still don't get it. Are you saying that I *can't* build the village or that I *shouldn't* build it, Damien? And what about all the clothes I'll need for our weekends in AC?"

He took a deep breath and put his hands up. "I'm saying that we are in this together. I've always made the decisions, and I've done really well so far, right? Just trust me, and we'll get there! I promise. And in the meantime, it would be a big help if you pulled your weight by being understanding and not investing in another project for a few years while we catch up. Can you do that? For us? For our future?"

"I don't like that you didn't tell me you were doing this. I really don't. You said we were a team," she said, pointing at him. "You have to tell me about this shit *before* you do it, or you know I'm gonna be pissed. You can't come home and say hey, baby, I just spent a million bucks and mortgaged the home and expect me to be happy. Oh shit, you didn't mortgage the house, did you?" She looked panicked.

"Linda," he said as he got up and took her into his arms, "of course I didn't. Stop worrying, it's all going to be great."

Chapter 18

The next day, Damien was sitting in his office trailer with his head in a pile of paperwork when he got a call from Elwood Wellington, skipper of Titan Fisheries boat 2.

"Hey, E, what's up?"

"Hey, *D.*" Elwood paused a bit long. "I got some real bad news. Dad and I were in a bad car accident yesterday, and we're really shook up."

Damien was listening. "What do you mean? You're okay, aren't you? How's E Senior?"

"That's what I'm trying to tell you. Me and Dad we were in a real bad car accident yesterday."

"A real bad car accident? How are you? Where are you?"

"See, that's the thing. Dad and I won't be workin' any time soon 'cause we both got real banged up."

Damien was losing patience. "Okaayyy. What does real banged up mean exactly?"

"See, that's the thing. Dad got it worse than I did. This other car just came out of nowhere and banged us all over the place. It's real bad, man."

Listening once again to dead air, Damien pushed again for the details. "Elwood, what kind of physical condition are you and Earl in?"

"Well, that's the thing. They still need to do some tests, but I think it's real bad. We won't be skippering for some time to come it looks like."

Christ, dead air again. These guys knew exactly what they were doing on a fishing boat and were good at it, but what a bunch of morons they were on dry land. "Elwood, are you in the hospital? Is Earl in the hospital?"

"See, that's the thing right there. We were in the hospital, of course, right after we got banged all the heck over the place. You should have seen it. I'm lucky to be alive, and that's the truth. The car though, that's a goner. You should see it. Really sad situation that is."

"Are you saying that you're not in the hospital and that Earl is not in the hospital either and that you're okay?"

"What I'm saying is that we got banged around, and we won't be able to skipper anytime soon. Now, I know that could present a problem since the crews are lined up to go out in the morning for a long run, but Dad and I, well, we're just too banged up. We can't go. No, sir. We can't."

"Elwood. What are your injuries? What are your dad's injuries?"

"Well, Dad's got a splint on one leg, and he can hardly walk. They think he's got a neck and back thing going on.

He's in a lot of pain. It's a really sad situation."

Dead air. "Ellllwooood, what about you? What kind of injuries did you sustain?"

"Well, I got about the same. And I'm having some trouble breathing too. They think maybe I got some bruised ribs. Not too sure just yet, but they got me wrapped up good, and me and Dad are *not* going to be skippering for a while, that's for sure."

"For how long? How long do they think it will be for you to recover?"

"Well, they just don't know. I guess we'll have to see how the body mends. In the meantime, I wanted to let you know that we won't be doing any skippering. Like I always say, nobody knows what's in store over the next wave. Now I gotta go. Squirrel II is calling, and she's skipper on land." He hung up.

Damien stared at the phone. Damn, he hated that little man. He hated having to deal with the uneducated rabble and listening to their lame-ass excuses. He thought these guys were above the farm labor/vomiters en masse. He could always count on them. They lived for the sea and for those ships. Even though they no longer owned them, it was still their life, and they were doing okay. They should thank him for helping them out! Now what was he going to do? Both of his skippers being out at the same time was a huge problem.

Fuck! Damien pulled out his desk drawer and grabbed a box of Cheez-Its. He dove his hand inside, grabbed a handful, and plowed them into his mouth. He crunched as he considered his problem.

He needed experienced captains, seasoned skippers, who not only had the proper licenses to operate his commercial fishing boats but captains who would take care of his ships and the crews too. Confidence in a captain is a real thing at sea, and mutiny and chain of command were really real out there as well. Both of his ships had a few quality and steady deckhands, and both ships had high-dollar deckhands who were mechanically inclined. That was another critical piece and not just while you were at sea. Stuff happened to equipment all the time, and it needed constant maintenance and repair, but more importantly, the boats needed someone to sail them. And someone who also knew how to fish.

Damien's insurance company had insisted that his captains be licensed with a minimum of three years of experience so he could qualify for the rates he received. That had been no problem for Damien because he inherited the Wellington boys, and they were born on the sea. Maybe he had taken them for granted because they had never called in sick or missed a voyage. If they hadn't gambled so much and had so much personal family drama, they would still own their own ships because they knew how to fish. And they always brought the boats home safely.

Damien had to make some decisions, and it sure didn't sound like Earl and Elwood were going to help him. He couldn't afford the boats to miss a scheduled voyage. The crews were already booked, the season was perfect, all the licenses had been filed, and the boats were in great shape. All he really needed were two skippers. By tomorrow.

Shit! Damien pushed a load of cracker crumbs off his shirt, threw the box on his desk, and paced as he thought about where he was going to find them. Could he afford to let one or two of his experienced deckhands skipper without a commercial license? What if they got caught? What if they came into rough weather or one of another billion problems came up on the voyage, and they couldn't handle it? What would the rest of the crew think about going out with a nonlicensed skipper? Would they do it?

It would be easier to temporarily use some of his seasoned deckhands. They'd been on board with the Wellington boys for years and must know everything there was to know by now. Damien knew at least one of them, what was his real name? Damien called him Captainitis John, referencing the guy's desire to one day be captain. Maybe the guy didn't like that. He had all their phone numbers...

Damien hopped into the car and drove like hell to the wharf. He called the lead crew and especially Johnny Captainitis and told them to meet him by the boats in two hours.

Chapter 19

Damien had a long session with the lead deckhands and explained the situation. They could go out and skipper the two boats on the voyage as planned, or they could all stay home with no pay. Samara had thrown together a document that he had his new faux captains sign, releasing Damien/Titan of any liability if tragedy should befall, yada, yada, yada. They signed them willingly and were both eager to captain, swearing to Damien on their lives that they would make conservative choices in the face of trouble and would keep him in the loop if something came up. Samara drafted a short announcement to the rest of the crew that their skippers wouldn't be the Wellington boys, and if they chose not to come aboard that would be fine, but they would be dismissed with no pay. If they chose to come aboard, they would adhere to their captains' plans and orders.

Everyone agreed. Damien stayed the night near the wharf and helped the crew launch in the morning in good spirits with all the traditions that drew them to the art of manliness and being a sailor.

Fingers crossed, Damien thought as he drove away. Another hole plugged, hopefully. Just as long as nobody found out.

———————

Charles Carrows got a fascinating call that evening from Earl Wellington.

"So, hey there, Mr. Carrows, it's me, Earl here. So, I'm calling to give you that update."

"Mr. Wellington, I'm pleased to hear from you. I understand that you were in a bit of a traffic accident. I'm so sorry to hear it!"

"Yup, we got delivered the loaner, thank ya, and the car accident, that went off without a hitch. They wrecked the car for sure, and then your guys set me boy and me up real good with all the medical stuff. I got splints and casts and something for my neck. He even gave me prescription bottles that say Oxy something on 'em, but of course, he said they just had aspirin in 'em, so that's fine there.

"Yessir, we really appreciate that new disability van you helped us get. Elwood's kid is gonna be able to drive now thanks to you, and we don't forget that. We couldn't afford that van, and it just about broke all our hearts for that boy. But now, he sits so proud and feels real good fer the first time in years. Yup, I can't thank you enough for that, Charlie."

"I'm glad to hear that the van is working out for him. I

really appreciate all the help you're giving me, too. I know this wasn't something you were comfortable with, and I admire you deeply for that ethic. I appreciate that you and Elwood understood that what we asked you to do was all about helping folks who are being used by Titan, just like you. We want to set that straight for you and your family, Earl. And I was just about to say, you can trust me, but I know those words have lost value to you recently, so I just hope the van helped to restore your faith as a promise of my future goodwill."

"Well, you were right about us not wanting any part of lying and scheming, wasn't how we were raised. We're gonna do our best to work around the lying, but you were right about standing up and taking action when action is deserved. I'm a man of the sea, and by God, what he serves up, I deal with. But I didn't expect this fella to lie to us so bold faced. Didn't see him coming. Don't know why. I've asked myself that, and I don't know why I didn't see him coming. He's a pretty good snake-oil salesman, isn't he, Charlie?"

"He is, Earl. But I'm better."

The next day as the Titan Fisheries boats left the harbor, Alex and Michael Macchi made a phone call to their buddy who worked for the Port Authority in New York. The buddy had a connection with the regional Coast Guard. The names on the boats were given as Titan 1 and Titan 2. They would be boarded.

Chapter 20

D amien!" screamed Linda. "Your dad just called, and he said he's been trying to get a hold of you all day. Would you please return his call? He said something strange happened at the lumber yard, and he needs your help. Give him a call!"

"Okay," said Damien as he sat in front of the home office computer. "I will. I got the message."

Damien got his father on the phone. "Dad, what's up? What's going on?"

Frank Miller was a big, scary, angry guy, or at least those were the primary characteristics Damien remembered of him while he was growing up. He had been a sweetheart with MaryLou, but he was bigger than life to Damien, who always felt like a kid again any time his dad spoke with him.

"So, I got some bad news. The bank called in my loan at the yard, and they want immediate payment. You ever heard of something like this happening before?"

"What do you mean they want immediate payment? Why would they make that move?" Damien made a sour look, confused.

"They said it was because of failure of something, something related to the fact that I have been late paying them."

"Why have you been late paying them, Dad?" he said, his fear and interest piqued.

"I don't know, I got behind, and then I needed some money to pay for some equipment that broke down, and I figured they wouldn't care as long as they eventually got their money, and I mean, I intended to pay them, but it's just been a struggle lately."

"Well, did you explain that to them? Did you call them when you couldn't make the payments and talk to them about an extension or anything?"

"Why should I? They've been working with me for years. I'll pay 'em. They know that."

"They might not know that. You need to call them. I'll bet they'll want to work something out with you. Just tell them what you told me, and they'll come up with a new schedule. Offer to pay a few bucks in penalties or whatever, they'll cut the deal. It'll be fine. Let me know what happens."

"Yup, I'll give 'em a call."

———

"Damien!" Linda screamed later that day as he was about to go outside on the porch and the phone rang. "It looks like your dad is calling. Answer that!"

Damien rushed to pick up the phone. "Dad! Hi. How did it go at the bank?"

"Well, they didn't go for it! They just said no to everything I proposed. I thought you said this would work."

"What do you mean they said no? Who did you talk to? Did you talk to the main guy?" he said as he walked into the kitchen.

"Well, I started with the regular loan officer and then asked to speak with his boss, and they sent me over to some VP of something, and he listened to me tell them that I was sorry I had been late a few times but that I would get caught up, and they could attach a penalty or something, but he told me that they wouldn't consider it. He said that I had broken faith or some crap and that they were calling in the loan and wanted full payment on it by the end of the week."

"What the hell? What the hell is going on over there? Did you say that you have done this a *few* times?" he said, sitting at the counter.

"Ya, two or three times I skipped a payment, but like I said, I thought they knew me over there, and they would give me a call if it were a big problem, but I didn't hear nothing from them bastards. Nothing. They should have called me if they had a problem."

"Dad, maybe you're right, they should have called you, but you should have called them too. You can't just keep skipping payments and expect them to ignore it."

"Don't tell me what to do!" he roared. "I know what I'm doing. I've been doing business fine at the yard for your whole life. We did okay. Look at you, bigshot, with all your toys. Who do you think helped you get all that started? Who gave you the money and support to get everything you have going on over there?"

"Dad, calm down. Calm down. I know you got me started, we don't need to go there," he said, as he got up to pace.

"Well, I wonder sometimes if you even think about your mother and me. We barely see MaryLou, and you're traipsing 'round the state and whatnot, and you never make any time for the two of us."

"Dad, I get it. I've just been really, really busy with the companies, and there is a lot going on, especially right now. There's actually some pretty exciting stuff too that I think you're going to get a kick out of. Maybe you can come out this weekend or next, and we'll throw some steaks on? What do you think? But right now, we need to focus on what the bank is saying to you. Did you get the impression that it was a final notice, or do you think it would help if I called over there for you?"

"Well, I don't suppose it could hurt for you to call over there, but they probably won't talk to you unless I give them permission, or if we go over there together."

"Okay, well, why don't I call them and make an appointment, and I'll call you back with a time, and we'll go over there together. How about that?"

"Yeah, okay, give me a call."

Damien called the bank and made an appointment for the next morning at 9:00 a.m. He called his dad and told him to meet him there.

Damien put on his best sports coat over jeans and walked into the bank the next morning with his dad. He could sell anything, this shouldn't be a big deal. The two of them walked over to a waiting area with chairs and potted plants and signed in. A woman approached, inquiring, and Damien told her that they had an appointment with Mr. Morrison. She smiled at them and walked them toward a glassed-in office where a man was working behind an almost empty desk. The glass door was propped open, and they walked inside as Mr. Morrison, a tall, serious-looking young man in a suit, came around his desk.

"Mr. Morrison, nice to meet you. I'm Damien Miller, and this is my father, Frank."

"Nice to meet you both. Have a seat, and let's take a look at what we have here."

Mr. Morrison went to his computer and began to pull up the files as Frank said, "You know, I find it difficult to believe that you guys didn't just give me a call when you saw there was a problem. I've been banking here for at least twenty years, and you could have given me a call if there was a problem. But *no one* called me. I want to make that crystal clear right now."

"Dad, I'm sure Mr. Morrison understands all that. I'm sure we can iron out this little wrinkle in no time," he said hopefully, smiling at Mr. Morrison, who was currently frowning at his computer screen.

"Ahem, well, it looks like we are asking for full payment of the balance on an outstanding loan for Mr. Frank Miller." Palm up, he gestured at Frank. "The balance of $103,500 is due at the end of business this week."

Damien couldn't believe this was happening. "Mr. Morrison, are you telling us that there is no room for negotiation? That there is no one here we can speak with who can work something out for us? I mean really, Dad missed a few payments as I understand it, but please, I'm sure we can work something out."

"Nobody called me," Frank said, grabbing the chair and leaning forward.

"Yes, well, Mr. Miller, it looks as if you missed more than a few payments. We gave you courtesy forgiveness for the first two over the last two years, but this year you've missed another two payments and the bank sees no alternative now but to collect the balance due to loss of good faith."

Damien glanced over at his dad. Was it true? Had he missed four payments? Frank was red in the face. They were heading into dark territory.

"Dad, okay, it's going to be okay. Listen, Mr. Morrison, so why can't we attach a penalty or fee and just settle this right now? You'll get your money. My dad's right, he's been banking here forever. Doesn't that count for something?"

"Damn right it should!" Frank said in a loud voice. Out

of his peripheral vision, Damien noticed a few heads turn their way.

It also got Mr. Morrison's attention. "Gentleman, please don't get hostile. The facts are that this loan has been deemed by our parent company now as high risk. It is the position of the bank that all high-risk accounts be closed or renegotiated immediately. Since the last banking crisis, it has been the position of this bank to earn the trust of its customers by assuring them that we will safeguard the assets of this institution, and what we say we mean, and our customers can count on us to act accordingly. They can trust us with our investments. It goes both ways. The account was flagged, and after it hit a certain number, someone decided it was deemed high risk. At that point, it was out of my hands. The loan balance of $103,500 is due in full by close of business this Friday or legal action will be forthcoming."

Damien was flabbergasted. He assumed there would be some wiggle room and a negotiation opportunity. This was unprecedented for him.

"But nobody called me!" yelled Frank. "Why didn't somebody call to tell me that they were going to make me pay it all back if I was late on another payment? I would have listened to that! *Nobody* called me."

"Mr. Miller, it is not the responsibility of the bank to call you and counsel you regarding your loan obligations. In the loan documentation, it clearly states our policy. I have seen some loans renegotiated, but your loan is flagged, and I will not, nor do I have the power to reverse that. It is final, I'm afraid," he said, sitting back in his chair.

Damien had to act before his dad leapt across Mr. Morrison's desk and beat him. He wouldn't put it past his father.

"Okay. Let's just all take a breath. Dad, look at me. *It is going to be okay.* Don't worry. Mr. Morrison, what would it take to get an extension? Can I cosign on the loan and get it back into good faith?"

Mr. Morrison glanced at his screen and shook his head. "I'm afraid not. This particular loan has been flagged not only for bad faith and immediate repayment but also as nonnegotiable. You will need to either repay this institution or the consequences will be enforced." He reached into his desk and took out some papers and handed them to Frank.

Frank grabbed them and started reading while Damien leaned over to take a look. This was going in the wrong direction. "Dad, would you allow me to speak on your behalf to Mr. Morrison privately for a moment?"

Frank jumped up out of his chair and stormed out of the office.

Holy shit. This was not good. "Mr. Morrison, I really, really can't believe you won't work with us. This is truly unbelievable. What can we do to come to an arrangement? I work with banks all the time, really, there has to be a way."

"No. There is not. I've given you the options. It is out of my hands and the hands of this branch. What you do when you leave here is up to you, but our business is concluded," he said and stood.

Damien stood as well. "I've never worked with this bank, and there may be a reason for that. You are completely unbelievable. In the future, you may regret your decision." He left to find his dad.

Well, shit, thought Damien. *Shit, shit, shit.* He knew he was going to have to bail him out. There was just no way he was going to allow his dad's business to go under. His stupid brother was useless. Dad couldn't depend on him for anything.

Damien also knew he was pretty tapped out at his local sources due to the boat financing and the home improvement loans. Maybe he could call John Wallace? He needed cash. He had to go somewhere, and he knew his dad didn't have the money.

He caught up with Frank in the parking lot. Damn, his father was a big man, and at that moment, he looked truly menacing. Damien walked slowly toward him, his hands outstretched in a calming manner. "Dad, okay, that was the weirdest thing in the world that just happened in there. Really. I mean, I work with banks all the time, and this is really, really surprising. I don't think you should take this personally. I think they have some kind of screw loose."

"No kidding! Mr. Asshole Morrison better watch himself because this isn't over."

"Dad, it is over. I'm asking you to calm down. I'm going to take care of this, and we'll just never do business with this bank again. Believe me, they will regret that one day. Do you hear me? I'll cover the loan, and you can just make payments back to me, okay? We don't need those assholes. Forget about it. We're bigger than they are. Let's just walk away. Right now. I'll get a check and get it over to them by tomorrow or Friday latest, but don't worry about it. Really, it's okay."

Damien saw Frank's temper slightly abate, his face less contorted. That was a start. "Dad, just get in your car and go back to work. I got this. What are sons for if they can't help their family out now and then? It's all taken care of. Did you talk to Mom about this weekend? Are you guys coming over? Come on, we'll burn some steaks and play a little pool and watch the video of MaryLou's dance recital that I missed so I can get out of that doghouse. You'll love it, right?"

That put a smile on Frank's face. Damien knew he loved MaryLou. Linda not as much, but MaryLou was their sunshine. "Yeah, we're coming. Why did you miss that dance recital again?"

"I don't know. I rolled over a spike or something in the parking lot on my way out, and my tire just popped. Shit happens."

Frank grumbled, "Yeah, it does. Thanks for helping me out here, I appreciate it. You get back to work, too. Let me know if I need to sign something stupid for these assholes."

"Yup! I'll let you know. Tell Mom that I expect her to

bring her Oreo cookie dessert on Saturday. MaryLou and I love it."

Again, the smile as he got in the car. Did Damien see tears in his eyes? Holy shit.

––––––––––

Damien had not intended to tell Linda about the loan for his dad's business, but as it turned out, he had to. The good news was that John Wallace had been extremely understanding about the situation and was intimately familiar with the financial constraints of Damien's funds. He also said he knew all about how important dads were too. He was totally awesome. John said he knew a guy at one of Damien's local Morristown banks and fast-pushed a loan through.

The bad news was, even though Damien had a power of attorney, the new bank insisted Linda's signature be on the loan. He hadn't seen that coming. It meant he was forced to bring her up to speed.

"What? We have to get a $100,000 bank loan to cover Frank's stupidity? Why do we have to put our name on the line? Why can't Frank go take care of this himself?"

"I explained that to you, Linda. Dad doesn't have the collateral, and if he doesn't repay the loan this week it will snowball, and he could lose his business. I'm not going to let that happen."

"Why do we always have to come up with the money? Why can't people figure out their own problems? First those stupid franchise farmers, and now your dad. Damn it, Damien, I don't feel awfully compelled to do this for him. He's never liked me."

"Of course he does, Linda. Let's not rehash that topic again. The loan is a done deal. We have to do this for my mom and dad, I mean, what are our options? If we don't help them and they lose their business, what's next, their home? Then what—they move in here with us?"

Linda's mouth was one big O. "Noooooo. Never. That just can n-e-v-e-r happen. That would be the worst thing ever. Damien, no kidding, I'd leave you before I would ever live with Frank."

"Wow, Linda, awfully sweet. Just get in the car, and let's get over to the bank and make this happen. Done deal. Move it."

And it was done. But then the phone rang for Damien.

It was Johnny Captainitis.

Chapter 21

What are you saying?" Damien shouted into the phone over the fairly bad connection.

"I'm saying that we were boarded by the Coast Guard. Never seen that happen, man, ever. We've always been good with them, and they know it. They said they were doing spot inspections, something to do with Homeland Security, and no offense, just routine. But then they asked where the E's were, the skippers, and I told them that I was captain, and they asked to see my license, and I told them I didn't have one, and they told me that it was against regulations, blah, blah, blah, and now they're escorting us back to port. The voyage is over, and we ain't got no fish 'cause we hadn't arrived at our first destination when they stopped us."

Damien slammed down the phone. This was the Wellington boys' fault. He was going to pay them a visit.

After Charles got confirmation that the Coast Guard was escorting the Titan boats back into the harbor, he called Earl and Elwood Wellington to let them know to be ready. There was a possibility that they might get a visitor.

———

Damien growled when he pulled into the parking lot of Madge's Market in Barnegat Light. He'd never been to either of the Wellingtons' homes before, but he figured he shouldn't show up empty-handed. He slammed the stupid Chevy's door shut and went inside. He walked down the aisles, trying to figure out what in the hell to bring Earl. Damien knew he was married, and he remembered that both the E's called their wives the same weird damn name of Squirrel.

Damien picked up some suspicious fruit and then reconsidered. He walked down another aisle, looking for candy. Disgusted with the selection, he swore as he grabbed a bag of Hershey's Kisses. At the register, he saw a sad bundle of flowers in clear wrap. "How much for those," Damien said, his wallet out.

"Twelve fifty," said the older lady at the counter, popping her gum. Her nametag said *Madge*. Damien gave her an angry look. "Forget it," he snarled and left with the Kisses.

When he drove up to Earl's house, he saw the wrecked car in the driveway. *Damn.* Damien flinched. *That looks bad.* He rang the bell. An extremely large, red-haired woman wearing a frilly apron and smoking a cigarette opened the door. She towered over him. Damien took a step back.

"Yeah, what can I do for ya?"

"Hi, ma'am, Mrs. Wellington? I'm Damien Miller, come to see how my captain is doing after the terrible car crash he and E had."

"E? Who's that?" she said, not inviting him in.

"E, er, Elwood." Damien smiled. "You know, nicknames? I call one E and the other E Senior." He shrugged.

The Squirrel gave him a dubious look while she inhaled her cigarette. She didn't move but took some time looking him over. Beginning with his shoes, she worked her way up slowly.

Eventually, she moved out of the doorway and said, "Uh-huh. Well, come on in."

Damien entered and handed her the Hershey's Kisses. "Thank you, ma'am. This is for you, just a little gesture," he said, nervous now.

She took the candy and guided him into the TV room. Earl was stretched out on a recliner, his leg in a cast. A cane sat by his side next to a card table filled with prescription bottles, coffee cups, and an overflowing ashtray.

The Squirrel followed him into the room.

"Well, look who's here. Big D. Whatcha doing here, Big D?" said Earl.

"Hey, Earl, I just thought I'd come over to see how you were doing. E told me about the car crash, and I was worried about you guys. How're you feeling?" He gestured toward Earl's cast.

"Well, D, it's like this. We got pretty banged up. Pretty bad stuff. I've been in a hurting kind of way here, I'll tell ya."

"Yeah, Elwood told me you had a splint on your leg. Is it broken?"

"Well, D, like I told you, we were pretty banged up. She hit us hard, she did, and she just about took us hook, line, and sinker."

Damien noticed no one had asked him to sit. He could feel the Squirrel behind him. He gave her a glance. She was lighting another cigarette. "She? A woman hit you?" Damien asked.

"Huh," said Earl. "Ah, no, I'm just thinking about her rig."

"Right, I see. Sorry that happened to you. Where did it happen? Who hit you? Were they drunk or something?"

"Drunk? I don't know about that. Maybe. Maybe. They might have hooked him for that. We sure did get banged up though."

Damien was getting impatient. "There would be a police report if he, or she, were drunk. Maybe I could take a look at that, give you a hand?"

Squirrel took the bag of Hershey's Kisses and threw it overhand past Damien's head onto a nearby couch. "We take care of our own," she said as he looked over at her and pulled his head back, startled.

"Right," Damien said, focusing again on Earl. "Did

they say how long you have to wear that cast?" Damien saw a cloud of smoke creeping over his face, falling from over his head.

"Damn if it don't itch already," Earl said, grabbing a stick and trying to manipulate it into the cast. "Squirrel there got me some talcum powder. She thought that might help my misery. And I thank ya. I do thank ya for trying." He gave Squirrel a smile as she inched closer into Damien's personal space.

"Earl, when do you think you'll be ready to come back to work? I gotta make plans, you know if you can't come back soon, I gotta make some plans," Damien said nervously, sidestepping a bit.

"I see, well, you know I hit myself a snag, that's for sure. Don't know how long I got to lie in this net. I guess we'll just have to see."

This was going nowhere. "All right then, Earl, I'll leave you. You take care, and I hope you feel better real soon." Damien walked backward out of the room, keeping an eye on the big redhead in the apron who looked like she might come for him. At the doorway, he said, "I'll be in touch, okay?"

Neither of them said anything to him. Damien turned around and walked quickly to the front door and leapt into the fresh air. *Damn them! Damn them, I just hate those boys! Now, what do I do?* Angry and frustrated as hell, he got back in the car to drive back to the office.

———————

Samara Poe chose that moment to call Damien on his cell. "Damien! I've been working like crazy, trying to delay the mediations to let the clock run out so the terminations could take effect, but their lawyer, like some kind of crazy miracle, got the judge to give them injunctive relief until after mediation. So, we're definitely going. It's the next step."

"Damn it, Samara," Damien exploded. "You were supposed to fucking take care of this and make it go away! What are you trying to tell me now? Do your fucking *job!*"

Samara Poe didn't like being yelled at. She used to be a demolitions expert in the army and enjoyed blowing things up, maybe too much, and now had to use all her energy and Zen to focus and visualize herself in a calm place. She had learned these techniques at some evening classes she had been attending, which her therapist felt would help her deal with her inner rage issues and self-hate. Even the army thought she was wound a little too tight. She knew this because they told her.

She really, really didn't like being yelled at. She gave him silence while she did some calming breaths.

"*Samara?* What the hell are you telling me? Are you there?" Damien screamed.

Close your eyes, Samara. Visualize the sea and a cool breeze. Now open them. Breathe. You are a lady, a professional lady, you will be treated with respect. Be calm, and calm will come to you.

"Damien," she said very softly. "Damien, you need to calm down. You need to remember that you are speaking with your peer, a professional. You should not raise your voice to me. It is not appropriate, and I will not be yelled at. Do we have an understanding now? Are you ready to proceed calmly or should I call you back?"

"The fuck!" he screamed.

Samara didn't respond but waited.

"Okay, Samara," Damien said softly, "you're right. I *apologize* for my behavior. I will try to control myself and not yell at you. I'm just having a bad day. Now, what is it you need to tell me?"

That's better, she thought. She enjoyed her job very much, but she wouldn't tolerate being yelled at. She'd gotten enough of that in the army. It was one of the reasons she had needed to leave and switch to law school. That had segued into her finding a nice legal niche she was good at. Terminating contracts. Prior to coming to work for Titan, she'd worked in a legal factory that was hired by companies strictly to get rid of problem franchisees. She found the work very satisfying but had needed a change of pace. After being introduced to Damien Miller, she eventually moved into the position of Titan in-house legal counsel. She had no regrets and was working on becoming more of the corporate head she visualized for herself, rather than the detonator and terminator from her previous lives.

But now she was back in the saddle, terminating contracts, and she realized she had missed it. It was cleansing to sweep away the rubble that was polluting a company's success. It was a righteous duty that companies needed to employ to protect themselves from the greedy and needy. Deadbeats all, she was happy to blow them away.

"Very well, I accept your apology. Now, I was going to say that I need to proceed with scheduling the mediations, and we will obviously need for you to attend them. I'll need your schedule and a commitment from you to attend those days."

"You need my schedule? Just check my Google calendar and plug them in. They're going to be held in Jersey, right? I mean, we don't have to travel for this, do we?"

"Okay, step one, I will access your calendar. Step two, I will work with the other attorney and the mediation group and find a mutually beneficial time for the mediations to take place. Step three, I will let you know after I put them on your Google calendar, and you are correct, they will take place at a location of our choosing."

"Okay then, Samara," he whispered. "Book it. Are we done?"

"Yes, that's all for now," she said and hung up.

Chapter 22

———

Damien, baby," Linda said early that evening. "Can we go to AC again this weekend? Carey called and wanted to know if we wanted to hang out and do some gambling."

He was so distracted by the recent events he wasn't even listening to her. He needed to hire new skippers, and fast, and he wasn't sure how he was going to make that happen. They were sitting on the porch having a cocktail, and Damien was just zoning out staring at the river. What was that lump over there in the yard?

"Damien! Snap out of it! Are you even listening to me?"

He spun his head around to her. "Yes! I'm listening, you want to go to AC. I told Dad that he and Mom could come out this weekend."

He got up and walked over to the rail and looked at the yard. Huh, there were several lumps around the grass.

"They can come over some other time, Damien. Come on. Carey said that she and Harley would love to celebrate with us now that we're owners. She didn't offer the plane this time, but still, it would be super fun, right?"

What was she saying? He walked off the porch to investigate the lumps in the yard.

"Where are you going? I thought we were talking about AC?" She got up and followed him. "What are you doing?"

"What are these lumps around the yard? Look, Linda." He pointed. "Look, there are several of them. Oh, wow," he said as he approached the first one and squatted next to it. Oh, man, *no*. He got up and took his shoe and kicked at the mound. It covered up a hole, and he knew what he was looking at.

"It's a mole hole. We must have a mole, for God's sake."

Linda stopped to stare at the hole in front of him as Damien looked out at the yard. The sun was shining at just the right angle to illuminate the yard leading to their porch, and Damien froze. There were dozens of mounds.

Linda saw them too and recognized the situation at the same time. "Oh my God! Damien! Do you see that? Do you see that? They're everywhere! Look over there and over there? Oh my God, we have rodents!" she screamed.

How the hell could this have happened? This wasn't the work of one mole; there must be a whole colony of them.

At that moment they both saw a small furry creature run from beneath a flower bed and into the cover of a neighboring hedge.

"Ahhhhhhhhhh!" screamed Linda. "Damien! We have rats!"

"Shut up, Linda! God, why are you always screaming?" he yelled as he ran toward the last spotted site of the varmint. As he approached the area, another one came running in a path directly in front of him, and even he started yelling. "Ohhhh, shit!" he said and jumped out of the way.

He saw Linda hopping in place behind him, wine spilling out of her glass with each hop. "We have rats, Damien! I can't live with rats!"

He had to get a hold of himself and deal with this. He approached the flower bed where he first saw the rodent and pushed back on some of the stems to get a look at the ground. He immediately let them fall back as he jumped back and then leapt farther out of the way. At this point, Linda made a beeline for the safety of the porch, and she watched Damien do what looked like a pee-pee dance and swear as he ran around the yard.

He was out of his depth here. What he had seen on the ground underneath the bushes was more than even he could bear. It was a whole nest of crawling fur and poop building *some kind of colony*. He ran after Linda onto the safety of the porch and past her into the house.

She ran after him and slammed the door shut. Puddin', so used to the screaming and hollering and banging, gave them a few exhausted barks and sat down, confused. MaryLou, also typically kept to her room when her parents were screaming, but something apparently felt different about this one because she rushed into the kitchen as her parents were running around it wild eyed and screaming.

"What's going on?" she yelled at them with a shaky voice.

Linda ran over to her and grabbed her in a tight hug like they were fighting for their lives.

"We have rats!" she screamed.

"Whaaat? Mommmy!" MaryLou joined in the jumping, and that's when Puddin' decided to lose his mind as well.

Damien thought his head was going to explode. He ran to the front door and ran outside and looked all around the ground to see if he was safe to stand before he got out his phone and called one of his guys to see if he could help.

The guy didn't answer the phone, and Damien left a panicked message for him to call him back immediately. He ran back into the house where the dog was still barking, and MaryLou was screaming while jumping up and down on the new sofa, which wasn't designed for that activity. Being a new, aesthetically pleasing modern design but not overly sturdy, one of the legs buckled, and MaryLou fell off the sofa and landed on the carpet.

Linda started screaming again, and they both ran over to MaryLou, who was crying on the floor.

"Honey!" screamed Linda. "Are you all right?" Linda threw herself on the floor to examine her daughter.

"Mommmmmmmy, I don't want rats in the house!" she wailed.

"MaryLou!" shouted Damien so he could be heard over the wailing and barking. "Are you all right? Did you hurt yourself?"

"Nooooooo, I'm okay!" She wailed harder from shock

and fear as Linda held her.

Damien couldn't believe all this drama and all the drama now in his life. He had to get everyone to calm down.

"Calm down! We don't have rats! We have some kind of mole or vole problem...outside! Not inside, so just calm down." He turned to Puddin' with an angry posture and yelled, "Shut up!"

He pointed at the dog. "Why didn't the damn dog alert us to something going on in the yard? You would think he would start digging or yapping out there or something?"

"We've been training him not to bark, remember? Don't blame this on him!"

"I'm not blaming the dog. I just can't believe he wouldn't have done something. The place is crawling with rodents out there!"

At this point, MaryLou started wailing again, and Linda crawled over to examine the damage to their new couch.

"Okay, that's it! I'm going outside to call someone. We gotta get someone over here to get rid of them."

"You cannot use poison, Damien. Puddin' will get into it and die! You know he likes to eat out of the garden. You can't use poison on the yard!"

"Well, what do you think we should do, Linda, let them colonize further and move into the house?"

"Damien! You're upsetting MaryLou. There just has to be another way, that's all I'm telling you."

Damien stormed out of the house.

Chapter 23

The next day, Damien jumped out of bed and made a list of the *problems* they were facing and a list of the *solutions* he knew would make them go away. He was going to tackle them, one by one, and he had the adrenaline and resources at his disposal to make that happen. He was a man of action and would *dominate* the situations one by one. By noon, after the exterminators left, he'd made several dozen phone calls delegating instructions to staff and associates to resolve every stinking little problem that had come up during the week. He was a fighter. He would take control, and he would control the situations and *prevail*! He was a winner, and winners didn't quit.

But still, he didn't like doing it. He didn't want to deal with the stupid crap anymore. He wanted to be above it and be in a position where people did things for him. People who would be proactive and didn't wait for crap to fall on them before they did something about it. People and staff who took control *for* him and protected him from having to deal with all *their* mess!

Linda had been overwhelmed as well. Lying on her bed, her phone on speaker, she was talking to Carey as Damien walked into the room to grab a stack of papers he'd left by the bed.

"I think we should burn the place down," Linda sighed.

Carey laughed. "Sweetie. Don't be ridiculous, I'm sure someone can fix it. What you need is a weekend away. Get out of the house. *Evacuate*, sweetie. Come on down. We've got the suite, you can stay with us. Throw some clothes in a bag and get in the car. We'll keep it casual this weekend. Come on, you can be here in two hours."

Linda gave Damien a look, searching for his approval.

With as much as he had to do, a part of him couldn't blame her for being upset over the infestation in the yard and wanting to get away. That problem was legit. Crazy legit. He never wanted to witness anything like that the rest of his life.

He nodded at her and whispered, "MaryLou goes to my dad's."

"Yay," said Linda, smiling. "Damien just came in and said we could go."

Damien walked out of the room. It was a good idea. Charles had also called this morning and invited him down to go over some casino business. He needed to pay attention to that part of his life now too.

Which was how, late Friday afternoon, Linda and Damien found themselves once again in the car on the way to Atlantic City to spend another weekend with the Carrowses.

And by God, they deserved it.

———————

Their arrival at the Atlantic Hotel almost felt like coming home. They dropped the car with the valet and instructed them to bring the bags to Carey's suite. Carey greeted them in the room with big hugs. "I thought we'd hang out here tonight," she said as she walked into the spacious, comfortable suite.

Harley and Charles were sitting on the sofas, watching a baseball game and drinking beer. Damien thought it looked like heaven.

"Hey," Charles said, toasting their arrival. "Glad you could make it." He gestured to the television with his bottle. "Yankees and Red Sox. You want a beer?"

"I'd love one," he said, flopping on the sofa and grabbing a cold one out of an iced bucket in front of them.

The bags came, and the women followed the bellmen into Damien and Linda's bedroom.

Charles leaned over the coffee table and took a handful of nuts. Munching on them, looking at the screen, he said to Damien, "Charlotte and Alex have a box at Yankee Stadium. We could take in a game sometime?"

Damien took a draw on his cold beer and said, "Sounds good." He relaxed. For the first time that week, he felt like he could breathe.

The next morning as Cadell, the butler, served them breakfast, they discussed the day.

"I've got the cabana booked for the weekend," Carey said as she sipped her chicory tea. "We've got the masseuse. Did you want to do that poolside?" she asked Linda.

"Yes, definitely," Linda said, mimicking her, taking a sip of her chicory tea.

"Mmm," Linda said, "so good. My liver will be ready for a little action by noon." She giggled. Carey joined her.

Charles, eating his eggs, said, "Damien and I have some business. Harley, did you want to come with us, or are you going down with the girls?"

"Do you need me?" Harley said, relaxed, legs crossed as he drank his coffee.

"No." Charles shook his head. "Just some casino business."

"I'll stay then," Harley said.

After breakfast, Charles and Damien headed out. Charles had a large black duffel bag strapped over his shoulder, and he threw it into the trunk before they pulled out of the parking lot in his Bentley Continental convertible. The car was powerful and sleek with a prominent grill. Damien rubbed his hands over the quilted golden leather interior. "This is beautiful, man," Damien said.

Charles smiled. "You like the color? Peacock-blue metallic. Just got it."

They talked about the car, its capacities, and exactly

what it had under the bonnet. Charles said, "We need to head over to Carrows, but I have a quick delivery to make. I hope you don't mind?"

"No, of course not," Damien said.

Charles relaxed. "So, D, now that you're in the club..." He gave Damien a sidelong smile. "I want to share some of the ways we handle our business. When I gave you the invitation to invest in Carrows, you need to know that I didn't take that lightly. As a businessman, I'm sure you understand about gut instinct. When it feels right, you do it. You don't ask permission. When opportunity knocks, you answer. I had a gut instinct about you. We know that you're sharp. You have had an admirable streak of success and innovative ideas. That's something you should be very proud of.

"But John and I talked, and we also know, or we're pretty sure we know, that you're really more like us. The ultra-successful. Someone who won't let anyone, or any obstacle, interfere with their plans and dreams. Were we right about you, Damien?" Charles glanced at him.

Damien felt so comfortable now in the surroundings of luxury, and with Charles and the Carrowses, he almost felt like family. "Damn right you were. I'm driven and successful. I've always been a winner."

Charles smiled and nodded as they cruised along. When they reached a light, he opened the car's top and let the sunshine warm them and fill them with a comforting sensual satisfaction. They were indeed men of the world.

Charles pulled into the private airfield of the Cross

Keys Airport. He parked next to a hangar and retrieved his bag from the trunk. Inside, a pilot and crew appeared to be conducting the preflight inspection of a Gulfstream G550.

A man by the flight stairs saw them arrive. He walked over to them and gave Charles a quick handshake and smile. "Mr. Carrows, so glad to see you again."

"Lloyd, you too. I want you to meet Damien Miller. Damien, this is Lloyd Greiner."

Damien and Lloyd shook hands.

"Lloyd and I go way back. Let's step into the office over there," Charles said as he gestured them toward a small room.

The three of them entered the empty room, and Charles heaved the bag onto a small desk. "Ooof, big one, Lloyd. Let's take a quick look."

Charles unzipped the bag. Damien's eyes grew large as he looked down at stacks of money. Hundred-dollar bills, bundled up and wrapped in cellophane.

"We got a mil and a half here, so it's pretty heavy. Do you think you can lift it?" Charles said as he smiled at Lloyd and played with his gold ring.

"No problem. I got this. Did you want a receipt?"

"No, we're going to take off. I trust you. I'll look at the account this afternoon after you get back."

Charles turned to Damien. "You ready to roll?"

Damien didn't know what to say. "Yup."

"All righty then, Lloyd, as usual, good to see you." Charles shook his hand, winked at Lloyd, and headed out the door.

Damien followed. *What was that?*

They got back into the car and drove away. As they left the airfield Charles said, "Lloyd and my family go way back, he's a good guy. We have a mutually beneficial relationship."

Damien didn't know what to say. He didn't know if a response was even required. They both knew that this wasn't something Damien ever did as a part of his day-to-day, so he didn't have much to add. He had questions, but he didn't know if it was cool to ask them.

"You okay, D?"

"Yeah, of course! I just didn't know what to say. I've never seen that much cash before. That was kinda awesome." He grinned.

Charles threw his head back and laughed. "Yes, it was awesome. I love money, and there's nothing like the feel and the smell of the real thing. We don't use cash all that much in our regular lives, always cards and paper going in and out. Cash is king though. What you saw back there is one of our secrets, but then I'm sure you realize that."

"Of course, sure," Damien said in deference to this great man.

"Well, D, big business brings in big money, and the bigger the business, the more money there is. Competition can be brutal, too, and my family and I didn't get where we are today by always playing by the rules."

"Oh, I get that. I'm in complete agreement." Damien nodded.

"Did you know that my grandfather was a pirate?"

Charles said, smiling as they hit the freeway and the wind. Charles reached over to the stereo and cranked up the tunes. They flew back to Emerald City playing "Pump It" by the Black Eyed Peas.

Chapter 24

It was with great reluctance now that Damien and Linda drove back to their *country home* in Morristown, New Jersey, still in their Chevy loaner. Life was so much nicer and easier when they were with the Carrowses. It was intoxicating. As usual, they were treated like kings and queens. Carey once again let Linda borrow an outfit and jewels, and Damien could feel that she was as sad to leave the privileged universe and go back to the real world as he was.

It wasn't that they didn't have a nice life, but the more time they spent with the Carrowses, the more they wanted to be like them. While that dream was probably impossible anyway, they were both fairly certain that their lives were on a trajectory toward something much, much bigger than what they were currently living. For now, that would have to be enough. The next step, a leap over the heaving bodies of the average, was sure to come.

Damien needed to refocus on his list of items to square

away. He was currently facing much more than he had ever had to deal with at one time and needed some help and some really good luck. He needed to make damn sure that the belts were as tight as possible over the course of the next few years. Everything had to be focused on high profits and repayment of the debt service. He needed to find some new employees fast, and he needed to make sure there were no holes in his system bleeding cash.

His first priority was finding captains for his boats. He needed to get them back on the water as quickly as possible so they would be making money rather than losing it. He was pressing everyone at Titan to work on the staffing problems full time. The problem was they were all stretched tight with the upcoming Titan Farm mediations. He'd tell Samara to phone it in. No reason for her to spend more time than necessary preparing for mediation if they had no intention of giving the farmers a dime.

He knew the farmers were all broke too. They couldn't hold out for much longer, and it would all go away. Maybe he would have Samara go after *them* and pierce *their* corporate veils and attach liens to *their* properties. That wasn't a bad idea. Samara was on salary. God knows she enjoyed her job.

But right now, he needed to focus on the ships and selling more farms and spending as little as possible. Maybe he could attach more costs of doing business to the farmers. They should help pay for the training school he was setting up to help them. After all, it was *their* business, not his that needed the training. He'd float that one past

Samara too. Maybe they should pay for the website too? Hmm.

He needed to get down to the docks and literally start knocking on cabin doors until he found some captains. He knew the Wellingtons weren't going to give him a hand finding replacements. He knew he could make this happen, he had to.

———————

By the end of the week, the rodent infestation was nearly eliminated. The exterminator cost a bundle with daily house calls, but the traps needed constant replacement, and neither he nor Linda wanted to do that gruesome job. The guy said he had never in his life seen such a concentration of voles in one yard. He thought maybe it had something to do with the warm weather and the river.

Damien managed to find a new foreman for his model farm but only because he paid him for what he was worth. Damien didn't like to do that, but he needed the production to run smoothly for the rest of the year, so it was the smart move. As long as the rest of his underpaid crew didn't find out.

The best part of the week had been when he got his car back. He groaned as he sat in it for the first time. He closed his eyes and absorbed the familiar feel of the seats. It felt good.

He had a couple leads on skippers too. They were coming in this weekend from the Carolinas. If they were even halfway decent, Damien needed to secure their hire.

He didn't want to give them too much money, just enough to hook them. Maybe he could offer them a weekend at his casino? He considered that option but then shuddered. If they were anything like the Wellington boys, he couldn't unleash *that* with his name attached to it at Carrows. The horror! He might have to offer them a larger percentage of the take. Promise them anything, and once they came on salary, he'd find cheaper skippers. He didn't care if they moved their families up from the Carolinas for the job. If they didn't take a pay reduction after the first year, he'd shit-can 'em.

Last weekend Charles had asked him to come back to Atlantic City, but at the time, Damien had been reluctant to commit. Now, as he drove back to the pier, he realized that he'd only be an hour away from Atlantic City. He decided to take him up on the offer.

"Hey, Charles, you still up for tomorrow? I'm gonna be at the docks for some business with the Fishery in Barnegat Light. I thought I'd come up to AC after I was finished."

"Damien. So glad you called. Sounds good. Barnegat Light? What's that, about an hour from here?"

"Yeah, the boats are tied up there. I'm interviewing new skippers."

Charles said, "You know I've always been interested in the fishing industry. My dad has some business in the Puget Sound area, and when I was younger, I used to tag along. Would you mind if I met up with you and took a look at your operation?"

"No, that would be great! I don't know if I mentioned this or not, but my boats, Titan 1 and Titan 2, are temporarily grounded until I get new skippers. I hope to hire a couple this weekend so I can get the boats back on the water."

"Maybe I can help with that. What time do you want me there tomorrow?"

"I'm meeting with them at noon at Pier 12. You want to meet up with me around 11:30? I can show you around?"

"Yup. Sounds good. See you then."

Having Charles Carrows at the interview could only work in Damien's favor. For one thing, it was totally cool that he was going to be there for the closing. It would give Charles an opportunity to watch him sell. He felt confident Charles would be impressed.

———————

Saturday morning, Charles Carrows pulled up in a Lamborghini to Pier 12 and met Damien on the dock.

"How many cars do you have, Charlie?" Damien reached out and stroked the car as he looked at Charles. He admired Charles's easygoing style, always smiling and high on life.

"Oh, a few. If I told you the truth, it might pain you; though, I know how much you love cars."

"Yeah, I do. Cars and boats really. I've always loved them both. Are you ready to go aboard?" He gestured up toward Titan 1. "We try to keep them clean, but obviously smells linger, and fish mean money, so I don't care."

Later that afternoon, Charles called Alex while driving back to AC. "I just met Damien at his Barnegat Light pier. He was interviewing new captains, a couple of newbies from the Carolinas who went through school together and were looking for their first job as skippers. Let me give you their names, and you can reach out to them next week after we close this operation down. Damien offered them all kinds of back-end promises with this huge contract that Samara Poe must have cooked up. I wanted to scream at them when I watched them sign."

"Ah, hell," said Alex. "Two more."

"I'm positive they wouldn't see anything coming their way on the back end, either. He sold them though, I'll give him that. If he wasn't planning to just use them and screw them, I might have approved, but he's such a scumbag."

"Well, good luck tonight. Carey and Harley are in a room down the hall from the suite. They're ready if you need them," said Alex.

"Yup. I'm as ready as I can be. Here's hoping it works."

Back in Atlantic City, Charles and Damien entered Charles's suite at the Atlantic Hotel and Casino. Damien threw himself, exhausted, onto the sofa in the living room overlooking the Atlantic Ocean and the boardwalk. It felt good to be home.

"Why don't you take the other room for the night and

head back in the morning, D?" Charles said as he went to the bar.

"That sounds reasonable. I've got a bag in the car. Man, I'm beat. Busy, busy week. I'm so tired of some of the *little* stuff I have to deal with."

Charles came over to Damien with a crystal tumbler filled with ice and scotch and turned to open the balcony doors. Damien got up and followed him out.

"You work hard, Damien, I'll give you that. Really nice interview with those newbie captains. You can sell!" Charles raised his glass in a toast to Damien.

Damien took a sip of his drink as they watched the sun setting out on the sea. It was relaxing and inspiring. "Thanks, Charles. I think they were halfway home just walking past your car. Thanks for that too." Damien raised his glass in return.

"No problem at all. Let's get out of here and celebrate. A big dinner and then I'd like to hit one of the clubs. There's this girl I've been seeing. She's in town with a friend of hers. You don't mind making it a foursome, do you? I mean, it'll all be aboveboard and everything. We'll tell them you're married, it's just, I'd like to see her if you get my drift."

"Right, no problem. Linda would be cool. I better give her a quick call before we head out," he said as he walked back into the suite.

Charles was staring out at the sea, and as usual, smiling. He really enjoyed his life.

Chapter 25

They hit the Palm Restaurant and had a few drinks with their surf and turf. After dinner, Charles declared it early and decided he wanted a respite before meeting the girls at the club. He suggested they go back to the Atlantic and play some blackjack.

Damien was uneasy about it but followed Charles onto the casino floor. They walked past the flashy slots and tables. The place was bustling and noisy with customers' chatter, the clanging of the machines, the casino staff, and watchful security. It was all a part of the excitement. Charles led the way until they reached the high-rollers room where Damien had burned through $30,000 a couple of weeks before. He was not interested in repeating that mistake tonight nor did he even have much money on him. As usual, he was used to Charles footing the bill for everything and only rarely did Damien put things on his credit card.

They stopped outside the door to the room with the

gold and red curtains, a velvet rope and security barring the way. Charles said quietly, "We both have to play if we go in there. You understand that, right? If you sit at the table, you've got to put some money down. Are you cool with that?"

Damien shrugged, considering.

Charles said, "Hey, you paid me back last time, I know you're good for it. If you need to borrow some cash, just say it, no problem, I know we'll work something out."

"No, I just don't want to lose any more. I don't have a lot of wiggle room right now, remember?"

Charles put his hand on his shoulder. "Listen, D, sorry if I was insensitive there, it's just me, sometimes I don't think, and I get it, I do. But hey, life's looking up for you now. We're business partners, and I can guarantee that will pay off. In the meantime, you've got your businesses to look after, and I get that. I wouldn't want you to do anything to jeopardize the health of your companies. But, listen, you really do have to put something down. Lay out two or five hundred bucks, and if you lose it, you're done. How does that sound? I just wanna play for a little while before we hit the club."

"Right, no, five hundred bucks is doable. Thanks for being cool about it."

Charles smiled. "Great. Let's go."

The pit boss in the room nodded to security to pull back the velvet rope and allow them to enter. The quiet, wood-paneled room had three tables, each in the classic half-moon shape. There were maybe five players total, and one of the gold padded tables stood empty. It was fairly early; there was a chance people were still at dinner. Charles walked over to the empty table; the dealer stood behind it, at the ready. Damien and Charles sat on the crushed gold velvet high-backed chairs as a beautiful woman appeared and asked them if she could bring them something to eat or drink.

Charles and Damien ordered drinks and turned their attention back to the table. The pit boss approached and said, "Gentlemen, welcome back. This is a no-limit table. The minimum bet tonight is $100. Will we be managing the credit lines through you again, Mr. Carrows?"

Charles glanced at Damien and said, "Yup. I've got him covered. Give him whatever he needs. I'll start with twenty."

Damien, flustered, realized Charles asked for twenty thousand in chips. He said, "I'll take five hundred— dollars," he added, to be certain they understood. He wasn't going to ease off the bargain. He needed to stay focused. The chips were counted out, and the drinks arrived. The beautiful waitress stayed beside them, smiling. Damien noticed Charles give her a $100 chip.

Damien was a little uncomfortable, but now that he and Charles were square about how much he could afford to play, he relaxed and placed the minimum bet. Very soon, his stack of chips grew, and he jumped deeper into the game. To his surprise, he was winning.

Maybe it was because this time he was playing relatively sober. Last time he had been very drunk. Damien suddenly felt he had a knack for the game. He was calling the shots just right, almost like he knew what was going to come out of the shoe. In a little over an hour, he'd made nearly $50,000. He was on fire and loving every minute of it.

Charles, at the same time, had been losing and losing big. He announced that he was ready to leave. "See, Damien, you got to spend some to make some! Why don't we stop? That way you come out ahead when you get home." Charles stood and gave the dealer a huge tip. "Let's cash you out and get out of here."

Damien felt high as he walked into the evening with his lump of cash. Fifty thousand large. He was surprised at how little room it took up in his jacket pocket.

They climbed inside the waiting limousine. Charles plopped down next to the bar. He picked up an empty glass and shook it in Damien's direction. "Don't throw that cash around on the girls tonight, D, or you'll have me to answer to. Not to mention Linda. Let's roll," he yelled at the driver.

As they pulled away from the curb, Charles said, "Hey, did you want to put it in the safe in the room?"

Already underway, Damien shook his head and said, "No, it's fine."

Charles smiled and handed him a large glass of vodka and soda, Damien's drink of choice.

"Congrats!" Charles exclaimed. "To you, Damien Miller, may we never go to hell but always be on our way!"

Damien laughed and raised his glass. "It feels good!"

Charles smiled and looked out the window. "The girls

we're meeting—my girl, her name is Lovisa. She and her friends work for Lufthansa, and she gives me a ring when she's got some extra time on her hands on this side of the world. They like to party, so don't be surprised."

Charles took a sip of his drink and lay his head back. "God, she's gorgeous. I told her I was in AC, so she said she'd come down."

"Is she your girlfriend then?" Damien had always been curious about Charles's relationship status. He'd made some assumptions, but it had never really come up before.

Charles shook his head. "I wouldn't call her that. She's someone—well, we enjoy each other when we get a chance to be in the same city at the same time." He raised his glass. "Not all treasure is silver and gold, mate." He threw his head back and smiled. "Captain Jack Sparrow." He finished his drink.

They cruised along, the LED coach lights softly illuminating the ride as Charles fidgeted with his phone.

"Catch this, D," he said, pointing to the small flat screen in the wall. "You like NWA? I was just a kid in LA during the riots, but man, this shit was everything to us out there when me and my buds were growing up."

Charles pulled up a video of the rap group and turned the volume up high as "Straight Outta Compton" cranked out of the speakers. He rolled his head and beat it, Damien along with him as the two of them drove through the night toward their next destination.

The limousine took them to a loud nightclub where they met up with the girls. Damien hadn't participated in big club evenings in many years and, of course, had never done them up in the style that they enjoyed that night. He was used to Charles being treated well, and he was accustomed to their glamorous evenings, but he had never seen Charles flaunt his money or throw it around like he did that night.

The girls were wild, and the drinks in the club's VIP area flowed. It didn't take long for Damien to get caught up in the atmosphere and raucous and bawdy party. The young, beautiful girls were everywhere. Charles's date clung to him, and when not dancing with either him or Damien, she and her friend danced provocatively with one another. Charles seemed to be very interested in his girl, and even though Damien had made it clear to her friend that he was married, she didn't seem to care and spent a great deal of time and effort flirting and dancing with him. Charles kept encouraging Damien to relax, and as usual, it was hard to resist his charms and influence.

That night, Damien was high on life. He wanted to be just like his new friend, and he watched his mentor roll through life with casual ease and abandon, which Damien tried mighty hard to emulate. They spent an obscene amount of money on liquor, and Charles took care to remind him several times to keep his own stash private. This evening would be on him. He assured Damien there would be others.

There were photographers around too. Damien knew one of Linda's fondest desires was to be photographed while she was out looking glamorous with the Carrowses.

To date, that hadn't happened, and Damien was pretty sure that he and Charles surrounded by gorgeous women weren't the type of photographs she had in mind. It was out of his control, however, and after a while, the photographers started to blend in with everyone taking selfies and pictures with their phones. Charles told him it was just a typical night in the fast lane.

However, Damien had never seen his friend drink quite so much before and realized after a while that at least one of them needed to be semiconscious. So, he became the wingman. Late that night, Damien practically carried Charles out of the club and into the limo for the ride back to the hotel. He dragged him through the lobby and up to the suite. Once deposited on his bed, Charles promptly passed out.

What a wild night. What a roller coaster his life was on. One minute he was worrying about voles and red-headed Squirrels, the next he was winning $50,000 in blackjack and being a wingman for Charles Carrows in the bars. He loved being Damien-fucking-Miller. He went to his room and fell asleep.

In what seemed like just a few minutes later, his phone rang. He looked at it through bleary eyes and realized it was 8:00 a.m. Charles was calling.

"D...man, where are you?"

"Charlie, where are you? I'm in bed."

"I'm in the next room, you gotta come here," he said and hung up.

Damien climbed out of bed. He threw on his pants and

walked across the suite to Charles's room. When he got there, he found the bed empty but heard Charles getting sick in the bathroom. He didn't want to go in there, but the man called him.

"Charles, dude." Damien knocked on the door and opened it, poking his head inside. "You okay?" He walked slowly into the large marble-lined and gold-fixtured bathroom.

Charles was lying by the toilet, his face damp with perspiration. "D...I'm so sick, man, how did we even get home? I don't remember anything," he groaned.

"Yeah, it was quite a night. I pulled you out of the club around two and got you back here. Lovisa and the girls said they were going to another party. You didn't look like you could handle much more, so I pulled you out. You weren't feeling any pain!"

"I am now," he complained. "Get me a cold cloth over there, will you? And maybe a Coke and some aspirin?"

"Sure." Damien ran around getting him the stuff. "So, I'm going to need to leave in a little bit, are you going to be okay? Did you want me to get you anything else?" he asked as he followed Charles out of the bathroom and watched him crawl back into bed.

"D, I need you to do me a big favor. I'm in really bad shape. No way I can drive. I'm probably still drunk too. Or maybe I just puked that all up."

"Sure, yeah, what do you need?"

"I was supposed to take another run out to the airport and meet Lloyd with some cash, but I just can't do it. You have to help me, it's all set up, and they're expecting me to show up at nine."

Damien thought he understood what Charles was saying but was once again stunned stupid at the thought that he was being asked to drive around with millions of dollars in cash.

"You want me to bring him the bag? To the airport?"

"Please, Damien. Yeah, I need your help. I can't do it. I could call and tell them to forget it, but it's a big hassle to schedule this shit, and I don't want to deal with it. You know what to do and where to go, you've been there. The bag's in the safe over there, will you do it for me?"

Damien looked over at the huge safe in the closet.

"Take my car. Just give the valet my card, and he'll bring it. I'll call him. Come on, man, please?"

Damien looked at his sick friend and knew that he would do anything for him. This was just another one of those weird things in the life of the super-rich. Not weird for the rich, but weird for him. Damien also puffed up that Charles trusted him with the job and all that money. It was a good feeling.

"At nine? Did you say, same place, same guy?"

"Yeah, it'll take you like two minutes, just give him the bag. The code to the safe is 009456. Bag is inside," he said and groaned.

Damien went over to the huge safe and opened it. Inside was another black duffel bag. He lifted it out. It was really heavy.

"Tell Lloyd there's two in there, and don't bother with

a receipt. Just give it to him and go. I trust you both."

"All right, you got it. I'll take my car though 'cause I gotta get home after the drop. I hope you feel better." He didn't know what else to say.

Charles raised his head, pulled the cloth away from his eyes, and looked at Damien holding the bag. "Yeah? You sure you don't want to take mine?"

Damien smiled. "I got my sweet baby back. I'll drive her."

"Whatever," Charles said and flopped back down.

———

Damien went back to his room and finished dressing. He grabbed his small overnight bag and the duffle of cash and left the suite.

———

The moment the door closed, Charles sat up and called Carey. "Damn, he's taking his own car. Stop him. He's on his way down. Where are you?"

"I'm in the lobby. I got him. Call valet."

———

The maître d' met Damien in the hallway reception on their floor and asked if he would like for him to arrange some breakfast. Damien was nervous holding a bag filled with two million bucks but stopped long enough to ask the man for a coffee. He took the drink and his bags and went downstairs. Carey Carrows walked toward the bank of elevators as he got off.

Surprised, he said, "Hey. Good morning."

"Damien," she said as she walked over and gave him a lingering hug. She whispered, "Kiss, kiss," as she air-kissed the sides of his face.

"Charles didn't tell me you were in town. Oh, dear," she said, stepping back, appraising him. "Linda called me last night, but I didn't get a chance to call her back. You're not being a bad boy, are you, Damien? Are the two of you arguing?"

"No," he said as he dropped the heavy bag, switched his coffee hand, and picked it back up. "I had some business with my trawlers in Barnegat Light. It just worked out."

"I see," she said, taking her sunglasses off the top of her head and spinning them. She had a small bundle of miniature white roses stuck through a headband by her ear. "What did you two get up to last night? Why didn't you call us?"

"Charles said you guys had checked into another place to evaluate the competition."

"True, but you could have called." She moved past him toward the elevator and pressed the button. "I was just going to pop up and see him. I take it he's awake. Is he alone?"

"Yeah, he's alone, but he's a bit green this morning," he said, hefting the bag again in his hand, redistributing the weight.

Carey looked down at it. "Hmmm, well, I'll just be going then. Check on the dear boy."

"Yup," Damien said as he turned to walk away. "See you later."

Carey came after him. "Damien." He stopped.

She pulled the headband off her head and extracted a flower. She tucked it through a buttonhole in his jacket and patted it. "There now," she said quietly. "It's not red, but..." She stepped back and smiled. "Damien, will you accept this rose?"

He got the reference to *The Bachelor*. He smiled, playing along, "I will."

"Good. We like you, Damien." She skipped back to the elevator as it dinged. "You're practically a *Carrows*," she whispered and smiled.

Damien hummed a bit as he walked toward valet, momentarily even forgetting about the cash. He was grateful when he got outside so he could drop it. He retrieved his ticket and gave it to the valet.

He drank his coffee with contentment while he waited. But after a protracted amount of time, he became impatient. Suddenly, the young man appeared, out of breath, but without his car.

"Sir, I'm afraid your car is not drivable. It won't turn over."

"What?" Damien yelled. "That's bullshit. I just got it out of the shop."

"I'm sorry, sir, I tried several times. I got nothing. Perhaps the battery is dead? We could call a car service?"

Damien didn't know what to do. He wanted to check on it personally, but he was holding a bag with two million dollars cash and needed to meet Floyd at the airport. He was in a hurry. He needed a car. He could take a taxi, but the thought of that somehow frightened him. He didn't know if that was a good idea.

"Sir, did you want us to call a car service and see if it needs a jump? You could wait inside. We're kind of backed up now, but it shouldn't take too long."

"Argh," he said and pulled out his phone. He called Charles. It rang several times. Charles picked up, and Damien explained the situation.

Charles said, "Give me the guy, you can take my car."

Damien handed the phone to the young man, who listened and walked with it over to a computer monitor. He looked at something and spoke to Charles, then returned the phone to Damien. "Sir, Mr. Carrows's car will be brought around immediately. We're sorry for the inconvenience."

"Just get it," Damien said as he looked at the time on his phone. He'd make it, but still, it was aggravating.

The young valet pulled to the curb with Charles's peacock-blue Bentley. The car gleamed in the morning sun, and Damien told the valet to pop the trunk. Damien hefted the duffle and his small bag inside. He closed the lid and walked to the door.

"Jump mine. I'll be back in about an hour. Or two." He got in the car, made a few small adjustments, and left the Atlantic Hotel.

On the road, he had a lot on his mind.

He was really nervous, for a variety of reasons. He

looked around Charles's immaculate dream of a car and got a feel for how it handled. It almost, almost made his sweet baby seem passé. His sweet baby, dead in the garage. The hell? Maybe it would never recover from the accident. It pissed him off.

His thoughts turned to the money in the trunk. Two million in the trunk and fifty thousand in his pocket. He shook his head in disbelief as he looked down at the console and turned on the stereo. A talk radio station came on, talking about financial investments and the stock market. Damien switched the channel until he found something he liked.

It felt good to have friends like the Carrowses. He smiled at the flower in his lapel as he cruised along.

Zipping down the tollway, he was enjoying the smooth ride but hit the brakes as he realized he was going much faster than he thought. What if he got pulled over? How the hell would he explain having two million cash to the cops? Wait. Why would they even look in the trunk? Why would it be their business? Is it against the law to have two million in your trunk? He didn't think so, but what did he know? What about the fifty large in his pocket? That was easier to explain, he was in Atlantic City.

Damien thought about all that money. Just sitting back there. He cautioned himself. *Don't even think about taking a little bit off the top. Shut that down, idiot.* In addition, he was worried that he was probably doing something illegal, but he didn't exactly know what.

Whose money was it? It was either Charles's or

someone else's money. They had to be laundering it. But it wasn't really laundering if it was from a legitimate source. Whatever they were doing with the duffels of cash, they obviously did it all the time. Cash must be safer than wire transfers. But where did the money come from? What kind of business had that much cash? Casinos did. It had to be from a casino. Carrows Casino wasn't open yet. It had to be another one they were involved with. Probably the Atlantic, which was why they always stayed there. Which only reaffirmed what Damien knew. The casino business was very lucrative.

Maybe there would be occasions for Damien to benefit from some cash opportunities now that he was a shareholder of the casino. That thought inspired him. He was a big believer in cash. It was one of the backbones of his success. Who knew? In addition to the straightforward profits, there might be many more ways to make money than he initially thought. Charles trusted him, and Charles was opening another casino in Vegas too. That was exciting.

He just needed to drop the money off, and Charles would know he was a go-to, stand-up guy, who understood that this was how money was managed in the real world. Playing by the rules was for idiots and losers, and he and Charles Carrows were not losers. They were partners now. Damien could see that.

Damien exited onto a side road near the airport and came to a stoplight. He looked down at the console and saw Charles's gold ring. He picked it up and looked at it. It was subtle, but there was an impression of a skull and crossbones. He smiled, thinking about Charles mentioning it was his grandfather's ring and that he'd said they were descended from pirates.

The light turned green. Damien continued onward. What about his 50K? Could he give that to Lloyd too and have him start an account for him? Not pay the almost $15K in taxes? If he was going to be in the casino business, it was probably a given that there would be a lot of cash opportunities, I mean, exhibit A was in the trunk! Damien had always been fond of cash opportunities. You had to cut corners and take risks if you wanted to get ahead. This strategy had always worked for him. And if he needed another crystal-clear example of the system working for the non-risk-aversive businessman and entrepreneur, he had Charles Carrows teaching him. If they were avoiding federal taxes on their money, they must know what they were doing.

He stopped at another light and picked up the ring again. It was laying next to a small, square brown envelope. He looked inside the ring and read the inscription. It said, "Live With Out Laws."

The hell? He smiled as he neared the entrance to the turnoff. He put the ring back on the console and picked up the small envelope. He turned it over, and his eyes popped wide as he saw *D—* written on it. What? Was that for him? He focused on the road but felt something solid inside. At the next light, he looked inside the unsealed envelope. It was a ring.

Shit. Damien felt his face flush with pride and

embarrassment that he had stumbled on something that wasn't meant for him to see. He held the ring up to the light. It had the same skull and crossbones on it but no engraving on the inside. Holy cow.

The light turned, and Damien continued. Wow. What an incredible gesture. He was moved. What was it about Charles and pirates? He knew his grandfather was descended from them, and Charles really seemed sentimental about it. Yo, ho, ho and a bottle of rum. Was that it? Pirates plunder, pillage, and live outside the law. Ah. It came to him. Live without Laws, or Live with Outlaws.

Damien smiled and placed the envelope face down again where he found it. Time to get on the bandwagon. He'd love to use the money for paying down some of his loans, but this might be the smarter move. He wouldn't even have to tell Linda. Come to think of it, whenever they cashed out, the money was always brought to them. No trail of a receipt. No paperwork. No IDs, just a beautiful woman handing them cash. Damn. The Atlantic and Charles must have a deal.

If he opened his own account, it would inspire even more confidence in Charles that he was the right kind of guy. Kind of like making a spit deal with a friend. But he was no kid now, and this wasn't Monopoly money. He liked it.

Damien pulled up next to the hangar. He looked around and saw it was a similar setup as the time before. The pilot and crew were doing another walk-around. Lloyd and another guy were speaking by the plane. Damien got out and opened the trunk. He unzipped the black duffel and stared at the cash. He grabbed the $50K out of his pocket and threw it on top of the rows of $100 bills. Really nervous now, he zipped it up and heaved it out of the trunk. He walked toward Lloyd in the hangar.

Lloyd came up to Damien with his hand extended. "I just got off the phone with Charles. He explained that you would be stopping by instead of him today."

Damien shook his hand, lifted the bag off his shoulder, and handed it to Lloyd. He took it and said, "Charles said there was two in there. Should we go into the office and take a look?"

"No, he told me to tell you that he trusted you. But I hope you don't mind, and I don't think Charles would mind, I also threw in $50K of my own money. I was wondering if you could open an account for me too."

"Are you saying this is your money?" Lloyd put his hand on the bag.

"No, I'm saying that there is $50K on the top that's mine, the rest is Charles's. I thought maybe I could open an offshore account in the Caymans or wherever, now that I'm in the casino business with him. Right?"

Lloyd gave him a long look and said, "Just a moment, please. I'll need to speak with my partner over there." He left him and walked toward the gentleman by the plane. Damien watched him speak into his ear, and the two of them went into the little office with the bag and shut the door.

Damien wasn't sure what to do, but Lloyd told him to wait, and he had his $50K. He waited.

It wasn't long before the two of them opened the door and walked toward him. Bagless.

"Damien, I'd like you to meet my business partner, Joe Roth. Mr. Roth works for the federal government, as do I."

Damien did not understand. The government? What was happening here?

"Damien Miller you are under arrest for attempting to defraud the US government."

"*What* are you talking about? I didn't defraud anyone! What is going on here? I didn't do anything wrong!"

"Mr. Miller," said Joe Roth, "we are conducting an investigation into a money laundering and tax evasion operation of incorporators out of Atlantic City and have been working alongside Charles Carrows in an attempt to break the group that operates out of this airport. By giving us your money and handing it over to an officer from the IRS—" Here he pointed to Lloyd. "You have willingly admitted attempting to defraud the US government by establishing an offshore account for purposes of tax evasion."

Damien's heart raced. "What are you talking about? I don't understand what you're saying! Charles is working with the government? You think I'm a criminal? I'm not a criminal! What the fuck is this?"

"Mr. Miller, we have an active investigation going on here, and I'm afraid I'll need to take you to our offices and secure a statement from you about your activities. Joe, can you Mirandize him?"

"Mr. Miller," said Joe. "You have the right to remain silent..."

Damien couldn't hear what they were saying. The words meant nothing as Roth handcuffed him and perp-walked him out of the hangar into a waiting car.

Chapter 26

What do you mean you were arrested!" screamed Linda. "Where are you? What did you do, Damien?" Linda's voice was an octave too high, her words drilling a hole through his already throbbing head.

"Linda, stop screaming at me! It's all just a big misunderstanding. I didn't do anything wrong. Nothing! I swear to God. It's really complicated, but it wasn't anything criminal, it's like a tax thing. I was with Charles. It's all a big misunderstanding, I swear."

"Charles? What has he got to do with it? What were you two doing all weekend?"

"Nothing! We had dinner and drinks, and then I ran an errand for him, and it just got weird, but I'm telling you, I didn't do anything wrong."

"Then why the fuck did they arrest you?"

"Damn, Linda, can you just support me and maybe be a little sympathetic for once? I said it was a big mix-up, and it's just going to take some time to figure it out.

Charles is on the way with an attorney, and I'm not sure when I'll be home. They'll probably let me go after the attorney gets here."

He had not wanted to call Linda, but he knew he didn't have a choice. It had been hours since he should have been home, and she'd wonder where he was. It wasn't like he was going to be able to hide this one from her.

"Damien, if you did something and you're not telling me, I swear to God I'm going to be so pissed. We had this conversation after you went out and got a loan for a million dollars and didn't even ask me. Remember that one?"

Damien looked around the large utilitarian government room with puke-green walls. He felt sick. His hangover, empty stomach, the bullshit at the airport, and now Linda. He couldn't believe any of it was happening.

"Linda, I gotta go. Charles just walked in, I'll call you later." He heard her screaming his name as he hung up the phone.

He looked over at Charles as he walked into the room with a guy he had never met. The two of them were speaking with Roth and Lloyd, who had also just arrived. Charles kept looking over at him, and Damien didn't like the looks of it, but he was certain Charles would be able to fix all of it. He was the one who had sent him to the airport, for God's sake. It was his money in the bag! The rich always got out of stuff. If nothing else, he brought an attorney who would probably kick all their asses.

Charles finally came over to him. "Damien, this is

Stanford Langdon, he's one of my attorneys who agreed to speak with you."

Stanford shook Damien's hand. "Let's all go into another room and have a word."

The three of them sat down in the small, private room, and Damien burst out, "Charles, I don't know what the hell is going on here. I did exactly what *you* told me to do and delivered the money that *you* gave me. To the *Feds?* I don't understand what's happening!" He pounded his hands on the table.

"Damien," said Stanford. "Would you like me to represent you as your attorney in this matter, or do you have another option you would like to appropriate?"

Damien looked at their two calm and serious faces and just wanted to scream with impatience that they had to go through legal niceties. "*Yes,* you can be my attorney. Now explain to them, both of you, that this is all a big misunderstanding. I didn't do anything wrong!"

Stanford held up his hand and said, "Just one moment. As my client, I need to ask you if you are willing to have Mr. Carrows in the room with us as we discuss your case, or do you wish for him to leave the room?"

"Christ! He needs to stay because this was all his fault!"

Stanford held up his hand for silence again. "Damien, as I understand the facts, you offered a federal officer and an investigator from the Internal Revenue Service money—cash money—to set up what you believed to be an illegal overseas account. Is that correct?"

"I didn't know they worked for the damned government,

I thought they worked for you, Charles!" he screamed.

Charles spoke, "Damien, I never told you anything about what Lloyd did for me. The fact is, the Carrows family has been helping them uncover these foreign incorporators, and they were using our money and our hangar and our plane as props to set up a sting on some guys. They just needed more cash, and I was supposed to bring that to them this morning at nine, but I was too sick to go. I didn't think you'd bribe them or anything."

"I didn't bribe them! I just gave them my money and told them I wanted to invest my $50K from last night too! I thought you had a thing going, and I wanted to show you I was on board, man!"

Stanford held up his hand. "Damien, whether you knew it or not, what you did was a federal offense, and they couldn't look the other way even if they wanted to. You just gave yourself to them in the course of their sting investigation. I'm sorry."

Charles said, "I can't believe you thought I was doing something illegal. I'm in the casino business. I'm a Carrows! I'm not a criminal. Why would I be a criminal? I've already got everything I'm ever going to need!"

Damien closed his mouth as he slowly began to realize that he might actually be in some trouble. He felt himself perspire, and a small wave of sickness on his empty stomach ran through him.

Damien screwed up his face in pain. "But what about the ring, man?"

Charles tilted his head and looked at him with confusion. "What ring?"

"Your ring. The ring in the car. The envelope with my name on it? The pirate ring!"

Charles got up from the table and pushed in his chair, his jaw muscles working. "You went through my stuff, *man*? That ring was for my dad, dumbshit. I gotta go."

Charles left the room. Damien stared at the closed door. *Shit.*

———

Stanford got Damien released that day as the Feds and the IRS didn't really want to deal with the unexpected idiot and the processing. What a mess. It satisfied them that Damien signed some documents saying he would appear at a later date and time. Charles had left hours before, apparently pissed that Damien had thought he was a criminal. Stanford drove him back to the Atlantic Hotel. They told him his car had been jumped and was in working order.

Damien drove home late that night and entered the quiet house. It was never a good sign when Linda was quiet. He threw his bag on the stairs and went through to the sitting room. He found her on the sofa, one broken corner of it now propped on a brick. She was perched there like a spider waiting for its prey.

"Hi, hon. Did you have a nice day?"

"Linda, I swear to God, I am not in the mood for a fight

with you right now. You can't believe the day I've had. I just want to go to bed."

"Well, gee, I'm tired too. But I think you need to tell me what's going on before you go to beddy bye."

He let out a long sigh and put his head down. Running his hands through his hair and down his tired face, he sat across from her. "Ahhhh, what do you want to know?" he said.

"How 'bout everything. I've been going out of my mind since you called and then you didn't even have the decency to call me back. Did you get my messages?"

Damien had seen she'd called about ten times. He'd deleted them.

"Yeah, I got them, I just didn't have a chance to return them since I was pretty tied up!"

"What happened?" she growled. "Tell me what's going on. I've tried calling Carey to see if she knew anything, but she hasn't returned my calls either."

"Linda! I'm here now." He threw his hands up in exasperation. "I'll tell you everything, just give me a minute to catch my breath." He got up and walked around. "Aaagh, okay." He launched into the story. He told her the truth about everything except the part about the dancing and the girls at the club.

"So, you won fifty thousand dollars gambling and then decided it would be a good idea to use that as seed money to open an illegal account in the Cayman Islands? But *instead,* you handed it to an undercover IRS agent and asked him to do it for you. Is that right?"

"Yup! That about sums it up! Didn't know what I was doing, obviously, and now I have a legal mess to figure out."

"Does this mean you're going to jail?"

"What? No. There won't be any jail time. I think it's just a misdemeanor, and this attorney, Stanford Langdon, that Charles brought in seems sharp. He told me not to worry, and he'll see if he can even just get it dismissed or something. He said he'd argue that I was misled or stupid or something."

"Well, yeah! That about sums it up!" Linda folded her arms across her chest.

"Okay, so now you know everything, all right? I've got to get some sleep. We'll talk about this more over the week. Let's just see what Stanford can do first, okay?"

"What's this mean about your relationship with Charles? And what about Carey? Maybe they're pissed at you, too, and that's why she wouldn't return my calls!"

"Geez, Linda, how many times did you call her?"

She stopped and looked embarrassed, trying to remember. "I don't know. Once, twice I think."

"Well, maybe you should leave her alone while this gets sorted out. It'll be fine. Everyone will cool off; it was just a big misunderstanding. Charles will eventually realize that too. I'm going to bed." He fled the room before she could say anything more.

Chapter 27

Damien was at Titan Feed when Stanford Langdon called two days later. He pulled up the call and walked outside into the parking lot.

"As your legal representative, I have been working with the IRS, specifically Lloyd Greiner, to reach some type of agreement to make this as easy for you as possible. As you know, Lloyd was in a difficult spot because of your overture at the airport hangar. He felt he had an ethical responsibility to report the activity.

"It wouldn't typically be Lloyd's job to follow up on your case, but I pressed him about the large and special circumstances surrounding the situation. You wanted me to make this go away, so I reminded them about the undercover work that was being conducted, the generosity of the Carrows family and their representatives, and here I included you, and the willingness of my client, you, to pay whatever penalties would be reasonable. They weren't initially sure how to manage this very odd case, but I kept

Lloyd personally involved, and they've decided it would be in everyone's best interest to wrap it up quickly."

"Stanford." Damien put his hand over his heart, his head back as he looked at the sky. "That's awesome. I'm so relieved. I really am innocent here, though, I was going to pay the taxes on that money. I didn't do anything wrong."

"I know you impressed this opinion on me many times over the course of our day together, but I'm afraid the Internal Revenue Service felt otherwise. I believe the deal that I have negotiated with them is the best offer you will be made. I strongly recommend that you take it."

"Okay, what are they offering?" Damien said, pacing the gravel lot.

"Well, they would charge you with misdemeanor tax evasion based on a statute and violation, which was frankly slightly twisted for the purposes of your case being so unprecedented and unusual. It would require an admission of guilt, and you would need to pay a penalty of $5,000."

"What about my money, the $50K that those punks still have? That's my money."

"Yes, they will refund your fifty thousand, I believe in a check format, after the plea agreement is signed."

"Well, yeah, all right, so I'm really only out five, and I'll get fifty back?"

"Yes, in addition to pleading guilty to the misdemeanor tax violation, and of course my legal fees."

Damien let out a big breath, which he hadn't even realized he'd been holding. "Stanford, this is really great news. I gladly agree to those terms. I just want it to go away, and even I'm not stupid enough to think I can win in court against the IRS. Talk about ironclad contracts!"

"Well, that's probably accurate. I should tell you that while this isn't a condition of the plea, you should probably prepare yourself and your businesses for future auditing. They may not have been looking at you before, but they are watching you now. I think it is reasonable to assume that you will receive that notification within the next six months."

This was not something Damien wanted to hear, but over the course of the last couple of days, he realized that he might have made himself a target to the IRS. His accountant, Ryan Foster, would need to be alerted, and he and Damien would need to discuss strategies for possible cover-ups on the books at all his companies. This could be bad but maybe not. The government would need to find proof, and they'd been careful.

"Make the deal, and send me your bill. I'll sign the document. Thanks for your help, Stanford."

That afternoon Samara Poe instructed Damien to review his calendar because the Titan Farms mediations had been scheduled. They would be held back-to-back on five consecutive days representing the interests of six contract farmers.

"As you know, we picked off another one yesterday who came crawling back begging for forgiveness and mercy," said Samara with satisfaction. "We'll get the other ones to bend either in mediation or very soon after. The penalty fees we've attached for this process was a genius move on my part, if I say so myself. They are running up further debt every day this stretches on. I'm very certain by the time we get to mediation, most of them will be broke, or broken by the process," she said with pride.

"Right," said Damien. "Ah, good work. Do I really need to attend the mediations if we're not going to be offering anything but a sword?"

Samara took a deep, cleansing breath. "Damien, as I've explained, your appearance will be necessary as a show of good faith in the face of opposing counsel and the independent mediators. It will fulfill the requirement of *participating* in the mediation process as well as the further breakdown of the farmers. You, as CEO and founder, would need to be in the room for show, if nothing else. You may conduct other business while the mediator consults with the farmers in the other room privately. When the mediator is speaking with Titan, you need to appear to be interested and participate."

"Fine. But try to piss them off so we can get out of there as quickly as possible."

"Yes, I would be happy to do that, but the longer the mediation drags on, the more legal debt the farmers will incur. If we spent the day just pretending to engage and keep them in hopeful negotiations, it will be more destructive. In addition, you should know that I picked the most expensive office venue in the city, and the daily rate of rent for those rooms is shared by the farmers and us. The point is, we won't experience the pain of these extra costs as much as they will."

"Okay. The calendar looks fine, I gotta go," he said and hung up.

———————

Damien had not spoken with Charles since the ill-fated IRS office scene. He thought it would be a good idea to let Charles have a chance to cool down, but Linda was still upset that Carey hadn't returned her phone calls.

"If you messed up my relationship with her, Damien, I swear I will be soo pissed at you!" she screamed at him. But pissed off might have been tolerable compared to the savage fury she unleashed as the next shoe dropped.

Linda's fondest desire had been to be immortalized in photographs with either one of the Carrows sisters while on the town looking glamorous. That gift had not come through for her, but she kept a beady eye on the Manhattan papers, columns, and tabloids. What she had not been expecting was a two-page spread of pictures in the *Post* capturing the "Wild Nightlife of Playboy Millionaire Charles Carrows," taken at an Atlantic City nightclub, which prominently featured Charles and her husband frolicking with extremely hot, scantily clad models. Dancing, drinking, laughing, and kissing. And sure enough, even though the pictures were focused on Charles Carrows, in the background of one photo, there was Damien in a hot embrace, the girl sitting astride him, making out with him.

"*You piece of shit!*" she screamed at him. "You crappy piece of shit. What the hell is this, D-Bag?"

Damien was horrified. He vaguely remembered the girl and the wild night in the bar. He remembered her kissing him but was unaware that the moment had been captured by someone's camera.

"What do you have to say, asshole?" she said, visibly shaking with rage in front of him.

"Linda," he began calmly.

"I want you out of here! I want you gone!" She wadded up the paper and began whacking it against the walls. "I don't want to see your stupid face again! You humiliated me and lied to me. How am I going to explain this to my friends? And family! And Carey! And MaryLou!"

"Wait now, MaryLou doesn't need to know about this. We don't need to tell her anything."

"Wake up, *D-Bag*! Of course she'll find out! Someone will only be too delighted to tell her or show her, and I guarantee it will be all over Facebook tonight!"

"Then we'll have to prepare her for it, Linda. I know it looks really bad, but I don't know how to explain it other than she came on to *me*! I *told* her I was married, *several* times, but she was totally hammered, and she lunged at me! I didn't kiss her, *she kissed me*. I swear to God, Linda."

"I don't think I can believe anything you say, D-Bag," she spat. "First you borrow a million fucking dollars without asking for my permission, then you open another business without asking my permission, then you win fifty thousand dollars gambling and try to hide it from me by opening an offshore bank account, then you're such an idiot you give it directly to the IRS, for God's sake, and now this!"

She marched to the kitchen counter and grabbed a letter off a stack of mail. "I also opened the mail. We got an invoice from a Mr. Stanford Langdon for legal work. Ten thousand dollars! You are unbelievable." She threw the letter in his face.

"I think you've lost your mind, Damien, I really do. I think you really do believe you are some millionaire playboy now, and you don't give two shits about any of us, the little people, as you are so fond of saying. Well, I guess little Linda in the country is now one of the *leetle* people. But I tell you what, Mr. Big Shot, I'll make sure you remember who you are dealing with. I know where all the bodies are buried. I can and I will take you down. Don't think I won't, asshole. Now get out!" she yelled as she ran from the room in tears.

My God, thought Damien. My God, what in the hell was it going to take to calm her down now? His second thought was wondering where in the world he would go.

Chapter 28

Damien didn't want to leave the house with Linda so upset, but he knew she needed time alone to calm down. He would give her a call later. Damn. This was going to be a hard sell, but he felt confident that he could get back into her good graces before long—though it might be expensive. He was intimately familiar with the money and gift scenario to secure her forgiveness. Damn, this was going to take some time.

He wasn't sure how he felt about the pictures. If he was honest, he'd admit that it was a bit of a thrill seeing himself in the tabloids alongside his millionaire playboy friend making out with an extremely hot girl. Most guys would think it was a dream come true. He might be inclined to agree with them. He smiled in satisfaction thinking about his notoriety with such exalted company. Who knew—this might actually lend to his image and legend.

He should probably reach out to Charles now that they were published in the papers together. That would be a good excuse to call. Maybe he could camp out with Charles in AC while Linda cooled off? He picked up his cell.

Charles answered the call.

"Hey, Charles! Thanks for answering. We haven't spoken in a bit, but I wanted to touch base. How are you? Listen, I need to apologize again about what happened last weekend. I was so totally out of line with what I did, and I'm sorry if I embarrassed you or put you out. Thanks for bringing Stanford Langdon to me though, he's been a big help getting me off the hook with the Feds."

Charles wasn't responding. Damien, uncomfortable, continued quietly with sincerity. "Charles, really, I hope you realize that I would have never purposefully hurt you, I just misread the situation, and I fucked up. I'm really sorry about everything. But we can get past this, right? We're friends, I hope, at least that's what it looks like in the tabloids." He stopped to give Charles a chance to laugh or react. "And we're business partners too." Nothing. "Charles, are you there, man?"

"Damien, I'm not so sure we are business partners any longer. I was going to call you today as well but only to tell you that you need to give John Wallace a call. He needs to speak with you about the shareholder's contract. Give him a call, or he'll call you. You should set something up to meet with him. Soon."

"What are you talking about? Why does he want to talk to me? What about the contract?"

"Give him a call, he'll explain. I gotta go," Charles said and hung up.

––––––––––

After spending the night in a hotel, Damien left Titan 1 with a parking attendant and walked a city block through the financial district of Manhattan to the headquarters of Atlantic Banks. He passed security and boarded the elevator for his meeting with John Wallace. An assistant eventually escorted him into John's corner office overlooking the Manhattan skyline. Seated at his desk, he did not rise when Damien walked in and sat down.

The shareholder and loan documents were spread out in front of John as he began. "Mr. Miller, it is my unpleasant duty as financial administrator and business adviser of Carrows Casinos to advise you that we are rescinding our offer of minor shareholder."

Damien's mouth dropped open. He sat forward. "John, what are you talking about? Why would you do that? Is Charles really that mad at me? Did he tell you about the mix-up at the airport with that thing? Do you know about that? It was a completely crazy misunderstanding, but I've taken care of it."

"Yes, I know all about the mix-up at the airport. I've been in contact with Charles regarding the situation, as well as a representative of the Internal Revenue Service. I have also been given, as now a public document, a copy of your signed confession to the tax evasion charges."

Damien held up his hands. "Misdemeanor tax charges! I just had to pay a fine, it was nothing. No big deal. It's settled and done with." Damien made a sweeping motion with his hands.

"I understand all that. You paid the fine, but you pled guilty to tax evasion, Damien."

"It wasn't tax evasion, I was setting up an account. I was gonna pay my taxes. They cooked up some disclosure statute and brewed it up with some attempted concealment baloney and came up with that!"

"However you got there, Damien, it is public record that you pleaded guilty to tax evasion, and that is something that we cannot have any of our shareholders involved in. There are laws in the state of New Jersey, and federal laws as well, which prohibit the owners of casinos to have entailments involving certain legal statutes while obtaining or holding a gambling license. I'm afraid this qualifies as such, and we will no longer be able to be in business with you at Carrows Casinos."

Damien threw himself back in the chair as he felt his dreams of Titan Casinos and the fantasies he had playing James Bond evaporate.

"I can't believe this," he said quietly. "I can't believe you would pull me out for something so stupid and trivial. It was nothing. Not important, and I'm *innocent*. I didn't do anything wrong, John, I just made a mistake."

"Yes, you did make a mistake, Damien, a very large one in our eyes, unfortunately. And now that you will no longer be a shareholder in the casino, we need to discuss the loan repayment."

Damien snapped his head back. "Loan repayment?

What? If I don't have the shares, I don't need to pay for them. There isn't anything to pay for."

"Once again, I believe you fail to grasp the situation." John reached for the huge contract, which attached the loan to the shares. He picked it up and continued. "The document clearly states that any illegal act or attempt to undermine the success of the casino and its obligations through illegal acts is a default of the contract and such terms of default would be enforced. The offer would be rescinded, the shares returned, and full and immediate repayment of the loan would be due."

Damien's stomach lurched. "What? John? What are you saying here?" Damien croaked.

John dropped the contract on the desk and picked up a large envelope. "Take a look at your contract. I'm sorry, Damien. I've prepared a notice of default and outlined the immediate terms of repayment—within a week."

The room began to spin as Damien watched John Wallace pick up his phone and say something to someone, then stood up and handed a legal-sized envelope to him. The door opened, and Damien turned to see a big man staring at him with a menacing expression. John gestured at the man and said, "William will show you out."

Damien shook as he stood, and huge William grabbed his arm to steady him. The big brute escorted him all the way out of the building. Damien walked down the street in a trance and retrieved his car. He got in his sweet baby and cried.

Driving through the Holland Tunnel toward Jersey, he

thought he was going to be sick. He was overwhelmed with a new feeling of fear and dread. What was going to happen to them? How was he going to repay the loan? A million dollars? Who was going to give him a million dollars? My God! There were attachments to his businesses and his home! Linda would never, never forgive him for any of this.

He had to think. He pulled into the parking lot of a Hilton Gardens in Morristown and got another room. He sat on his bed trembling. My God, this might destroy them. He could lose his business, his home. Who would satisfy the new loan to cover his dad's business?

He spent the night staring at the ceiling of his hotel room, trying to come up with a solution, but he couldn't find any easy answers. He might be ruined. He realized he had assets in the business, but the sale of his equipment and farm would put him in the position of not earning money, and he needed to earn money to repay his debts! He could sell the boats, but again, he would need time to find buyers, and they were attached as collateral to Titan Farms.

Maybe he could work something out with John Wallace. He would have to give up something, but okay, he was ready to make the hard choices. He would live to fight another day. The next morning, he placed a call to John.

John's assistant answered. "Mr. Wallace instructed me that if you should call to refer you back to Stanford Langdon. He thought you might already have his number?"

"Yeah, I have his number. Thanks."

"Stanford Langdon."

"Stanford, it's Damien Miller. I need to speak with you about a matter that came up at Carrows Casinos. John Wallace asked me to give you a call."

"Good morning, Mr. Miller, what can I do for you?"

"What can you do for me? Well, actually I've been giving it some thought over the last twelve hours and realize that you've probably already done enough to screw me over."

"Mr. Miller, I don't have any idea what you're referring to."

Damien got up from the small desk in the corner of his hotel room and paced in front of his unmade bed. "The hell, Stanford, you were the one who advised me to sign a guilty plea for the bullshit IRS case, and if that hadn't happened, I wouldn't be in the mess I'm in now! John Wallace and Carrows Casinos are taking back my shares in the casino and demanding immediate repayment for a loan of one million dollars because I violated some clause that says something about casinos can't have owners who committed certain illegal activities, and apparently tax evasion, *even though it wasn't tax evasion*, is one of them! What do you have to say for yourself, Mr. Ten-Thousand-Dollar Lawyer?"

"Mr. Miller, I hear that you are very upset right now, and I am going to ask you to respectfully lower your voice and refrain from cursing at me. As to your allegations on my legal advice, I was solely representing you and your particular case with the IRS and was not aware of any attachments that would follow you as a result of a guilty plea in relation to your business with a casino in the state of New Jersey. You didn't mention it. Had you, I might have approached the negotiations from a different angle, or perhaps not, but you advised me to settle it, and settle it quickly, which is exactly what I did."

"Stanford! You don't seem to understand the bind I'm in now! John Wallace wants me to pay him a million fucking dollars—within the week! Where am I supposed to come up with that kind of money?"

"I'm confused, Mr. Miller. Why are you asking me about your finances?"

"I don't know either, except when I called Mr. Wallace's office to see if I could negotiate something, the stupid secretary told me John said to call you!"

"I see. Okay, Mr. Miller, may I make a phone call and call you right back?"

"You'd better! I'm waiting by the phone!" Damien disconnected and threw the phone on the bed. His fists clenched, he let out a scream of frustration as he looked at himself in the mirror.

––––––––––

Damien lay on the bed, his eyes wide, trying to calm himself after drinking a terrible pot of coffee and waiting for nearly an hour before Stanford finally called.

He shot up. "Stanford! What have you got? Did you

talk to John? Can we negotiate something?"

"Mr. Miller. I did speak with John Wallace regarding the default on your contract with Carrows Casinos as I informed you I would."

Damien ground his teeth. "Well? What?"

"Mr. Wallace thought you might need legal representation for the negotiation and referred you to me."

"What? Are they willing to negotiate?"

"I didn't say that. Again, he thought you might need legal representation during the process and suggested that you reach out to me. However, I'm not wholly comfortable with this arrangement. There could be a conflict of interest."

"I don't have time for this legal bullshit. You said John said he would negotiate? I need to do that. Can you represent me or not?"

"I've spoken with my colleagues. They don't technically see the conflict, but I'm not comfortable going forward."

"For Christ's sake," Damien said, rubbing his temple. "I'm not using my business attorney for this. I need some help here. Who do you got? Give me a goddamned name and number!"

Stanford gave him the number of another firm and wished him luck.

It took all damned day. His new attorney, Dash Scanlan, contacted John Wallace and got a copy of the contracts for review. He was on it. Damien got his credit card out and sent him the requested legal retainer. He lay on the bed staring at the popcorn ceiling, his head spinning, and waited.

The next day Dash Scanlan called him back.

Sitting in his underwear on his unmade bed, a box of congealed pizza beside him, Damien said, "You're killing me, man. What have you got?"

"Okay, this is what I have ascertained regarding your legal and financial situation in the matter of John Wallace and Carrows Casinos versus yourself. As it happens, they do seem to be willing to enter into discussions but not directly. Somewhat irregular but still to your advantage I believe—you have been directed to take a meeting with Mr. Henry Carrows. Mr. Carrows is currently in Manhattan and is able to meet with us tomorrow at 10:00 a.m., if that is all right with you."

"Yes! That's all right with me. I can meet with him. I know him! I went to his daughter's wedding at Oheka. Okay," he said with some relief. "Set it up."

Chapter 29

The next morning, Mr. Dash Scanlan and Damien Miller were escorted into a monstrous conference room of a legal firm in a midtown Manhattan office building. There was a stack of the legal pads and pens in the middle of the highly polished table next to a carafe of water and glasses. Damien grabbed a glass, poured it halfway full, and took a sip. Dash unloaded his briefcase, and they waited several minutes before Mr. Henry Carrows and another gentleman entered the room.

Damien gave Henry Carrows a hopeful smile. He didn't know if he should stand and shake the man's hand or what. He was only glad that he had gone home before he came to the meeting to put on a suit. Linda had mercifully not been there.

Henry Carrows took a seat directly in front of Damien and silently appraised him.

Damien felt a small flush to his face as he spoke first, saying, "Mr. Carrows, thank you for meeting me here today.

I don't know if you remember me from your daughter Charlotte's wedding? I was so honored to be there for such a wonderful occasion. I had the great privilege of meeting the rest of your family, Charles and Carey, whom my wife and I have become great friends with over the last couple of months. Finn Laferty and I are also business partners in my organic farming business. I really appreciate you meeting with me here today. I'm sure we can reach some understanding with our business."

Henry Carrows said nothing.

Damien didn't know how to interpret that and looked over at Dash to say something.

"Mr. Carrows, we've never met before. I'm Dash Scanlan of the legal firm Morgan, Bird and Scanlan, representing my client Damien Miller during these transactions."

An elegant, older man sitting next to Henry Carrows introduced himself. "I'm Mr. Lane Matthews of the firm Baach, McKenzie & Blake, representing Carrows Casinos, John Wallace and Atlantic Banks as lender, and Mr. Henry Carrows as an interested party. What we say in this room is acknowledged now as confidential, and I, therefore, ask you to review this contract of confidentiality I put before you and ask that you sign it before we proceed." He slid copies of the documents to each of them.

Dash took his time and read every line apparently several times because it wasn't terribly long. He eventually advised Damien that he saw no impediment of a binding nature or detriment to him by attaching his signature to the document.

"Okay then, we may proceed," said Mr. Matthews. "I am now giving you a document that outlines our proposed agreement and terms. You may take some time to review it." He slid copies of two extremely large legal documents to Damien and Dash.

Damien was tremendously uncomfortable. Henry Carrows had yet to say a word, and the document before him was huge. Were they going to watch them while they read? He opened it up and began.

It was an offer for Henry Carrows to repay the loan of $1,000,000 to John Wallace. In return, Damien would immediately sell him outright the businesses of Titan Farms, Titan Feed, and Titan Fisheries and its related equipment and brand. Damien could keep his home and his original flagship poultry farm but would conduct that business with Henry Carrows as owner under a similar contract to the current farmers of Titan Farms. That familiar document was also attached. Damien's head jerked up and his eyes locked onto Henry Carrows, who stared through him.

Damien wiped sweat from his forehead as he put his head down and finished a quick overview of the documents. He looked over at Dash, who was going through it with a thoroughness that was exasperating. Damien took another glance across the table. Henry Carrows was still staring at him.

"Dash," Damien whispered. "Just get an overview."

Dash did as instructed, finished reading, and looked to the wall of stone that was Henry Carrows and Lane

Matthews sitting across from them.

"Gentlemen, I believe we have an idea of the broad arrangement of the proposal, but I believe we will need some time to discuss and consider the arrangement as outlined and let you know what terms we might agree to."

Mr. Matthews said, "All right then. Mr. Scanlan, Damien, you have one hour. After that, the offer will be taken away, in full, in perpetuity."

He and the silent Henry Carrows stood up and left the room.

———

"Dash! Read faster! What am I going to do? They only gave us an hour? Should I do something like this? Can I do something like this? Should I sign? The *fuck*! What the fuck should I do? I spent years of my life building this company and now what, I'm just supposed to sign it over to these assholes? Why would I do that? Can we fight this? Is this even legal? Is it? I mean, what are my options? What is going on here? I could be ruined! They're asking me to give up these companies that I've invested all my life and money into. I've been working 'round the clock. I put everything I have into them, and now they think they can just take it away? Buy me off? My name is attached. The Titan brand! They can't just take that from me. I have a family, employees, customers, vendors, contracts. Tell me what to do!"

Dash shook his head and gave him a puzzled look. "Mr. Miller, I don't have ready access to your financial picture so that's something you'll need to consider. You may share that information with me if you'd like so I can help you make a decision whether this would be a palatable or reasonable offer. Without those numbers, I would have no idea if what they are offering is something you should consider."

"The first thing to *consider* is if I even need to pay back the $1,000,000! I bought shares of a casino that wasn't even open yet. I owned those shares for about three weeks. Why would I pay them $1,000,000 if I didn't buy anything?"

"Okay, well I think I can help you with that. I've reviewed the loan documents that you signed with John Wallace and the Carrows Casino shareholder agreement. I recognize the section in the document that pertains to illegal acts being relative to the agreement and the attachments of your home and businesses as collateral of the loan/agreement. I believe they, Carrows Casinos, are very serious about their exposure and legal obligations as it pertains to them securing a gaming license in the state of New Jersey. I believe I can counsel you with certain authority that this is an accurate and legal standing that they must adhere to, to secure a gambling license. Their release of you as a shareholder was legal and necessary."

"Well, what about the stupid money I spent for being a shareholder for only three weeks? They can't charge me $1,000,000 for three weeks!"

"Again, according to the documents you signed and the contracts you agreed to, if certain illegal acts were perpetrated by you at any time over the duration of the contract, they could rescind the offer. Whether you owned the shares for ten hours or ten years makes no difference. You purchased them, you defaulted, and because of the nature of default, no compensation for the shares would need to be awarded to you. As I read this document, which you signed, you gave them as loan collateral Titan Farms, Titan Feed, Titan Fisheries, and your home in Morristown. They have the power to obtain any or a portion of those assets as payback for that loan.

"That is why we are here today. They want you to either pay back the $1,000,000 in two days' time, or they want to obtain Titan Farms, Titan Feed, and Titan Fisheries as payment. As I said, I do not know the value of these businesses, so I cannot counsel you as to whether this is a fair price or settlement. You would need to decide that, and they have given us, in my opinion, an extremely unreasonable amount of time with which to make this decision."

Damien pounded his fist on the table. "I blame Stanford Langdon for this. If he hadn't let me sign that admission of guilt, we wouldn't be here right now looking down the barrel of a goddamned shotgun. God! I can't believe this is happening to me!"

"Mr. Miller, may I suggest that you put pen to paper, quickly, and make an attempt to tally the worth of your companies. While I believe it is unreasonable for Mr. Carrows and Mr. Matthews to put you under this time constraint, it is ultimately their prerogative. If this is their offer, but it is attached to the clock, then you have a choice to take it or leave it. I suggest you at least begin the process of calculation. In the meantime, I will go out and speak with Mr. Matthews and ask for an extension of time. Excuse me," he said and left the room.

Damien grabbed a legal pad from the center of the table and started writing. His hand trembled as he listed his best guess at debt versus equity and assets. He had no idea how to put a number on his brand. The name he had built. That alone should be worth $1,000,000, but then again, what was Titan Farms worth? Not including his model flagship farm, the assets were based on the future projected earnings of his farms, selling more franchises, building the brand, and the end dream of the ultimate sale. But he wasn't near that finish line. The Fisheries, he probably had $300,000 in equity and loans out on the rest. His home was heavily mortgaged with no equity at all.

On paper, it didn't look like much. His biggest asset was his flagship poultry farm, but they didn't want that. Why didn't they want that? What the hell was he going to do? If he didn't accept this offer, where in the world would he come up with $1,000,000 in two days' time? No bank was going to give it to him unless he gave them his businesses, and Titan Farms was only showing a modest profit, and Fisheries was in the same struggling position. That left his flagship farm and his home. Another bank would want to take his home for sure. But hell, it was already attached as collateral to this loan.

Dash Scanlan walked back into the conference room

and sat next to Damien. "They said they would give you an extra ten minutes. Frankly, I'm shocked, Mr. Miller. I believe them when they say they will walk after that time and not return. I think you should believe them as well. Have you come any closer to a decision?"

Damien felt sweat run down his back. "I hate them. How can they do this to me?"

"You signed the contract, Mr. Miller. They have the right. You could take Carrows Casinos to litigation, but that could take years, and I believe they have rather deep pockets. I'm not sure you would prevail since there is no room for argument regarding your crime and their gambling licensure. While it may not look like it right now, I believe at the end of the day, they are bailing you out of a difficult position. I'm sure you do not feel grateful for that right now, but you may in time."

"I hate you too."

"Yes, well, if you lack confidence in my abilities, you should fire me or seek different representation, or I could recuse myself and allow you to seek more palatable representation. But due to the time constraints, which are ticking as we speak, I am willing to stay in this room with you as your counsel if that is your decision."

"I really, really hate you, but you can stay."

"Thank you, Mr. Miller. Have you reached a decision?"

Henry Carrows and Lane Matthews opened the door to the conference room and returned to their previous seats across from Damien and Dash.

Mr. Matthews began. "Are you prepared to sign?"

"For the record," began Dash, "I will tell you that I have counseled my client that this negotiation is not only unusual, but a situation of duress is being perpetrated against him."

"We'll admit to no duress whatsoever. Either your client is interested in the deal before him or he is not. If not, then we remove it from the table and excuse ourselves. His business with John Wallace and the repayment of the loan is entirely up to him, we are simply offering a solution."

Dash turned to Damien. "What do you want to do?"

Damien glared at everyone at the table, picked up a pen, and signed the document. "I'll get it back. You can't stop me. I'll get it all back, gentlemen." He got up and left the room. Dash gathered his things, and he and Lane Matthews followed him out.

Henry Carrows sat back in his chair and gave a deeply satisfied sigh and smiled. It felt good to be a pirate, but sometimes it felt even better to be Robin Hood.

Chapter 30

Dash Scanlan called Damien a couple hours later. Damien had been told that they would need him as he made a rush to the exit of the law firm. He stayed in the city and walked the busy streets with no direction and waited.

"Damien, the documents were signed and notarized. You need to meet with me at my office so I can have your signature notarized as well. I have also been instructed by the new owners of Titan Farms, Titan Feed, and Titan Fisheries that you may not approach your office without their presence. You may not contact your employees, who are no longer your employees, but are the employees of Henry Carrows, the new owner of the companies, via phone or email to disclose the negotiations and sale of the companies. In addition, upon final signature of the documents this afternoon, you are to surrender your car with the vanity plate TITAN 1, which is an asset belonging to Titan Farms."

Damien did as instructed. He met with Dash at his office and had his signature notarized. The meeting concluded, Damien stood to leave.

"Mr. Miller." Dash held out his hand. "I'll need the keys."

Damien glared at him. He reached in his pocket and put them in his hand.

"I've arranged for Enterprise Car rentals to meet with you. I believe there is an agent in the lobby who brought you a loaner."

Damien gave him a smirk and went to the lobby. In the parking lot, he glared at the budget Chevy sedan with hatred but got in and drove away. Going home, he faced Linda and her bombardment of indictments as he gave her the unvarnished details of what happened.

She threatened to divorce him, and this time, she had almost literally thrown him out of the house. He'd barely kept his temper as she chased him through the house and watched him pack a bag. He'd left and driven to the small marina on Lake Hopatcong where they kept a sailboat.

Damien went below into the ridiculously cramped space of his old twenty-five-foot Catalina. He threw his bag onto the small forward V-berth next to some life preservers and tools. The place smelled like mildew, and dust had accumulated on everything. His phone began to vibrate. It was Samara. He turned it off and threw it onto the foam mattress next to his bag and sat on the short narrow bench in the galley. He put his head in his hands and noticed a trail of ants crawling across the floor. He sat up and groaned as a sourness built in his stomach.

He looked around his new home. How the hell did he end up here?

Samara Poe was incredulous that Damien wasn't returning her calls. She knew he often acted in an irresponsible and rude manner toward people he didn't want to deal with, but Samara thought they had a special unspoken agreement. She thought she was in a different class. She needed to go over some details and last-minute strategies for the mediations with him, but she couldn't even reach him. She was very, very angry.

That morning was the official start of the mediations, and Samara unloaded her car with documents and wheeled them into the beautiful office complex where they had rented space for the mediations to take place. It was a beautiful day, and although Samara was experiencing anger issues toward Damien, she was prepared and looking forward to a wonderful week. It would be so refreshing to sweep away the obstacles that were mucking up the vacuum filters of her personal kingdom at Titan. She assumed Damien would arrive soon. She didn't think he was completely ignorant about the importance of his role this week.

She obtained the keys from the leasing office and rolled herself to the elevators and then to the top floor of the building. She opened up the two identical conference rooms overlooking the city and hummed a satisfying tune while she unpacked the boxes. She had thoughtfully copied lunch menus from a local deli for the prelunch orders, which could be placed before the mediations began, and fanned them out on the table in the farmers' room. She had also arranged for coffee and water services to be supplied to the rooms by 8:00 a.m. She now availed herself of a fresh cup and sat down with her documents neatly organized in front of her, perfectly prepared in expectation of a highly satisfactory day.

The elevator dinged, and Samara looked up to see the first contract farmer from Ohio, Russ Rhode, and his attorney arrive. She didn't say anything, but as they got closer to the rooms, Samara got up and gestured them to the room across the hall from her. They didn't say anything to her either. Shortly thereafter, the appointed mediator arrived, and Samara asked him to join her in her conference room. He declined and said he would remain in the hallway until all the parties had arrived.

The next group was the Titan Farms staff of Walter Wilson and Ryan Foster but no Damien. Walter and Ryan came into the room, and she closed the door. "Where is Damien? Have you heard from him?"

Walter looked at Ryan and said, "I haven't heard from him in several days. I thought it was kind of odd that he hadn't returned my calls, but I figured he was busy with you."

"I haven't heard from him either," said Ryan.

"Well, where is he?" Samara hissed.

"I don't know, have you called him?"

She looked at them under hooded brows. "Of course, I have. I've been trying to reach him for days, but he hasn't returned my calls either."

At that moment, the elevator dinged again. Samara opened the door and looked out. But rather than Damien, she was surprised when three strange men stepped off and approached the rooms.

One of them put his head in the conference room with the Ohio farmer and told them to come out into the hallway.

"Good morning, everyone. I know this is irregular, but I have some news. If we could all arrange ourselves into one room, I will explain." He gestured for the Ohio farmer and his attorney as well as the mediator to enter the Titan war room.

"What is this? Who are you?" said Samara. "Are you in the right place? This is a private mediation between two parties, and you are not invited to attend. Who are you?"

"Yes, you must be Samara Poe. I will explain everything. Please, everyone, take a seat. My name is Lane Matthews, and this is my legal associate, Mr. Jeff Carpenter. We represent Mr. Henry Carrows." He gestured to Henry.

"Is this about Damien?" Samara asked. "He's not here yet. I believe any announcement is inappropriate until Damien Miller arrives. I cannot believe you would interrupt the sanctity of our private business today. Your interruption is inappropriate."

"Samara Poe," began Henry Carrows, "as of Friday last, I am the new owner of Titan Farms, Titan Feed, and

Titan Fisheries. Damien Miller sold to me outright the rights and assets of the brand Titan and those businesses. My attorneys will be happy to share the negotiated legal documents with you pertaining to the sale. Therefore, you are an employee of *my* company, and it is with great delight to say this in such distinguished company." He gestured to Russ Rhode, the farmer from Ohio, and looked back at Samara. "You're fired."

They watched Samara's face turn from pale to beet.

"Yes, absorb it, Ms. Poe. And as for the rest of you, I assume you to be Walter Wilson and Ryan Foster." Henry gestured at the other two sitting with their mouths open next to Samara. "You are fired as well. You will find the offices of Titan Farms off-limits and the locks changed within the hour. You will not return there unescorted. My associates will retrieve all company property from you now, including cell phones and laptops. Mr. Matthews, I believe you have more to add?"

"Ms. Poe, Mr. Wilson, and Mr. Foster, I have spent a great deal of time reading up on your company and absorbing the financial information you use to sell farms for Titan. I am giving you notice that we intend to litigate each of you personally and hold you responsible for the fraud that has been perpetrated against the small business owners who purchased the farms with goodwill and to their singular detriment were instead given a perilous and illegal business model literally made up by criminals. We intend to pursue these claims with the full backing of the inexhaustible resources of Mr. Henry Carrows. Please give your devices to Mr. Carpenter and leave the building. We will be in touch."

While the looks of horror on the faces of the skanky filth that was the Titan inner circle was a rewarding pleasure to observe, Henry Carrows was more moved by the crying that had erupted from the farmer from Ohio at the end of the table. His head was in his hands, and his lawyer had his arm around him as he openly wept.

Henry approached him. "Mr. Rhode. We haven't been formally introduced. I understand that this is all very shocking, but I give you my word that I will make certain that you enjoy the profitability that you had every reason to expect upon the purchase of your farm. That is if you choose to remain in the poultry farming business. If you choose not to, you have my assurances that I will buy you out and let you leave freely, in peace, with plenty of money in your pocket, making you whole again. I'm sorry for the pain that has been perpetrated against you and your family."

Tears ran down the Ohio farmer's face, his body shook.

"I understand your wife has some medical concerns. When you call her, I hope she feels relief and that the shock won't be too great. I'm sure this day will feel like a roller coaster for all of you.

"Mr. Matthews and Mr. Carpenter will spend as much time as necessary going over your desired outcomes and see to it that you leave here today satisfied. I will be making these same overtures to the rest of the Titan farmers by the end of the day."

Henry Carrows smiled at the farmer from Ohio. "No more worries, Mr. Rhode. It's over. It's going to be okay."

They waited until the ragtag bunch of crooks left the room. Henry turned to Lane Matthews and said with a joyous smile, "It's time to call the Wellington boys."

Epilogue

One year later

Isabella and Finn Laferty sat with their guests around their new firepit at Laferty Organic Poultry Farms in upstate New York. Russ Rhode and his wife, Cathy, sat near them, enjoying the brisk autumn air as the sun disappeared below the horizon.

"It feels so good," marveled Russ, referencing the perfect fall day and a bit more. "He's bankrupt. Bit by bit, they broke him." Russ smiled sideways at Finn. "Yup, the last Titan standing, Damien Miller, has fallen."

Cathy raised her water bottle in a toast. "Long live Sovereign Cooperative Farmers!" The other three followed suit.

Russ laughed. "God. Just a bit at a time. First, they bring in an accountant and force all payroll, invoices, and expenses to be managed by them rather than by Damien. Then they force him to buy those horrible shacks and install the rancid blackout curtains, then they make him start a hormone injection protocol because his birds were too skinny. Shit, the only ones I feel for are the birds. Not like ours anymore, right, Finn?"

Finn looked over his farm, completely reconfigured now and wholly organic and clean. The best part was that they were finally profitable. Henry's team had completely restructured the seven farms remaining from the Titan debacle. Each one was now a separate entity but a part of a powerful, successful cooperative. They had each other's backs like no farming community in the country. Each farmer's loan was forgiven and the numbers crunched to discover what it would really take to put each on a path to success—they were all definitely on their way. Buying power, a fortune in guaranteed loans waiting for them if they should need capital, a CPA and law firm managing all the numbers and equipment to keep everyone on track—it was a dream come true.

"It's what I've always dreamed of." Finn smiled at him.

Russ grinned. "God, Samara, Walter Wilson, the whole gang has been investigated and ended up with enough legal fees to bury them. Then the IRS swooped in on Damien...I gotta ask myself what's sweeter sometimes, my success or that prick's downfall?"

"Our success," said Cathy. "By far."

Russ nodded at his wife, who was feeling good again, thanks to the extraordinary health insurance financed by the cooperative with the help of Henry Carrows.

Russ laughed. "I heard Damien was looking at an offer as a manager of a timeshare condo sales operation in Florida. Can you imagine?"

Finn smiled. "Almost makes me want to travel that way and see if we can get a meeting with him so he can tote us around. Think about all the rich people he'd have to kowtow to!"

They had fun joking about the sweetness of that dream a bit more, then sat in companionable silence. Russ leaned on his elbows and clasped his hands.

"But, Finn, I ask myself all the time why the man did it. You know? Was it because his daughter is married to Isabella's brother?"

Finn shook his head. "Nah, he just saw the potential that Damien missed. He wasn't greedy about it, he's in it for the long-term. I also don't think he liked the idea of someone putting his foot on our necks while lifting himself up. It didn't sit right with him. That's all."

"Yeah, I suppose." Russ kicked the dirt around at his feet. "But you've spent some time with him, I mean, I just met him that once, then his staff took over. He's like a dream. Like smoke. He's invested so much. Do you think we can trust him? Are you worried about shenanigans coming our way?"

Finn and Isabella met each other's eyes and smiled. Finn looked at Russ. "We can trust him."

Russ threw up his hands, looking for more. "What makes him tick, man? I mean, what's he really like?"

Isabella reached out and held Finn's hand. "He's our hero, isn't that enough?"

Russ sat back and looked at the sky. "Our hero." He

smiled and mused. "Yup, and one who sure knows how to kick the shit out of the bad guy."

Acknowledgements

I'd like to thank my family and friends for slugging through the raw material and for the endless discussions and support for my work.

To my editors, Alida Winternheimer and Erin Liles, your professionalism and dedication were a blessing to me. Thank you for all your hard work and patience.

I'd also like to thank the wonderful writers of the Western Suburbs Writers Group for all the feedback you gave me helping the work come to life. Your comradery means the world to me.

About the Author

Annabelle lives in Minneapolis with her husband and children.

You can reach Annabelle at:

Annabellelewisauthor@gmail.com

Follow Annabelle on Facebook at:

https://www.facebook.com/AnnabelleLewisAuthor/